———————— ★ ————————

"Is it time?" Isaiah asked.

"Time for what?"

"Am I going to die now?"

In answer, the voice reached over Isaiah's right shoulder with the hand holding the knife and swept it under Isaiah's neck in one smooth, hard, sharp movement.

Now the voice stood before him. Isaiah felt wetness on his chest and looked down. The front of his shirt was drenched with blood.

His head began to swim. He felt hot, lightheaded. His vision began to dim. "Am I dying?"

Frowning in puzzlement again, the voice watched Isaiah closely, then gave a simple nod.

Isaiah sank to his knees among the weeds. It was over. He wouldn't have to run from the voice anymore.

His last fleeting thought was that if anyone could have helped him, it was Anna.

———————— ★ ————————

DEATH
IS
DISPOSABLE

EVAN MARSHALL

W🌐RLDWIDE®

TORONTO • NEW YORK • LONDON
AMSTERDAM • PARIS • SYDNEY • HAMBURG
STOCKHOLM • ATHENS • TOKYO • MILAN
MADRID • WARSAW • BUDAPEST • AUCKLAND

To Frank Corso, who thought of it

Recycling programs
for this product may
not exist in your area.

DEATH IS DISPOSABLE

A Worldwide Mystery/March 2012

First published by Severn House

ISBN-13: 978-0-373-63620-4

Copyright © 2008 by Evan Marshall

Printed in U.S.A.

Acknowledgments

My love and thanks to my wife, Martha Jewett, my sons, Justin and Warren, and all my friends for their continuing support.

I am also grateful to my agent, Maureen Walters at Curtis Brown, and to Edwin Buckhalter, Amanda Stewart, Megan Roberts, and Piers Tilbury at Severn House for making the publishing process such a pleasure.

Finally, I would like to thank Robin Geuer, and at the New York City Department of Sanitation, Deputy Chief Keith Mellis, Executive Officer, Public Information and Community Affairs, and Supervisor Jack Pisano, for generously sharing their expertise.

To him the porter openeth; and the sheep hear his voice: and he calleth his own sheep by name, and leadeth them out. And when he putteth forth his own sheep, he goeth before them, and the sheep follow him: for they know his voice.
—*John* 10:2–3

ONE

SANITATION SUPERVISOR Anna Winthrop drove slowly along West Fifty-First Street. In the middle of the block between Broadway and Eighth Avenue, she pulled out of traffic and parked in front of a vacant lot flanked by red-brick apartment buildings.

Not far from the sidewalk, Sanitation Police Officer Izzy Martinson stood gazing down at a heap of debris. Anna got out of the car and walked over to him, giving him a smile and a nod. The junk consisted of plaster, drywall, insulation, and broken concrete. Izzy took a drag on his cigarette and shook his bald head.

'Contractor, looks like,' Anna said, running her fingers back through her shoulder-length ash-blonde hair. 'You want me to have my people clean it out?'

'Not yet,' Izzy said, flicking his half-smoked cigarette on to the pile. 'We'll stake it out, see if we can nab 'em in the act.'

Since her promotion to supervisor two years earlier, Anna had worked with the Enforcement

Division's Illegal Dumping Task Force several times in an effort to catch offenders in the act. Only a few of the stakeouts had resulted in arrests, but Anna didn't say anything about that to Izzy.

She watched him drive off and cross Eighth Avenue toward Ninth. Then she got back into her own car, a white Ford Taurus sedan with a red-and-blue stripe and the department logo on its side, and SANITATION printed on its side and rear. She took a last look at the pile of debris in the lot, then pulled away and headed back to her garage.

That's how she'd thought of it for the past two years: *her* garage. As a supervisor for the New York City Sanitation Department's Manhattan Central District 13, overseeing her section's garbage and recycling collection, street-sweeping, and snow removal, she used the garage as her center of operations.

Not that the garage was much to speak of—a drab, two-story, tan-brick building wedged between the ugliest brownstone on West Forty-Fourth Street and the fenced-in playground of an elementary school—but it was *her* drab, two-story, tan-brick building, and she'd grown surprisingly fond of it.

She drove through the garage's chain-link gate and into the cavernous building itself, parking to the side near several rows of tires waiting to be disposed of. Getting out, she crossed the vast, dimly lit space in which Manhattan 13's roughly 150 vehicles and pieces of equipment were parked or stored. Ahead of her, behind widely spaced cinder-block columns that formed a corridor, were the garage's offices, their large rectangular Plexiglas windows darkened by closed venetian blinds.

About a hundred feet from her office, three men from Anna's crew stood in a cluster, a small mass of green uniforms and steel-tipped safety boots. As soon as they saw her, they grew quiet, watching her. Winston Avery sniggered. Jay Rapchuck turned to look at something on the garage floor, and Anna followed his gaze.

In the middle of the floor, someone had arranged garbage to spell out the message 'WE ♥ ANNA'. She looked back at the men. Now Jay was laughing wholeheartedly, his flabby frame shaking. He jabbed Winston, who let out a snicker.

'This had better be gone by the time I come out of my office,' she told them, 'or I'll write up every one of you.'

As she approached her office door, she saw Kelly and her partner Brianna coming toward her across the garage floor. They had seen the men's handiwork. Kelly was shaking her head in disgust, her bobbed honey-blonde hair swinging from side to side.

Dark-haired Brianna looked hostile. 'They're like little children,' she said, looking over. The three men were already sweeping up the mess. As if sensing they were being watched, Jay turned and winked at Brianna. He had the hots for her and made no secret of it. Winston looked at Kelly, the object of *his* affections, and wiggled his eyebrows suggestively. Both women looked away.

'Just finish your route?' Anna asked them.

'No, we've been back about half an hour,' Kelly said.

Nodding, Anna put her hand on the knob of her office door.

'Wait,' Brianna said softly. 'You've got company.' When Anna raised her brows enquiringly, Brianna said, 'Santos.'

Anna smiled. She and Santos Reyes, a beat cop from Manhattan's Midtown North Precinct, had met twice before—once when he was following up on a complaint about the noise the sanitation trucks made, and once when a purse-snatcher had been seen running into the garage. She was glad he had a reason to come back. She'd always had a thing for Hispanic men, and this one was especially handsome.

When she entered the small room, he was standing in silhouette between her desk and the wall, reading the notices on her corkboard. He was tall, slim but muscular, with a nice tight rear end…and when he turned to her and smiled, she felt herself melting again.

She wished him a good morning and he gave her a sweet smile and a nod. 'Ms Winthrop—'

'Anna—please.'

'Anna. And I'm Santos.'

'Agreed,' she said, walking behind her desk. 'What can I do for you today?'

He looked down, frowning in embarrassment. 'This is pretty much a formality, something I've got to follow up on.'

She waited, smelling his peppery cologne.

'It's about a neighbor of yours, a Mrs—' he checked a small notepad '—Dovner.'

Anna let out a groan. Mrs Dovner, who lived in the apartment below hers, was the bane of her existence. She had already complained to Anna about playing her music too loud and cooking with too much garlic. Now what?

'Mrs Dovner has complained that you've been, um, encouraging a homeless man who frequents your neighborhood. In fact, she says it's because of you that he's there so much.'

Anna's mouth dropped. 'You mean Isaiah?'

'Yes,' he said, looking a little scared. 'I believe that's the name Mrs Dovner gave. According to her, you give him bottles and, well, speak to him.'

'Oh, are those crimes now?'

'No—oh, no,' he said, eyes large. 'It's just that she says by doing these things you're creating a disturbance.'

She slammed her hand down on her desk. He jumped. 'A disturbance! Listen,' she said, leaning forward, hating to be yelling at him because he really was so incredibly cute, 'Isaiah is a sweet, elderly, mentally disturbed homeless man who trades in my cans and soda bottles for the deposits. Other people on my street give him bottles, too. And yes, we sometimes talk to him, the way we would talk to any human being. I think that's what Mrs Dovner doesn't realize—that Isaiah is a human being. Something I'm starting to think Mrs Dovner is not.'

'Like I said, this is just a formality.' He flipped his pad shut. 'Now I can say I spoke to you.'

'And just what is it you want me to do?'

His gaze traveled around the small room. Then he looked at her and burst out laughing. 'Darned if I know!'

Laughing along with him, she shook her head. 'I appreciate the visit…Santos. But since, as you say, I'm not doing anything wrong, I'm afraid you've wasted your time.'

'Maybe not,' he said.

She looked at him.

'I was wondering,' he said, lowering his voice, 'if maybe I could have your number...call you sometime?'

She'd wondered how many times they would have to meet before he asked her that. She grabbed his notepad from him, found a pen on her desk, and scribbled out her number. 'Not a problem,' she said, businesslike, as she handed back the pad. When he smiled like a little boy who's been given candy, she couldn't help smiling with him.

'Thanks,' he said at the door, holding up the pad.

Then he was gone, the smell of his cologne lingering above Anna's desk. She inhaled deeply.

WHEN ANNA EMERGED from her office at two-thirty, all traces of the garbage message were gone. She felt a small, secret sense of relief. Asserting her authority wasn't always easy. Heck, this *job* wasn't easy for a petite woman with a pretty, heart-shaped face, full lips, high cheekbones, and big, long-lashed green eyes. At twenty-nine, she was younger than eight of the ten men she supervised. Most of them showed her a grudging respect, but it was a battle she never stopped fighting. Kelly and Brianna, on the other hand, were never a problem. They liked and admired her.

On her way out, she passed the office of Hal

Redmond, supervisor of section two. Still at his desk, he gave her a broad wave. Next door was the office of Gerry Licari, who supervised section one. His door was closed and beyond the venetian blinds the room was dark. Gerry had two small children and rarely stayed much beyond the end of their shift at two o'clock. The last office belonged to Allen Schiff, the district superintendent. His door was open but the room was dark.

As if in compensation for Anna's earlier irritations, it was a glorious May New York day, the sky a high, hard blue, the slightest hint of a breeze in the air, the temperature a perfect seventy degrees.

Manhattan 13's garage was on Forty-Third Street between Broadway and Eighth Avenue. Anna lived on Forty-Third between Ninth and Tenth avenues, a five-minute walk west. At the corner of Ninth and Forty-Third, Mr Carlucci was neatening displays of apples and pears outside his grocery store.

'Hey, Mr Carlucci, what's with the fancy presentation?' She loved busting his chops, and it was mutual.

'Mind your garbage!' he said with a big smile, then gave her a wink.

A few minutes later, Anna entered her building and found herself face-to-face with Mrs Dovner, who lived in the front apartment on the first floor.

Anna gave her a little smile and started to pass the older woman.

'Not so fast, missy.' Anna hated it when Mrs Dovner called her that and had told her not to—which, Anna now realized, was exactly why Mrs Dovner still did it. 'I told the police what you've been doing, luring that dirty old bum here with all your bottles and smiles. I'm on to you.'

It occurred to Anna that Mrs Dovner, with her flyaway blue hair and ancient clothes, would herself have made quite a convincing street person. Anna drew a long breath. 'I've told you before—I have every right to speak to Isaiah and give him bottles, and I will continue to do so. If you bother the police about it again, I'll have to get in touch with them about you.'

'Me!' Mrs Dovner placed a deeply lined hand on her bosom, like some grande dame.

'Mm-hm. You're harassing me. It had better stop or I'll see you in court.' Anna went up the stairs, Mrs Dovner muttering below. Anna could only imagine the old bat's reaction if she knew Isaiah sometimes slept in their building's courtyard.

Suddenly the older woman let out a cry. 'There he is now! See what I mean? There he is!' She had her face pressed to the glass of the front door.

Anna hurried down the stairs. 'You leave him alone!' She ran in front of Mrs Dovner and out the door to the front stoop. She heard Mrs Dovner scramble out after her. Sure enough, Isaiah was across the street, making his way toward her. She gave him her kindest smile. Smiling back, he started toward her.

'Shoo! Scat!' Mrs Dovner squawked, standing at the edge of the sidewalk as if afraid to let her feet touch the street. 'We don't want you here.'

That did it. Slowly Anna turned toward her and got out her cell phone. She punched out some numbers, then pretended to hit the dial button. 'Yes, is this the police station?' she said into the dead phone. 'Good. I want to report a case of harassment.'

Mrs Dovner's eyes widened in horror, then narrowed to slits. 'OK for now, missy,' she said, as if vowing to return for another battle, and turned and stormed back into the building.

Anna turned back to Isaiah. 'I didn't expect to see you this week,' she said with a smile. 'You said you would be away.'

'Ah, yes. Trip postponed due to illness.' His voice was low, a little gravelly, pleasant to listen to.

She wondered where he had planned to go, with whom, and if he had really planned to go anywhere at all, but she knew not to ask. 'How are you today?'

'Fine, Anna, just fine.' He wore black jeans

and an oversize light blue Mexican wedding shirt, which Anna now realized looked new. His usually scraggly neck-length brown hair was clean and combed. And, she realized now, he was without his rusty shopping cart.

She looked at him more closely. He was different, she saw that now. Then she realized he'd been different the last few times she'd seen him—better dressed like this, his manner more…sane. His watery hazel eyes looked deeply into hers.

'The fact is, I'm doing really well now. I—I see a way out, a way out of…' He struggled to express himself, looking around him as if the right words were floating in the air. 'A way out of this life.' His eyes brimmed with sudden tears.

She understood what he meant and nodded. 'That's wonderful, Isaiah. Has something happened?'

He frowned in thought, then lowered his gaze and said, 'No cans or bottles anymore.' He locked his gaze on to hers as if trying to will his meaning into her. 'I just came to say thank you.'

He turned and ambled away. Anna watched him until he reached Tenth Avenue and disappeared around the corner.

EARLY THE NEXT MORNING, Anna stepped out of her building into a gray, drizzly rain. A rivulet of water in the gutter carried a Mars Bar wrapper and an empty Marlboro pack, reminding her she needed to finalize her street-sweeping schedule.

Walking east, she crossed Ninth Avenue and continued along Forty-Third Street. Ahead and to the right, on the south side of the street, three police cars sat at the curb and a small crowd had gathered.

She approached a man standing at the back of the crowd, craning his neck in an attempt to see into a brownstone. 'What's going on?' she asked him.

'Woman was killed. Murdered.'

Anna's eyes grew wide. 'Murdered? Who was it?'

The man shrugged. Two people away, an older woman wearing a flowered kerchief on her head turned toward them and said, 'Maria Trujillo.' She made the sign of the cross.

Anna had never heard the name. 'Anybody know anything about her?' she asked no one in particular. 'How it happened?'

No one replied. Two female cops, one tall with red hair, the other heavy and blonde, approached the crowd. 'People,' the blonde one said, 'please move on. Nothing to see here. Let us do our work.' No one moved. 'I'm not gonna say it again.'

Everyone moved. Anna continued east, casting a glance back at the brownstone. Two more cops, male, emerged and descended the steps to talk with the two women.

At the garage, Anna ran into Bill Hogan. He reeked of liquor and his skin was a wan yellowish color in the harsh fluorescent light. 'You see the commotion on Forty-Third?' he asked her.

She nodded. 'Any idea what happened?'

'Overheard two cops talkin' to each other. Woman strangled, one of them said. Don't know more than that. Figure we'll read it in the papers. Probably a robbery,' he said, and headed across the garage floor toward a collection truck beside which his partner, Fred Fox, was already waiting.

'Bill—' she called after him. He turned. 'Come and see me when you're done with your route, please.'

Looking stricken, he nodded and continued toward his truck.

'I knew her,' Kelly said from behind Anna, who turned. 'Not well, though. Her name was Trujillo. Maria Trujillo. Husband died years ago. Nice lady. Did charity work. You remember that children's benefit I helped out with last winter? She was the volunteer coordinator.'

'Really upsetting,' Anna said, entering her office.

Kelly stood in the doorway. 'Hey. It's New York.' She shrugged and gave a weak smile, as if that explained it all.

TWO

AROUND ONE-THIRTY, Bill Hogan knocked on her office door. 'You wanted to see me?'

'Yes, come in.' Indicating the chair beside her desk, Anna closed the door, then took her own seat.

Before she could begin, he said, 'I know what this is about, and you don't need to worry.'

'What is it about?' she asked levelly.

'My drinking,' he said, lowering his voice.

'I smelled liquor on your breath yesterday, and you've been drinking again today. This is a definite problem.'

He gazed down at the floor. His skin was still that odd color, a pale shade almost identical to his crew-cut sandy hair.

'This is an isolated incident,' he said at last. 'Fran and I have been having some problems at home and yesterday they kind of came to a head.'

'I'm sorry to hear that,' she said, knowing not to ask what the problems were.

He told her without being asked. 'Kevin, our

oldest—we found out he's been using again. Told him he could either go to rehab or move out.'

'And what did he choose?'

A look of pain came over his face. 'He moved out. Said rehab hasn't worked for him before and he didn't want to waste his time.'

'I'm sorry,' she said softly. 'But I think it's precisely at times like these that you need help not reaching for a drink.' She opened the bottom drawer of her desk and rummaged around in a file. 'Here,' she said, handing him a sheet of paper. 'I want you to call the medical division again to set up some alcohol counseling. The number is on there.'

He looked at her. 'I don't suppose I have a choice.'

'Why would you want a choice?' she said, trying to understand. He had just thrown his son out for refusing to go to rehab, yet he didn't want to put himself back in counseling.

He gave a little shrug. 'You're right, I guess. I'll call them.'

'Please do, and soon. I'll follow up with them to see how things are going.'

He glanced at her sharply. She knew he knew what she meant: to make sure you really did it. She rose. 'Good luck. You know we're all behind you here.'

He nodded, moisture coming into his eyes. Then he walked out of her office, shoulders slumped, like a schoolboy who has just been reprimanded by the principal.

Oh, well, if that's what it takes...

That night, Santos called her at home. They made a date for the following night. As far as Anna was concerned, it couldn't come soon enough. She hoped work stayed busy on Friday so the day would pass quickly.

She got her wish.

When she arrived at work the following morning, Ernesto and Pablo were waiting to speak with her. They'd just finished night-shift duty and had had a problem with a resident they wanted to tell Anna about before she heard it from someone else—namely, the Citizen Service Center, better known as simply 3-1-1.

'We was just minding our own business,' Pablo said, a look of extreme agitation on his good-looking face. Standing beside him in Anna's doorway, Ernesto nodded quickly in agreement with his partner.

'Tell me what happened,' Anna said calmly.

'OK.' Pablo took a deep breath. 'We pull up in front of this building, a brownstone on West Forty-Fourth, and we see this guy standing on the front stairs, throwing bags of garbage at the front door.

Middle o' the night and he's hurlin' garbage! Man, it was flyin' everywhere. Come to find out, this crazy guy thinks a woman who lives in this building has been putting her garbage in his cans.

'After a few minutes, the lady herself comes out with a baby in her arms and the two o' them start screamin' at each other. At one point the guy gives the woman a push and the baby starts screamin', too.'

'So what did you do?' Anna asked them both.

Ernesto spoke up. 'Hey, we didn't want to get involved, you know? So Pablo grabs the garbage from in front of this building, throws it in the hopper, gets on the back of the truck, and I start to drive on. All of a sudden this woman is down on the street near my door, with the baby in her arms, running alongside the truck and screamin' at me! I stop the truck and she starts cursin' me out for not protecting her from this guy! Hey, believe me, Anna, this lady didn't need no protection. More like the other way around.'

'That's nonsense,' she said. 'What do you think you should have done?'

The two men looked at each other, knowing now that what they did was not what they should have done.

'Break up the fight?' Ernesto ventured.

Anna said nothing.

'Call the police?' Pablo said.

'Bingo. You were right not to get involved, but whenever you see something like that going on, you should call the police.'

They both nodded.

Pablo said, 'Long as you understand, if this woman calls three-one-one or something and complains about us, that's what happened.'

She gave them a reassuring smile. 'I appreciate your telling me. Now go home and get some sleep.'

'OK, thanks,' Ernesto said, his normally sour face having relaxed into a smile. Watching them walk away toward their cars, she shook her head.

She spent the rest of the morning entering her section's daily statistical data on the department's twenty-year-old computer system, SCAN (Sanitation Control Analysis Network). Finished with that, she started on her time book and was halfway through when she got a call from one of the transfer stations at which the department tipped its garbage for shipment out of the city, usually by truck. According to the foreman at this facility, located in the South Bronx, a worker noticed clear plastic bags soaked with what appeared to be blood coming out of an EZ-Pack truck. When he and a coworker opened the bags, they found used syringes and blood-soaked gauze.

'These two guys said they were from Manhattan Thirteen. Terrence and Art, they said their names were. Just thought you oughtta know.'

Anna thanked him and said she would look into it. Hanging up, she gazed at her bulletin board, thinking.

It was illegal to dispose of medical waste with regular solid waste. Doctors were obliged by law to arrange with private companies for medical waste disposal. Not long ago, the department had instituted the ProFee (Professional Fee) Program, in which doctors could pay the Sanitation Department to take away their regular garbage. Was a doctor somewhere in her section sneaking medical waste into regular garbage to save money? She'd seen things like that happen before.

She would tell Art and Terrence to keep a sharp eye out.

AT SIX THAT NIGHT, she changed into cream-colored trousers and a pretty pale-green silk blouse and emerged from her building into a soft golden New York evening. It felt good to get out of midtown, to put her job aside. She and Santos had agreed to meet for dinner at Cubano, a restaurant he liked on Christopher Street in Greenwich Village. She took the subway downtown from Times Square.

He was there when she arrived, waiting in a

booth toward the back. He glanced up and smiled brightly when he saw her. He looked younger out of uniform, handsome in a white short-sleeve shirt open at the neck.

They found they both loved Cuban food. They ordered *ropa vieja*—'old clothes': thinly shredded beef seasoned with red wine, tomato sauce, garlic, and peppers. It came with rice and sweet plantains. They each had a glass of red wine.

'Absolutely,' he told her when she asked if he was Cuban. 'All four of my grandparents came over from Havana. My family? Castro haters right down to my brand-new six-month-old nephew.' He laughed, sipped his wine. 'We'll have to go dancing. Salsa, rumba, merengue. What about your family?'

She smiled. 'What about them?'

'Where are they from?'

Oh, boy. 'Um…Connecticut.'

'Connecticut?'

'Greenwich. Several generations now, actually.'

He gave her a shrewd look. 'Winthrop… Is that some old Pilgrim name or something?'

'Yeah, I guess it is,' she admitted. 'John Winthrop. I'm descended from him.'

His jaw dropped. 'Wow, that's back to the sixteen hundreds. Just what kind of family are you from, anyway?'

'OK, the jig is up. A rich old Connecticut family. My father is Jeffrey Winthrop. He cofounded Winthrop and Carnes Medical Products.'

'We have all that stuff at the station.'

'Yeah,' she said with a sigh, 'it's pretty much everywhere. About twenty years ago my father and his partner sold the company to Johnson and Johnson.'

'For a ton of money, I'll bet.'

'You don't want to know.'

'And your mom?'

'Mathilda Winthrop, née Pratt. Tildy. Active in various charitable organizations.'

'Never worked?' he asked, and quickly added, 'Outside the home?'

'Nope, not inside *or* outside.'

He took a bite of his food, then gave her a sidelong look. 'So what on earth are you doing in…'

'Garbage?'

'You said it, not me.'

She set down her wineglass, grew thoughtful. 'I don't think about this very often. I guess I try not to. It was a rebellion thing at first. I was embarrassed by my parents and all their money. I knew what they expected of me and I didn't want to give it to them. I thought, Let my sisters and brother do that. Me, I was going to be different. Got out of U. Penn, came to New York to look for a job, and just for laughs took the Civil Service exam with my roommate. I got offered a job as a sanitation worker. Garbage collector. She didn't.'

His eyes grew wide. 'Forgive me, but were you able to do that? I mean, lift those trash cans and everything?'

'It was hard at first, but it got easier.' She flexed her muscles. 'I may be small but I'm strong—one of "New York's Strongest".'

He was looking at her but not smiling. 'So what are you doing, slumming?'

'What do you mean?'

'Oh, come on. A deb like you. How many people do you know from rich Greenwich families who work in garbage?'

'I don't just work in garbage,' she said peevishly. 'I'm a section supervisor.'

He put his palms up. 'OK, OK, didn't mean to offend.'

She shook her head. 'Sorry I took it that way. I guess it's a sensitive subject for me. My sister Gloria's going to be a doctor in a year, and Beth is a lawyer with a high-powered white-shoe firm. My brother, Will, is an investment banker. Except for Will—the only person in my family who accepts me just as I am—everyone thinks I'm throwing my life away, and they're not afraid to tell me so, every time they see me.'

He scrunched up his nose. 'Not very pleasant for you, huh?'

'No, it isn't. I dread going home.'

'Then don't go home,' he said simply.

She gave a small, rueful laugh. 'I can't just do that. How would your family react if you did that? Besides, they're my family, the only one I've got.' She shook her head. 'We're having a party for my mother's sixty-first birthday a week from tomorrow. I'll be there, wouldn't miss it. I love my mom. I just wish she and my dad—and my sisters, for that matter—would accept me as I am, garbage and all.' Her gaze wandered, eyes unfocusing. 'The worst part of it is that they've gotten *me* wondering.'

'You like what you're doing, right?'

'Absolutely.'

'Then what's the problem?'

'I don't know... Sometimes I wonder if I really belong in this world. Some of the guys I supervise resent me. I'm younger than most of them; I'm a woman; and they know my background. Kelly and Brianna, they're another story. They admire me, I think. I don't mean to sound like a snob, but they're both from families who consider them pretty successful. It's likely those two will find, well, people right for them in this world.'

'Ah, so that's what this is about. You don't think

you'll find that special someone in the Sanitation Department.'

She looked down. 'Right.'

Gently he covered her hand with his. 'Who says that's the only place to look?'

She met his gaze, returned his smile. 'True. Now, what about you? What's your story?'

'My story? Real different from yours, I'll tell you that. I grew up in the projects in Washington Heights. When I was six years old, my parents had a terrible fight. At the time I had no idea what it was about, but later I realized Dad had been having an affair. I remember Mom crying and saying to him, "Make your choice—her or me. And if it's her, leave now and don't ever bother coming back." He walked out the door and we never saw him again. Mom raised me and my five brothers and sisters by herself. The family considers me pretty successful.' He winked at her. 'Hey, I could use some more wine. You?'

'Yeah, definitely.'

He hailed the waiter. 'U. Penn, huh? What did you study there?'

'Finance. Thank goodness Will doesn't want to change me, or he'd be trying to get me to work for his bank.'

'I don't want to change you, either,' Santos said. The waiter brought their wine. 'Speaking of which, I'm sorry about that visit I paid you on Wednesday.'

'Don't worry about it.'

'The fact is, I think it's pretty cool your helping that homeless guy out like that.'

She lowered her gaze. 'Poor Isaiah. He's the gentlest man you could ever hope to meet. He'd never hurt a soul. And all mean old Mrs Dovner has to do with her time is bother the police because I give him my cans and bottles.'

'We get lots of calls like that. We don't take them seriously. Like you said, there's no law against giving somebody your cans and bottles.'

She looked up, narrowed her eyes. 'Then why did you come see me?'

He blushed a dark red, twirling his fork on his plate. 'Now I'm busted.' He burst out laughing.

She smiled. 'Well, I'm glad you did. Now that we're telling the truth, I've got a thing for cops. And Hispanic men.'

'Oh, yeah? And I've got a thing for cute little blondes with green eyes.'

'Then I guess we're well suited.'

A police car passed in the street and a darkness overcame Anna as she suddenly remembered the cars outside Maria Trujillo's brownstone, imagined a woman being strangled.

'You know about the murder, right? Maria Trujillo?'

His expression grew serious. 'Of course. It's my precinct. Terrible thing.'

'Have the cops got any leads?'

He looked at her in good-natured surprise. 'You don't really think I can talk about that, do you?'

'Of course you can! It's me—Anna Winthrop, Section Supervisor at Manhattan District Thirteen Garage. We're practically colleagues.'

He gave a little laugh, met her gaze. 'If we're going to be seeing more of each other—which I hope we will—we've got to work out some ground rules.'

'What kind of ground rules?'

'About what we can talk about. Either we never talk about police business—' he glanced quickly around the restaurant '—which I admit wouldn't be very interesting. Or,' he went on, lowering his voice, 'we agree that whatever I tell you must never, ever go any farther.'

'Guess which rule I like better.'

'Yeah, me too. So we agree on that, right?'

'You didn't even need to say it.'

'OK, because if—'

'Santos, I've got it. Really.' She leaned forward, lowering her voice. 'Now tell me what you know about that poor woman's murder.'

'A widow. Husband was a rich importer/exporter, died years ago. Maria owned the brownstone, lived there alone.'

'Job?'

He shook his head. 'Charity work, volunteering, that kind of thing. Hey, maybe she knew your mother.'

'Not funny.'

'Sorry.'

'She was strangled in her bed.'

She nodded.

'Looks like an aborted burglary. Perp jimmied a window in the alley. No grate on it—big mistake. As far as we can tell, nothing was taken or disturbed. He probably hadn't expected her to be there. She screams, he strangles her and runs out by the back door. From the looks of things, Maria had a boyfriend. We found new men's clothes in one of the closets. We're looking for him. We're also trying to find people who knew Maria, but it appears she was extremely private, kept to herself. She had a cleaning lady—she's the one who found her. We've already talked to her, scared little mouse from Little Italy. She said she'd only started working for Maria recently and never saw her with anyone. No luck tracking down previous cleaning people. Maria has a daughter, Esperanza, lives two blocks from her mother. She said she and her mother hadn't spoken in over a year. Guess they had a falling-out...'

After dinner, they strolled through the narrow, winding streets of the Village. Santos gave Anna his arm, and it felt good. Secure. They took the subway uptown to Times Square and walked to her building.

'Well, this is me,' she said. She realized she had no idea where he lived, and asked him.

'East Thirty-Fifth Street. Tiny place, but it's all mine.' He put his hands around hers. 'I had a great time tonight, Anna.'

She let him kiss her goodnight. Through the window in the front door she watched him walk away. She heard a noise and turned around in time to see Mrs Dovner's door close with a firm click.

THREE

SHE KNEW IT WAS SILLY, but when she got to Maria Trujillo's brownstone on her way to work Monday morning, Anna crossed to the other side of the street. The building looked different somehow, as if it knew a violent crime had been committed inside it. It didn't help that it was a gray day with a sharp wind that blew her hair in front of her face.

When she was nearly opposite the brownstone, a woman emerged from the front door and descended the steps. Her arms were loaded with clothes, some on hangers. She heaved it all into a trash can at the curb and headed back up the stairs.

Anna turned around, went back to the corner, and crossed to the other side of the street. She made a point of walking slowly toward the building, and her patience was rewarded when the woman re-emerged carrying another load of clothes.

She looked around forty, maybe late thirties. Nice navy linen pantsuit. Expensively cut dark hair and generous, pretty features, though at the moment they were fixed in a hard scowl. She looked up and saw Anna, who gave her a smile. The woman gave a tight, artificial smile back and was about to go up the stairs when Anna approached her.

'Morning. I hate to bother you, but do you know anything about what happened here last week?' When the woman just stared at her, Anna said, 'Oh, are you her daughter? I'm terribly sorry.'

'It's OK.' Esperanza shook her head in a way that said, Don't bother with the niceties. She waited, as if to see if Anna had more to say.

Anna pointed to the trash can overflowing with clothes—good clothes, she saw now, expensive. She remembered what Santos had told her. 'I understand your mother had been a widow for some time. It seems odd that she would have kept your father's clothing for so long.'

Esperanza gave her a frank look of surprise. 'What are you, nosy?'

Anna opened her mouth to speak but didn't know what to say.

'I'm sorry,' Esperanza said quickly, 'forgive me.' She smiled and put out her hand. 'Esperanza Trujillo.'

Anna shook her hand. 'Anna Winthrop. I live on the next block. I didn't know your mother, but I still feel as if we've all been violated in a horrible way.'

'I'm afraid I didn't know her very well, either. We hadn't spoken in over a year. But I'm her only family, so the police called me.' Esperanza shook her head. 'From what I hear, she was asking for it.'

Anna's eyes widened. 'What do you mean?'

'She was a volunteer.' Esperanza said it as if a volunteer were a filthy, revolting thing. 'No place was too squalid or dangerous. What did she think was going to happen?'

'But they don't know who—did this, do they?'

'No, not by name, but what do you think? What kind of people do you think she came in contact with at these shelters and soup kitchens and who knows where else? I'll bet you anything it was someone she met that way. Lucky son of a gun.' When Anna looked puzzled, Esperanza said, 'These clothes aren't my father's. They have to belong to whoever she was seeing. I have no idea who it was. There was a whole closet full of clothes like this, all new. So obviously whoever it was had at least partially moved in. Had himself a nice little sugar mama. Clothes, trips, money… Guess things got out of hand.'

'So you think it was her boyfriend who killed her?'

'Isn't that what I just said? Some lowlife from the soup line.'

Anna was about to ask about the jimmied alley window but remembered Santos had told her about that in confidence. 'Do you think it could have been a burglar?'

Esperanza gave her a sharp, speculative look. 'A window had been forced, but I think that had been done by someone else at another time. I begged her to put a grate on that window, but she didn't think it was necessary. Anyway, nothing's been taken as far as I can tell, so whoever jimmied the window was probably planning to come back. So she wasn't killed in a burglary.'

Clearly at a loss for more to say, Esperanza gave Anna a little smile, thanked her for her condolences, and went up the stairs. Anna continued thoughtfully down the sidewalk toward work.

OFTEN ANNA INVITED Brianna and Kelly into her office first thing in the morning. They were there now, Kelly working on her second cup of black coffee, Brianna drinking tea. They had tried to get Anna to talk about her date with Santos on Friday, but she resisted, saying nothing much had happened, which was true. She had changed the subject by telling them about her encounter with Esperanza Trujillo.

'That's a switch,' Kelly said. 'You know, the daughter disapproving of the mother like that.

Anna, you got any more of those Stella d'Oro cookies? I'm on a diet but those have no calories, right?'

Kelly, a size eight, was always on a diet. 'Not many calories, no,' Anna said. 'And no, I don't have any more. It wouldn't kill you to bring something in once in a while.'

Kelly's jaw dropped. 'I just brought in doughnuts!'

Brianna blinked once. 'That was a month—no, two months ago.'

'Anyway,' Kelly said, 'try to remember to bring in some more of the Stella d'Oros.'

Anna laughed.

'Now,' Brianna said, 'you were telling us about the murder.'

'That's all I know,' Anna said.

Brianna, who liked her tea dark, dipped her teabag up and down several times quickly. 'You ask me, this whole neighborhood's goin' to the dogs. Murders, muggings…'

'Nothing new,' Kelly said.

'Gives me the creeps,' Brianna went on. 'Nobody's up to any good. Around one o'clock last night I was walking home on Forty-Fourth after my shift and I saw this guy running like a maniac through the alley straight toward me. Must have been coming from the back of a house on Forty-

Third. Now you gotta believe he'd just burglarized somebody or who knows what. I mean, here's this guy running, all out of breath, hair soaking wet. And you know who it was? That homeless guy who's in the neighborhood a lot—Isaiah, I think his name is. I got out of there fast, I'll tell you.'

Anna looked at her in surprise. What could Isaiah have been doing there, and at one in the morning?

At that moment Winston Avery appeared in the doorway. 'Ladies,' he said with exaggerated gallantry, 'good morning.'

'Good morning,' Anna said pleasantly. She was, after all, his boss. 'What can we do for you, Winston?'

The man's eyes, a watery green in his pasty face, were fixed on Kelly as if she were a fresh, warm cream puff in a bakery window. 'Just wondered if you've got a cigarette.'

For a moment Kelly just looked at him, as if trying to figure out what he was. Then she shook herself slightly and reached into her purse. 'Here,' she said, holding out a pack of Virginia Slims. 'Take two.'

His eyes widened. 'Don't mind if I do. Thanks… Kelly.'

She looked away. He continued to stand there.

'Was there something else, Winston?' Anna asked him.

'No, no,' he said, coming to. 'No. Goin' on my route now.' Looking preoccupied, he walked slowly out into the corridor.

'There's gotta be a rule against this,' Kelly said.

'Against what?'

'Being a letch.'

'Not unless he actually does something inappropriate to you, which he hasn't.'

'Give him time,' Brianna said dryly. 'He's jonesin' for you, girl.'

Getting back at Brianna, Kelly said, 'So what are you going to do now, look for your boyfriend Jay?'

Brianna picked up the Virginia Slims pack from Anna's desk and threw it at Kelly, who laughed. But Anna wondered how lighthearted she really felt. Four months earlier, another sanitation worker in Anna's section, Garry Thomason, had volunteered to fight in Iraq. Though Kelly had never said so, she had a serious crush on Garry—Anna had been able to see it quite clearly and wondered how many others in the garage had as well. Since Garry's departure, Kelly was often preoccupied— wondering, Anna was sure, how Garry was doing.

Toward the end of her shift, around one forty-five, Anna bumped into Pierre, Garry's replacement. Pierre and his partner, Tommy Mulligan, had just finished their route. While they were out, Pierre said, they'd been approached by a man on West Forty-Fifth Street—not part of their route—who complained that his building's trash hadn't been picked up the previous Wednesday night.

'What did you tell him?' Anna asked.

'First I explained that he's not on our route. Then I asked him if his trash was picked up on his next scheduled day, and he said yes. But I said I'd let you know anyway when I got back to the garage.'

'All right. Thanks,' Anna said, and watched him walk away. West Forty-Fifth was part of Jay and Winston's route. They'd been on the four-to-midnight shift that day. She went to see if they had come back yet. She found them upstairs in the break room, watching a rerun of *The Simpsons* on an old TV someone had thrown out. She asked them to come to her office and they followed her down the stairs. Standing in Anna's doorway, Jay said, 'Problem, boss lady?'

'I've told you not to call me that.'

'Sorry.' He gave her the leer. She remembered the message written in garbage. *Don't react, Anna. Don't give him the satisfaction.*

She told them what Pierre had said.

'Reason for that,' Jay said, 'is that I had a little problem that night. I was going to tell you.'

'A problem?'

'Yeah. You see, there's this old lady on West Forty-Fifth Street, Mrs Intile. Sometimes Winny and me take big stuff down to the curb for her—big stuff she's throwin' out, like chairs and what-not.'

'Hold it,' Anna interrupted him. 'It's not our job to take bulk items down to the curb. You know that.'

'Aw, have a heart, Anna. She's an old lady.'

'You don't take money for it, do you? You know that's against the rules.'

Jay held out his empty hands while Winston shook his head vehemently.

'No way,' Jay said. 'We're just trying to help out where we can, improve community relations, so to speak. Do a good deed.'

Anna regarded him dubiously. 'All right, go on.'

'Yeah, well, anyway, this Mrs Intile, she's hangin' out of her apartment window waving a handkerchief when we come around the corner in the truck. Yells down that she's got this dining room chair she wants us to take down to the curb for her. So I go up, and what do you think happens?'

Anna waited.

'I get stuck in the elevator.'

'Stuck?'

'Right you are. Thing just stops, *kerbang. Two hours* I'm stuck on that thing, callin' to the old lady to get the super.'

Anna shook her head, not understanding. 'Why didn't you just call the garage on your cell phone?'

Jay looked sheepish. 'Left it at home.'

Anna looked at Winston. 'And where were you while this was going on?'

'First I was waiting for Jay to come back down. After a while I figured something was wrong, so I went into the building. I pushed the button for the elevator, but nothing happened. Then I heard Jay yelling to Mrs Intile and I figured out the elevator was busted. I called to Jay and he told me he was stuck and I should get the building's super. So I go looking for him. Guy named Gomes, lives in an apartment in the basement. So I go down there. He's not there but his wife is. She tells me Gomes will be right back.'

'So what did you do?'

'I waited.'

'Why didn't you call me?'

Winston frowned. 'No offense, Anna, but what could you have done?'

'I could have called the police, for one thing.'

Winston looked as if this was a radical new

idea. *Idiot,* she thought. 'No one else in the building heard this?'

Winston shook his head. 'Anyway, Jay got the elevator going somehow before Gomes got back.'

'I don't understand why Mrs Intile didn't call the police,' Anna said.

Jay threw out his hands in frustration. 'I kept yellin' to the old lady to call the cops or call the garage, but she must not have understood me or somethin', because she kept yellin', "Hello? Hello?" She's nutty,' he said, twirling his finger next to his head. 'I had a hard enough time just tellin' her my name. All these years we've been carryin' stuff out for her, she never knew our names.

'Anyway,' Jay went on, 'like Winny just said, I kept fiddling with the elevator controls and suddenly it started up again. And you know what the old lady asks me when I get to her floor? "Are you gonna take my chair?" I says, "No, lady, not tonight," and she makes this big stink. I tell ya, no good deed goes unpunished.'

Anna refrained from pointing out that in this case, he hadn't performed a good deed. She just wanted to get these two jerks out of her office. 'Thank you for explaining what happened. And remember, it's not our responsibility to get bulk items down to the curb.'

She saw them out. Turning to go back into her office, she saw Tommy Mulligan jogging toward her across the garage floor.

'Anna,' he said, 'Pierre and I were just getting ready to head out and we found an old lady near the trucks.' He pointed to the long row of white collection vehicles parked slantwise against the garage's back wall.

'An old lady?'

He nodded. 'Wandering around. Said she wanted to talk to "the supervisor of her collection route".'

'Why?'

Tommy gave a deep shrug. 'She wouldn't say. Should I get Allen?'

'No, I'll take care of it. Where is she?'

She followed Tommy across the floor. In the narrow space between two collection trucks, facing partially away from them, stood an elderly woman, petite and frail-looking, in enormous sunglasses and a white turban that made her look like Norma Desmond in *Sunset Boulevard*.

Anna approached her. 'Ma'am,' she said softly so as not to startle her, but the woman jumped anyway.

'Oh, my heavens.' Her voice was low and reedy. 'You nearly gave me a heart attack. Are you the person in charge of this facility?'

'One of them, yes, ma'am. Your collection route is in my section.'

'A woman?'

'That's right. I'm Anna Winthrop. Is there something I can help you with?'

'I'm Alma Intile. I live on—'

'West Forty-Fifth Street.'

'How did you know?'

'I was just speaking with Jay Rapchuck, one of the sanitation workers on your route. He told me about getting stuck in your elevator.'

'Oh, yes,' Mrs Intile said, waving that away. 'He never took my chair.'

This girl's definitely dropped a stitch. 'Why don't you come inside where we can talk?' Anna said, and showed the woman to her office. 'Would you like to sit down?'

'No, I would not. I want Mr Rapchuck to come and get my chair. He said he would.' Mrs Intile tried to place her immense Louis Vuitton knockoff handbag on the edge of Anna's desk but missed. The bag flipped over as it fell, expelling its contents as it hit the floor. 'Oh, dear.'

'Don't worry about it,' Anna said, and knelt to pick everything up. Change purse, hairbrush, facial tissues, a lipstick, a tube of expensive Clinique hand cream, loose change, and at least a dozen pill bottles, which explained a lot.

'Here you are.' Anna smiled warmly as she put the last of the items back in the purse.

'When will he come?' Mrs Intile asked.

'I'm afraid he won't, ma'am.'

'Why not?'

'Ma'am, it's not our job to carry bulk items out of residences. You'll have to arrange for that yourself.'

'But they've done it for me before,' Mrs Intile argued. 'A number of times.'

'Well, they shouldn't have.'

'What am I supposed to do?'

'As I said, you'll have to make your own arrangements to have the chair carried out.'

'Preposterous,' Mrs Intile sputtered. Tucking her bag under her arm, she wandered out of the office toward the exit. When she was out of sight, Jay Rapchuck materialized at Anna's side.

'Was that who I think it was?'

She nodded. 'Mrs Intile.'

He rolled his eyes in exasperation. 'Hey, can't she cut me a break? I was stuck in her elevator.'

'I know, Jay. She's…not rational.'

He grunted and walked away.

ANNA SPENT THE REMAINDER of the morning writing reports, including one about Jay and Winston's mishap on Wednesday night. At lunchtime she decided to walk to a deli she liked around the corner and was heading out when her phone rang. She grabbed it. 'Anna Winthrop.'

'Is this the Sanitation Department?' a soft, wispy female voice asked.

'Yes, who is this speaking, please?'

There was a brief silence, then, 'I...I want to report a dumping.'

Anna looked at the receiver. 'I beg your pardon?'

'Some concrete and construction stuff. Someone dumped it in a vacant lot on my block.'

'Ma'am, to report illegal dumping, you need to call three-one-one.'

'I did. They kept me on hold too long. So I called you.'

'How did you get this number?'

'Someone in my building gave it to me.'

'What is your address, ma'am?'

'I don't want to say exactly. I don't want any trouble. I live on West Fifty-First Street between Broadway and Eighth Avenue.'

Anna sat up straight, remembering the heap of rubble she and Izzy Martinson had inspected on Wednesday.

'So can you do something about it?' the woman asked.

'Absolutely. I just need a little more information. When did this dumping occur?'

'Uh…Tuesday night. Late Tuesday night.'

That fit.

'I was walking Bruiser—he's my Pekingese. The guy dumping the stuff didn't see me, though. Bruiser and I hid behind a telephone pole.'

'What kind of truck was it?'

'A…dump truck, I guess.'

'Did you get the license plate number?'

'No.'

'The make of the truck?'

'No.'

'Color? Words? Markings?'

'No.'

'What did the man look like?'

'It was dark. I couldn't see him very well. But I could tell it was a man.'

Anna tapped her pen on the desk. 'Ma'am, without more information I'm afraid there isn't a lot we can do at this point, but I would appreciate it if you would let me know if you see something like this again.'

'I thought you wanted me to call three-one-one.'

'No, that's all right. Please call me, Anna Winthrop. I'm a section supervisor here at Manhattan Thirteen. That lot is in my section. Just remember, if you see this man dumping again, do not make your presence known.'

'Don't worry, I won't.'

'Take down the license plate number, a description of the vehicle, what kind of material is dumped, and the date and time.'

'Do I get money?'

Anna smiled. 'You mean the Tip Program. You would have to fill out an Illegal Dumping Tip Form, and to do that, you'd have to give us your name. But if you do give us your name and the dumper you reported is apprehended dumping at that location again, you're eligible to receive up to half of any fine collected, or five hundred dollars if there's a criminal conviction and no fine is paid.'

'But what if I give you my name and the guy who's doing the dumping finds out I was the one who reported him and comes after me?'

Anna frowned, surprised. 'That can't happen, ma'am. Your report is kept in complete confidence. How would he find out?'

'I have to think about it.'

'No problem. But either way, if you see the dumping again, you'll give me a call?'

'Yes,' the woman said, and hung up.

Before leaving for the deli, Anna called Izzy Martinson and left him a voicemail message about the woman's call.

When Anna arrived home that afternoon, Isaiah was sitting on the stoop. She hurried toward him, eager to avoid a confrontation with Mrs Dovner.

'Isaiah?'

The eyes he turned up to her were no less than crazed. Gone was the calmness she'd seen in him the previous weeks. Several days' worth of white stubble covered his face, his hair was matted and tangled, and he stank.

'Isaiah, what is it? What's wrong?'

'Anna, I need to speak to you about something. Something urgent.'

'Yes, of course. What—' Her cell phone rang. 'Sorry, one second,' she told him, flipping it open.

'Anna?' It was Kelly. 'Anna, you've got to do something. They've really gone too far.'

'Who?'

'Who do you think? Jay and Winston!'

'What have they done? Wait—hold on, Kelly.' She gave Isaiah a kind smile. 'Stay here and I'll be right back. I need to take this call inside.'

He nodded obediently.

From the sidewalk, Isaiah watched Anna turn and hurry into the brownstone, her cell phone pressed to her ear. Frantically he looked all around him to see if anyone was coming. Not yet. He hoped Anna would come back out soon. He desperately needed to speak to her, get her advice. She was the only one left he could trust. And he didn't know how much longer he could keep her from hearing the voice.

She can't help you, Isaiah! the voice suddenly screamed. *You're goin' to die! You deserve to die!*

He slid his eyes to each side without moving his head, then spun around to face the street. Three cars passed in a row, the middle one a yellow taxi. Its driver was watching him. *Following me,* he thought. *Another one.* Soon they would all be after him. If only he could speak with Anna…

He turned back to face her building. He could see her just inside the door, her back to him, still talking on her cell phone. *Please hurry, Anna.*

I told you, you're wasting your time. She can't help you. You're going to die!

He pressed his hands to his ears but it did no good. The voice grew even louder, shrieking again that it was time for him to die.

Something sharp pricked the skin of his back, just under his right shoulder blade. He let out a yelp of pain and twisted around.

So the voice had caught up with him. 'You're the voice, aren't you?'

'What?'

'Am I going to die?'

'Only if you don't do as I say.'

His gaze fixed on the blade of the knife, Isaiah nodded in resignation. He knew the voice was lying. He waited for instructions.

'We're going into the alley right over here.' Indicating. 'Now walk in front of me, and don't make a sound.'

As Isaiah turned, he felt the stinging pain in his back again. It didn't matter. Soon he would be dead. The voice gave him a shove and he walked to the side of the building and into the narrow alley.

When the alley opened out into a small courtyard, Isaiah hesitated, unsure of what to do. Once again, he awaited instructions.

'Don't stop. Keep walking.' A hand, the one not holding the knife, pointed. 'Over there. Near that wall.'

Slowly Isaiah walked to the right, his feet dragging in the tangled weeds, and stopped at the wall of the building that formed this side of the courtyard.

'Turn around.'

Isaiah obeyed. As he turned, the voice moved behind him, so that now the voice was between Isaiah and the wall.

You're going to die! the voice said from far away, which was odd, because the voice was right behind him.

'Is it time?' Isaiah asked.

'Time for what?'

'Am I going to die now?'

In answer, the voice reached over Isaiah's right shoulder with the hand holding the knife and swept it under Isaiah's neck in one smooth, hard, sharp movement.

Now the voice stood before him. Isaiah felt wetness on his chest and looked down. The front of his shirt was drenched with blood.

His head began to swim. He felt hot, lightheaded. His vision began to dim. 'Am I dying?'

Frowning in puzzlement again, the voice watched Isaiah closely, then gave a simple nod.

Isaiah sank to his knees among the weeds. It was over. He wouldn't have to run from the voice anymore.

His last fleeting thought was that if anyone could have helped him, it was Anna.

FOUR

In her building's vestibule, Anna yelled into her cell phone. 'Kelly, calm down. Just tell me what happened.' She heard Kelly take a deep breath.

'I was in the break room and I passed Winston's chair and he patted my bottom!'

'What!'

'I know, can you believe it? Then he laughed, and so did Jay, and then Jay gave Winston a high five. They're like children. No—worse. You have to do something.'

'I will, Kelly, I promise. First thing tomorrow.'

'No, now, or it won't mean as much. He needs to see how badly he's behaving. This is sexual harassment. Please come back and deal with him.'

Anna gave a little cry of frustration. 'Fine. But I've got something to do first. Give me an hour.' She snapped her phone shut, shot an apprehensive glance at Mrs Dovner's door, and hurried back outside.

Isaiah was gone.

Glancing up and down the street, she shook her head. He would return, she was sure. And when he did, she would ask him what he'd been doing in the alley on Forty-Fourth Street the previous Wednesday night.

With a shrug, she headed back to the garage.

IN HER OFFICE, Anna stood looking at Jay and Winston. Kelly stood beside her.

'Your behavior is unacceptable,' Anna told the two men. 'I'm writing you both up first thing in the morning.'

Jay and Winston both raised their eyebrows in innocent objection. 'What did we do?' Jay demanded.

'You know what you did,' Anna said, feeling like a kindergarten teacher. 'Apologize to Kelly, both of you.'

'I'm sorry,' they muttered in unison, heads down.

Once the men had gone, Brianna came into Anna's office. 'How did it go?' she asked.

'They apologized,' Anna said. 'But I'm still writing them up.'

Kelly looked troubled. 'It's not enough, Anna. I'm thinking of filing a complaint with EOO,' she said, meaning the Equal Opportunity Office.

'I think you should,' Anna said. Brianna was nodding. 'They're not going to stop until they're forced to.'

The two women left Anna's office looking determined. Before Anna could get out again, a call came in from a man at the Citizen Service Center. It had received a report from a member of the mayor's new SCOUT (Street Conditions Observations Unit) Team—fifteen inspectors on three-wheeled scooters whose job it was to report adverse street conditions—about garbage in a vacant lot on West Fifty-First Street.

'...and Allen Schiff, your district chief, told me that's in your section,' the call center representative said.

'Did he also tell you I'm aware of the problem?' Anna said. 'I thought the SCOUT people were supposed to report *street* conditions.'

'Supervisor Winthrop,' the rep said patiently, 'if a team member goes the extra mile and reports debris dumped in a vacant lot, isn't that in the best interest of all of us?'

'Yes, well, as I said, I'm aware of the debris, and so is Enforcement. They're working on trying to catch the illegal dumper, and until they do, we've agreed I won't have my crew clean the lot.'

There was a pause on the line. 'I don't know if that will be acceptable...'

Anna felt the heat of anger rise into her face. 'Acceptable to whom?'

'To the team.'

That did it. 'Frankly, sir, I don't care if that's acceptable or not. We're on it. You just take care of your potholes.'

She ended the call, fuming, and gazed across her office at the framed photograph of the mayor hanging on the back wall. She often thought that if he would let the city's agencies do their jobs, and stop instituting new and improved programs that duplicated the agencies' work, everyone would be a lot better off.

She headed back home. As she turned the corner on to her block, she wondered if Isaiah had come back. He hadn't. What, she wondered, had he wanted to speak to her about?

WHEN SHE ARRIVED AT the garage the next morning, Brianna told Anna not one but two cops were waiting for her in her office. 'What's up with you, girl?' Brianna asked, only half joking. Anna shrugged.

One of the cops, tall and lanky with red hair under his cap, turned to her, his expression grave. Beside him stood a female cop, petite with olive skin, attractively exotic features, and a lot of dark hair stuffed up under her cap. 'Anna Winthrop?' she said.

Anna nodded, indicated two chairs facing her desk. They remained standing.

'Ms Winthrop,' the female said, 'I'm Detective Rinaldi, and this is Detective Roche.' He gave a curt nod.

'What can I do for you?'

'We're not sure there's anything you can do,' Rinaldi said. 'We're investigating the murder of a Mrs Maria Trujillo on West Forty-Third. We've learned from a Mrs Iris Dovner, who I believe is a neighbor of yours—' Anna couldn't believe her ears. Mrs Dovner again! '—that you are acquainted with a homeless man by the name of Isaiah. We don't know his last name.'

Now it was Anna's turn to frown. 'What does he have to do with this?'

Rinaldi said, 'He's a person of interest in this case. A number of people have reported seeing him in the neighborhood.'

Anna remembered Brianna's story of seeing Isaiah running through the alley. But she said, 'You don't think—*Isaiah?* He's the sweetest, gentlest soul you could ever hope to meet. What possible connection could he have had to Maria, anyway?'

'That's not for you to ask, Ms Winthrop,' Roche said, finding his voice at last.

'You still haven't answered our question,' Rinaldi said, looking impatient. 'Do you or do you not know this man?'

'Yes, I do. He comes around and I give him my cans and bottles.'

Roche had opened a small notebook and was jotting something in it.

'When does he "come around"?' he asked.

'No particular time. Once or twice a week, I guess.'

Rinaldi didn't seem to like the vagueness of this answer. She inhaled strongly through flared nostrils. 'We are asking,' she said, removing a man's wallet from her back pocket and taking out a business card, 'that you contact us immediately the next time you see him. And you are not to tell him that we are looking for him.'

Rinaldi held out the card. Anna found herself not wanting to take it, but forced herself. 'All right,' she managed. 'But I'm telling you, this is ridic—'

'You understand?' Roche said.

Pursing her lips, Anna gave one nod.

Roche flipped his notebook shut and followed Rinaldi out of the office.

Anna stared at the corkboard. She had to warn Isaiah. Which was going to be difficult, since she had no idea when he would appear in her neighborhood next.

Going home to find him didn't make much

sense, she knew that, but she had to try. If the cops got hold of him, he wouldn't stand a chance.

As she approached her building, Anna saw Mrs Dovner standing at the curb in front, as if waiting for her. The older woman wore a violet housecoat, an apple-green cardigan, and flip-flops with plastic flowers on them. When she saw Anna, she turned toward her and waited, her hands on her hips.

'I saw your bum again,' she said with an expression of repulsion, as if she knew why Anna had come home.

Perhaps, for once, Mrs Dovner could actually prove useful. 'When was this?'

'Yesterday,' Mrs Dovner answered suspiciously. 'Yesterday afternoon.'

'Where?'

'Where do you think? Right here!'

'And did you see where he went?'

Mrs Dovner let out a snort of extreme exasperation. 'Listen to you, Miss Innocent. You know perfectly well where he went.'

'What? What are you talking about? The last time I saw him was yesterday afternoon. He said he wanted to talk to me about something, but when I came back outside, he was gone.'

'Of course he was gone!' Mrs Dovner shrieked.

'That's because you told him he could sleep in our courtyard again. Don't think I don't know about that.'

So she did know. 'What makes you think he was going to sleep in the courtyard?'

'Are you dense or just pretending? Because as soon as you went inside, he and the other man headed right into the alley. I was coming back from shopping and saw the whole thing. This time *I'm* going to call the police. Wait till they hear that now you're letting *two* bums sleep in our courtyard.'

'What did this other man look like?' Anna asked.

Mrs Dovner shrugged her shoulders violently at the silliness of the question. 'I don't know—like a man!'

'Young? Old? Fat? Thin? Tall? Short?'

'I don't know. I was just turning on to the block and I can't see that far even with my glasses. But it was a man, that much I know.' Mrs Dovner smiled in triumph. 'Where are you going?'

Anna was already starting down the narrow alley between their building and the one to its left. Her foot caught in the tough weeds sprouting from cracks and holes in the concrete. She yanked it free and hurried to the back.

She couldn't remember the last time she'd been

back here. Everyone referred to it as the court-yard, but it was really just a space that existed because the building didn't extend all the way to the backs of the buildings on Forty-Fourth Street as its neighboring buildings did. The sunless square felt cold and claustrophobic. High above, somewhere in a steely gray sky, a plane droned.

More of the same weeds that tangled in the alley grew here, partially hiding dented soda cans, crumpled brown bags, and an old rolled-up carpet. She looked up. Seemingly hundreds of windows looked down on this space from the four buildings. Many of the apartments' owners had blanked out the windows with shades or curtains, and Anna, whose apartment was at the front of the building, couldn't blame them.

Isaiah may have been here, but he was gone now. She turned to leave, her gaze passing over the rolled carpet under the weeds.

She stopped. It wasn't a carpet at all. She took two steps closer. No, it wasn't a carpet, but a man—sleeping, it looked like. There were his dirty gray trousers, his blue poplin windbreaker... Now her gaze traveled to the man's face and her breath caught in her throat.

It was Isaiah. He lay with his head slumped against her building. His peaceful expression was obscenely at odds with the slice that opened his throat from ear to ear, like a huge displaced smile. From this gash a prodigious amount of blood had flowed, staining Isaiah's white T-shirt a deep crimson.

Vomit rose into her throat. Turning suddenly, she bent and retched violently.

'You're not going to find him here now,' came Mrs Dovner's voice from behind her.

'Mrs Dovner, don't—'

But the older woman had already stepped far into the space and stood only feet from Isaiah's body. Knitting her white brows, she bent forward slightly at the waist, trying to make out what it was. Then her eyes grew round, her jaw dropped, and she brought a crumpled tissue she'd been holding to her mouth. With frantic, jerky movements, she ran back through the alley toward the street. It was only when she was out of sight that Anna heard her high-pitched shriek.

ANNA HAD NEVER SEEN Mrs Dovner's apartment. Jammed to overflowing with heavy furniture of dark polished wood, every surface covered in doilies, knickknacks, and framed photographs, it was a cleaning lady's nightmare. Then again, Anna was pretty sure Mrs Dovner would never have allowed anyone else in to clean.

Mrs Dovner sat beside Anna on a loveseat upholstered in chintz in a wild pattern of crimson cabbage roses and green vines. Actually, Mrs Dovner had positioned herself as far away from Anna as possible, which was fine by Anna, because Mrs Dovner reeked of patchouli, like some demented geriatric hippie.

On a sofa facing the two women sat officers Rinaldi and Roche. Once again, Rinaldi had taken over, asking the questions while her partner took notes.

'Now, Mrs Dovner,' Rinaldi said, 'tell us again about the two men you saw going into the courtyard yesterday.'

Mrs Dovner cast her eyes heavenward while putting out her hands in supplication. Her right hand still clutched the crumpled tissue. 'Why are you upsetting me like this? I've already told you everything there is to tell. There's no more.'

Roche piped in gently, 'Please tell us again.'

Mrs Dovner took a deep breath. 'I was coming back from shopping. At the Food Emporium on Tenth Avenue. I bought milk, liverwurst, and some rye bread. I don't eat much and I'm certainly not going to buy so much that I need one of those Spanish boys to bring up my groceries whenever they feel like it and then ask me for a huge tip.'

Rinaldi said, 'When did you first see Isaiah?'

'As I was coming around the corner from Tenth on to this block.'

'And what exactly did you see?'

Mrs Dovner threw a disdainful glance at Anna, her gaze traveling down her body in clear resentment that she occupied half of her loveseat. 'This one. I saw this one.'

'Ms Winthrop.'

'Mm.'

'And what was she doing?'

'She was standing on the steps, talking to the bum.'

'Then what happened?'

'This one must have gotten a call on her cell phone. I saw her take something out of her pocket. I assume it was a cell phone.'

'Yes?' Rinaldi prompted.

'She said something to the bum and then went inside.'

'And what did the—*Isaiah* do?'

'Nothing. He stood there. Which didn't please me, let me tell you, because I certainly wasn't going to come any closer until he cleared out.'

'And did he finally move?'

'Of course he moved. When the other man came.'

'Tell us about this other man.'

'I couldn't see him from so far away. I told this one that.'

'Where did he come from?'

'The other side of the street. He just kind of… appeared.'

'And he approached Isaiah and what happened?'

'The man put his hand on the bum's back and said something to him. Then they both went into the alley.'

'Did you hear any of what the man said?'

'No, of course not. I was way at the end of the block.'

'What did you do then?'

'Now that the bum was gone, I walked to the building and came inside.'

Rinaldi said, 'Now, you told us that Isaiah has gone into the back before. To sleep, you said.'

Mrs Dovner said, 'I assume that's what he was doing back there. Not much else to do. This one—' she turned to Anna '—encouraged him to sleep there.'

'Mrs Dovner,' Anna said impatiently, 'I did not *encourage* him. I only—'

'That's enough,' Rinaldi said, putting up a hand. 'The point is, he'd gone back there before.'

'Yes,' Mrs Dovner replied, 'many times.'

Now Rinaldi turned to Anna. 'Have *you* ever seen Isaiah with this man before?'

'No, never.'

'With anyone?'

Anna shook her head.

'Any idea who it could have been?'

'Not a clue.'

'Anything else you can tell us about Isaiah? His last name? Where he lived? Anything?'

Anna was embarrassed that she had to say no. 'He was a sweet, harmless man who came around a couple of times a week with his shopping cart, and some of us on the street gave him our cans and bottles.'

'Harmless,' Mrs Dovner muttered. 'Hardly. A blight on the neighborhood.'

They all ignored her.

'He never told you anything about himself?' Roche asked Anna.

'No—no, wait. The second-to-last last time I saw him, he said he was doing really well. He seemed pleased. And he looked different. He was clean, nicely dressed. He didn't have his shopping cart. He said, "No cans or bottles anymore."'

Roche's brows lowered over his eyes. '"Really well"—what did he mean by that?'

'I asked him what had happened, but he didn't answer. He just walked away.'

'When was this?' Rinaldi asked.

Anna thought. 'Last Wednesday.'

Roche looked at Rinaldi. 'Trujillo was killed that night.'

Rinaldi nodded and they both rose.

'So what are you going to do?' Anna asked, also standing.

The officers looked at her as if she'd been impertinent. 'We'll conduct an investigation,' Rinaldi said. 'Though it doesn't look like there's much more to learn.'

'What do you mean, much more to learn? Maybe someone in one of these buildings saw something. A lot of windows look down on the courtyard. Have you thought of that?'

Roche held up his notebook. 'Already on the to-do list.'

'And we don't know why he was killed,' Anna went on.

They waited for her to explain.

'For example, was he robbed?' Even as she said it, she knew how silly it sounded.

'Robbed?' Roche said. 'Of what?'

'Another reason, then. There's got to have been a reason.'

'Of course there was a reason,' Rinaldi said. 'I can tell you that in most of these cases, it's about drugs.'

'What do you mean, "these cases"?'

'Homeless killing homeless. Happens all the time.'

'What makes you think Isaiah was into drugs? He never seemed that way to me.'

'It's easy enough to find out,' Rinaldi said. 'The

body's already been taken away and the medical examiners will be able to tell from the autopsy.'

She and Roche turned and started for the door. They looked unutterably bored.

A fury suddenly rose in Anna and she blurted out, 'I hope it won't put you out too much.'

Rinaldi spun around. 'What's that supposed to mean?'

Mrs Dovner was looking at Anna as if she were insane.

'It's just that you don't seem to care. A man has died. Been murdered.'

'Who said we don't care?' Rinaldi said. 'We're here, aren't we? We're going to canvass the residents of all the buildings that look out on the back. What more do you want?'

Anna couldn't think of a response. She shook her head, her gaze cast downward at Mrs Dovner's pink-and-gray Oriental rug. Then she thought of something. 'Is he still a "person of interest" in Maria Trujillo's murder?'

Roche gave her a pitying look. 'Just because he's dead—been murdered himself—doesn't mean he didn't kill her. Why don't you just leave all of this to us?'

She half expected him to pat her on the head. She followed them out of Mrs Dovner's apartment to the foyer.

'One more thing,' Rinaldi said, turning. 'If you

see anyone else going into the back, call us. You have our cards.' She looked up at Roche. 'They really shouldn't be able to get back there. Make a note to speak to the landlord.' She turned to Anna. 'What's your landlord's name?'

'Vickery. Asa Vickery. Good luck getting anywhere with him.'

As if not hearing this remark, Rinaldi and Roche went out and down the steps to their patrol car.

'Happy now?'

Anna turned around. Mrs Dovner stood just outside her door, a nasty smile on her face.

'Happy about what?' Anna replied, eyes narrowed warningly.

'It's your fault he's dead. If you hadn't let him sleep back there, he'd still be alive.' The smiled widened.

Anna felt herself suddenly grow hot and advanced menacingly on Mrs Dovner, whose smile evaporated as she turned with surprising speed, ran into her apartment, and slammed the door.

Two HOURS LATER, Anna sat in her living room with a cup of tea, watching a soap opera without seeing it. She'd called Allen Schiff and told him she wouldn't be coming back to work today.

There was one sharp rap on her door. She got up and looked through the peephole. It was Mr

Vickery, looking angry. Inwardly groaning, she opened the door.

Mr Vickery, a small, painfully thin man in his late sixties, had his hand on his completely bald head, a gesture that indicated he was furious.

Anna forced a smile. 'Hello, Mr Vickery. Would you like to come in?'

He didn't respond to that. 'I've just come from Iris Dovner. I know all about what happened. I should evict you.'

'Evict me! Why?'

'You know why. You've been letting that hobo sleep in my courtyard. What's the matter with you? Why would you do such a thing?'

'Why wouldn't I?'

This only seemed to make Mr Vickery madder. 'You think you can do anything you want because you work for the city. That's it, isn't it?'

'What are you talking about?'

'You…liberals,' he spat out. 'Bleeding heart, ready to help anyone. Easy for you. You don't own this building.'

Anna put her hands on her hips. 'What do you care if someone sleeps in your courtyard? What possible difference could it make to you?'

'I don't need the cops all over me, asking me questions.'

Then she understood. She gazed down her nose

at him. 'Why, because you don't want them looking too closely at your buildings?'

He narrowed his eyes and gave her a sideways look. 'Why wouldn't I?'

She shrugged. 'No idea. But you clearly don't. Some building code violations, perhaps?'

His hand went back to his hairless pate. 'I'm not going to say it again. If you tell another of those hobos that he can use my yard for a flop house, I'll have you evicted.'

She bent forward so that her eyes were level with his and only inches away. 'And if I find any violations in your buildings—and believe me, I'm going to look—I'll see you in court or worse.'

In actuality she had no intention of looking for violations or doing anything else having to do with Mr Vickery, but her threat had the desired effect. Like a vampire coming face-to-face with a cross, he shrank back, practically hissing. Then, wordlessly, he turned and headed for the stairs.

She watched him go, wondering now just what, exactly, he was afraid the police might find. But that didn't concern her. Finding out who killed Isaiah did.

FIVE

WEDNESDAY WAS A relatively quiet day, for which Anna was grateful. It seemed a moment didn't pass during which she didn't think about poor Isaiah.

She hadn't heard from Santos since their date on Friday. Had he been turned off by her curiosity about Maria Trujillo's murder? By their vastly different backgrounds? She hoped not. She liked him very much. Should she call him? She would rather he called, but...

She spent most of the day at her desk, catching up—making note of the number and types of summonses issued in her section since the beginning of the month, finishing a report on the condition of the vehicles used by her crew.

On Thursday, her day off, she forced herself to get out, taking a book and a bag lunch to Central Park. In the afternoon she went to a high-priced shop on Madison Avenue that her mother liked and bought some expensive stationery for her birthday. Anna was not looking forward to Saturday.

Returning home late in the afternoon, she

averted her gaze from the alley beside the building that led to the courtyard in the back.

Friday's highlight was when Art and Terrence came to see her after their route and asked her to come and see something they'd brought back.

At the side of the garage floor sat five large clear-plastic bags. Immediately she saw that the insides were soaked with blood.

'Should I open one up?' Art asked. When Anna nodded, the handsome seventy-five-year-old reached into the pocket of his uniform and brought out a pocket knife. He slashed open one of the bags and its contents poured out: used hypodermic needles, bloody gauze pads, soiled bandages, IV tubing, and tongue depressors.

'Whoa,' Art said, standing and moving away from the bag. 'Stinks.'

'Where did you get these?' Anna asked them.

'Place on Park Avenue between Fifty-Fifth and Fifty-Sixth.'

'Number four-twenty-four,' Terrence said. 'Fancy apartment building.'

'With a fancy doctor's office in it, right?' Anna asked.

'You got it,' Art said. 'On the first floor. A Dr Sheldon Warner, plastic surgeon.'

'But we don't know for sure that's where these

came from,' Terrence said fairly. 'They were in the Dumpster.'

Art gave him a look that said, 'Gimme a break.'

'He's right,' Anna said. 'We'll find out for sure.'

Just before the end of Anna's shift, Santos called and they made a date for the following night. When she hung up she was smiling.

LATE SATURDAY MORNING, Anna steered her red Mini Cooper from Route 9A on to the Cross Bronx Expressway. Though her older brother and two younger sisters all lived in New York City, Anna had found it was easiest to make the forty-five-minute drive to Greenwich on her own. Her two sisters never failed to seize an opportunity to lecture her about her 'bizarre' career choice.

Beth, though the youngest at twenty-six, had been convinced for as long as Anna could remember that she knew what was best for everyone. It didn't help that she had just joined Schutz Fine Kovner, one of Manhattan's most prestigious law firms, and *the* pre-eminent firm for immigration law.

Anna merged on to I-95.

Gloria, older than Beth by two years, was even worse, possessing none of Beth's tact. Only a year Anna's junior and similar in appearance, she identified strongly with Anna. The last time Anna had seen her, Gloria said it pained her to think that in a year she would be finished with her medical residency and ready to join a practice, while Anna was still 'floundering' in her 'work for the city'. Gloria had never been able to actually speak the words 'New York Sanitation Department'.

With a pang in the center of her stomach, Anna remembered that Gloria's wedding to Donald, a surgeon, would take place in only two weeks. She would start mentally preparing for that, she decided, once she got today out of the way.

The only member of the family who made these visits bearable—no, more than bearable— was Will, dear Will, the eldest of the siblings at thirty-one. Though his profession was as lofty as their sisters', he accepted Anna unconditionally and always had.

Getting on to the Hutchinson Parkway, she girded her emotional loins.

PULLING ON TO THE LONG brick drive of her parents' seven-bedroom, seven-and-a-half bath, 15,000-square-foot, ivy-covered fieldstone mansion, Anna thought of Santos. What would he think of this? What would he think to learn she had grown up here, played hide-and-seek in the endless hallways and closets, built snowmen on the back terrace while one of the maids prepared hot chocolate.

But how far would her relationship with Santos go, anyway? Though they'd gone out only once, she liked him, liked him a lot. More than any man she'd met in a long time, that was for sure.

She'd told him about Greenwich, but would he be prepared for this? She remembered she had a date with him that night and smiled.

As she pulled up in front of the house, her father and Donald, Gloria's fiancé, emerged from the six-car garage, also built of fieldstone, that stood at a right angle to the house. Seeing her, they walked over to the car. She grabbed her bag from the passenger seat and got out to greet them.

Jeff Winthrop, handsome as ever in his trademark khakis, navy polo shirt, and boat shoes without socks, captured her in a tight hug. Despite his seventy-one years, he was in superb shape. She felt the hardness of his chest muscles through his shirt.

She breathed in his familiar scent of cigars and 4711 Cologne. 'Hello, Daddy.'

He released her, stood back to look at her. 'So good to see you, darling.' He was smiling fiercely, a gleam of mischief in those brilliant blue eyes set off all the more by his closely cropped white hair. He turned to Donald, who was just catching up.

'Anna,' the younger man greeted her, suddenly remembering to give her a kiss on the cheek. Sweet, clueless Donald. Beth maintained that Gloria would never have given him a second thought if he weren't so handsome, with his blond hair, jewel-green eyes, and perfect features. She said it was as if God had given him good looks and then gotten tired, forgetting to give him a personality. 'My sweet nerd' was how Gloria referred to him with her sisters. However, Gloria pointed out, her sweet nerd was, after all, a highly successful surgeon, and a kind man who loved Gloria more than she had a right to be loved.

'Come into the house,' her father said, taking Anna's hand. 'We need help cheering up your mother. You know how she gets on her birthdays.' They entered the marble foyer with its sweeping double staircase. 'Says she feels as old as dirt.'

Anna rolled her eyes. 'Sixty-one-year-old dirt. That's hardly old, especially these days.'

'Tell your mother that,' he said, leading the way into the kitchen, the family's favorite gathering place.

The kitchen actually consisted of two rooms— the vast kitchen proper, with its expanses of granite countertops and many softly gleaming stainless steel appliances, and a great room adjacent to it. Tildy had furnished this room with overstuffed chairs, sofas, loveseats, and a sprinkling of low tables. Tildy herself sat at the end of one of the loveseats, laughing as she listened to Beth, who was gesticulating wildly. When Anna entered the room, Beth looked over, her shoulder-length chestnut hair swinging, and a look of pure pity came into her dark brown eyes.

'Anna…' she said, hurrying over to take her older sister into her arms. 'How are you?' she asked, sounding as if someone had died.

The feeling of dread Anna'd had in the car had returned. 'I'm—terrific!' she said, far too enthusiastically, and inwardly kicked herself. 'Why wouldn't I be?'

Beth gave her a knowing little smile, as if to say, Naughty girl.

'Yes, my daughter *is* terrific.' Tildy rose from the loveseat and came over for her own hug. 'As always. You look wonderful, dear. Thanks for coming to my dirt party.'

'Oh, Mother!' This was said by Gloria, tall and elegant in a simple linen sundress, her blonde hair falling loosely down her back. She gave Anna a kiss, then stood back to study their mother. 'Have you ever seen better-looking dirt? Look at her!'

She was right, of course. Tildy was and always had been a beauty, and she knew it. Was that why she joked about her age—fishing for compliments, for assurances? Anna had always suspected so.

Tildy wore tan slacks, a white silk blouse, and no jewelry. She never wore jewelry. The story in the family was that when Tildy was a little girl, her father caught her playing dress-up in her mother's jewelry box. He'd swept her up in his arms, twirled her around, and said, 'It's a sin for a girl as beautiful as you to wear jewelry. There's no improving upon perfection.' Whether this story was true or not, no one had ever seen Tildy wear even a wristwatch.

'Come over here and talk to me,' she said softly to Anna, and led her over to one of the bow windows overlooking the back terrace.

'Gloria's in rare form today,' Tildy whispered. Anna glanced over at her sister, who was watching them. Their eyes met and Anna turned quickly back to her mother. 'About what?'

'About *you.*'

'Oh, no.'

'Oh, yes. She's been on about some friend of hers with a job for you.'

'What? I have a job I like very much, thank you.'

'I know,' Tildy said. 'Tell your sister that.'

As if Anna hadn't told her countless times before. She decided to take the bull—her sister—by her horns. Better to get it over with. She walked over to her.

'So,' she said, forcing a smile, 'Mother tells me you've got a job for me.'

Donald had sat down in a nearby chair and Gloria gave him a frown, as if it were he who had spilled the beans. Then she looked over at her mother, but Tildy was now busying herself at the kitchen counter, helping the maid arrange fresh fruit on a platter.

Gloria faced Anna with a purposeful expression. 'I do,' she said, straightening her shoulders. 'That is, a friend of mine does.'

'Gloria,' Anna said patiently, 'as I've told you more times than I can count, I have a job. A job I like.'

At this, Gloria lost it. 'Oh, for Pete's sake, Anna, stop pretending. It's gotten real old, hasn't it?' She looked around for support, but everyone seemed to be looking down. She persisted nevertheless. 'Let's be honest. You did this as a rebellion thing. Heaven knows what you had to be rebellious about—it must have been some phase you were going through. Whatever it was, you actually went through with it and now you won't admit it was a mistake.'

'Embarrassed?' Anna's smile was long gone.

'I'm a garage supervisor. I worked hard to get to where I am.'

'Where you are,' Gloria repeated, giving Anna a pathetic look. 'Where you are is a dirty little building full of garbage.'

'There is almost never any garbage in our facility,' Anna corrected her. 'We have trucks, plows, mechanical brooms...the garbage is taken to transfer stations.'

Gloria just glared at her, appalled. 'Aren't you embarrassed? Look at us! Beth, who's just joined one of the top law firms in New York. Me—in a year I'll be joining a medical practice. Will—'

'What about me?' Will, tall and handsome in jeans and a moss-green sweater over a T-shirt, held his wife Lisa's hand on one side and two-year-old Nina's on the other. Lisa and Nina looked bewildered. Glancing quickly around, Anna saw that everyone else looked positively alarmed.

Gloria didn't seem to care. 'You're an investment banker,' she said to her brother.

'Yes,' he said with a perplexed smile, 'I am. You're just figuring that out?'

'Don't be foolish,' Gloria scolded him. 'I'm not joking.' She turned back to Anna. 'We've tried to help you before and you've thrown our help back in our faces, but we're not ready to give up on you.

Good sisters and brothers don't give up on one another. So I'm trying again. I have a friend—'

'That alone is surprising,' Will said, throwing an arm around Anna and sweeping her out of the room. It took her breath away. She laughed, gave him a hug when they were safely away. Then she looked up into his wise old features and burst into tears.

'Not surprising,' he said, taking her back into his arms. 'Why do you do it, Anna?'

'Do what?' she said, her voice muffled in his sweater.

'Subject yourself to this?'

'Because this is my family,' she replied, wanting him to understand. 'They're supposed to—'

'Accept you are who you are?'

'That's right.'

'I don't know what families you've been looking at, but I don't know many like that, if any.'

'*You* do.'

'Do what?'

'Accept me as I am.'

'That's right, I do,' he said, feigning surprise, and gave her a big white-toothed smile. 'Let's find somewhere to talk.'

'Where?'

'Hm, don't know,' Will said, 'this house is so small. Come on.'

He reminded her of when they were kids, the way he bounded up the curving staircase ahead of her. At the top, on the landing, he beckoned her to follow and ducked into their father's study. He threw himself down on one of the tufted leather Chesterfield sofas, and she plunked down next to him, resting her head against his shoulder.

'Now,' he said, 'what's Gloria on about?'

She told him what their sister had said.

He rolled his eyes, gave his head a little shake. 'Poor, silly Gloria. She means well…and those are the worst kind. Now *you* tell me, how are things going in your life?'

She told him how happy she was at the garage, how good she felt about having been promoted to supervisor, but she also admitted that sometimes she did wonder if Sanitation was the right place for her, if she was in a position to ever meet her special someone. Then she told him about Santos.

'There you are, then!' he declared happily. 'Your special someone. A cop. Whoa. Wait till Gloria hears that.' He laughed good-naturedly and Anna gave him a playful swat on the head.

'Actually, that's terrific,' he said. 'This Santos sounds like a good guy. What else is new and exciting in your life?'

At that moment a picture of Isaiah, lying among

the weeds with his throat slit, flashed into her mind and she shivered.

'What is it? You look as if you've seen a ghost.'

'Close,' she said, and told him the whole story—Isaiah telling her things were better, then asking urgently to speak to her…the police saying he was a person of interest in Maria Trujillo's murder…Mrs Dovner making trouble and seeing Isaiah with another man…and finally finding the poor man dead—murdered—among the weeds.

'Sounds as if you'd grown fond of this man.'

She'd never thought of it that way. 'Yes, I suppose I had. I feel so guilty. He needed help and came to me, and I—'

'Took Kelly's call instead,' he finished for her. 'Because if you'd listened to him first, told Kelly you'd call her right back, he'd be alive. That's not what I think,' he hastened to add, 'but you do. Am I right?'

She looked into his kind face and burst into fresh tears.

'Oh, now,' he said, tightening his arm around her shoulders. 'You couldn't possibly have known what would happen if you spoke to Kelly first. It was a call from work—you had to deal with it. You've got to let go of that guilt because it's just not your fault.'

She gave a little nod and sniffled. 'I don't know

what's the matter with me today. Yes, I do. It's being here, and Gloria, and…oh, I don't know.'

'About what?'

She hadn't put these thoughts into words, not even to herself, not until now. 'Isaiah needed me in those moments before he was killed, and now he needs me again. The police don't care, not really. Oh, they'll go through the motions, follow procedure, but they'll hit the dead ends they already know are there and move on. Then no one will know why Isaiah died. Not unless I do something.'

He looked at her in surprise. 'You? What do you mean? What can you do?'

'The police never even said anything about trying to find out where he lived.'

'I thought you said he was homeless?'

'Everyone lives somewhere. Shelters, those encampments the city is always trying to tear down. There's got to be someone at one of these places who knew him, who can shed some light on what really happened to him.'

He was still watching her curiously. 'So what are you going to do?'

She hadn't known until this minute. 'I'm going to try to find out.'

'You mean, who murdered him?'

'Well…yes.'

For a moment he didn't speak. Then he said, 'Just be careful, Anna. I know, you work for the Sanitation Department, you used to haul garbage, you're tough and all that. But be careful.'

'You don't think I should do it?'

'I never said that.'

'Then what do you think?'

'I think, dear sister,' he said, his gaze meeting hers, 'that you should follow your heart. It's the best one in the family.'

She smiled. She could always count on Will.

'And now we'd better get back downstairs,' he said, 'before Gloria comes after us.'

She laughed. 'I must look terrible.'

'Not if you like running mascara.'

'Go down and tell them I'm coming,' she said, and at that moment their father's voice came to them from the foyer.

'Anna! Will! Birthday cake!'

'Don't be too long,' Will said with a smile, and left the room. Anna remembered there was a bathroom off her father's study. She went in and closed the door.

She looked in the mirror and had to laugh. Blotches of mascara dotted her lower eyelids, and her lipstick was nearly gone. She'd left her purse in the kitchen. She'd put on more makeup downstairs. In the meantime, she washed her face with soap and water, dried it with a towel from the rack, and opened the medicine cabinet over the vanity, looking for a comb.

There was no comb, but there were a lot of pill bottles, a surprising number of them. They worried her at first, all those bottles, but then she reminded herself that her father was, after all, seventy-one years old, and some medications were to be expected. Idly she began to read the labels, taking in the strange names.

'Anna!' It was Will this time. 'Coming?'

She opened the door and called out, 'Coming!' Then she raced across the study to the foyer and down the stairs, feeling better than she had felt in this house for a long time.

IT WAS NEARLY SIX when she reached the parking garage a block from her apartment where she kept her car. She hurried home and got ready for her date with Santos. At seven, he rang the bell.

She blinked. He was in uniform. Smiling, she sidled up to him. 'Oh, Officer,' she said in her best Mae West voice, 'you positively arrest me.'

He gave her a kiss on the cheek and walked wearily past her into the apartment. 'Got anything cold to drink?'

'Sure,' she said, and got him a Diet Coke from the fridge. 'Sorry—I don't have any beer.'

'This is perfect,' he said, sinking into the sofa and putting his hat on the side table. 'What a day.'

The police dispatcher had called Santos to a ten-floor apartment building at Fifty-Sixth and Madison. A crowd had gathered in front of the building, looking up. When he followed their gazes he saw a young man in his underwear sitting on the edge of the roof with both feet hanging over. A young woman—the man's sister, the police later learned—was lying on her stomach trying to convince her brother not to jump. Santos radioed back that the man was a confirmed jumper and asked for help. The Emergency Service Unit arrived a few minutes later and set up an inflatable mattress on the sidewalk. In the meantime, Santos had hurried to the roof. It was up to him to keep the man on the ledge.

'It was really only a few minutes,' he said, 'but it felt like hours. I had to get him to believe he had a lot to live for. He had psychiatric problems, obviously. I talked to him, kept him distracted.'

Santos had lain on his stomach next to the man's sister and crawled slowly toward him. The man started to get hysterical, and in that moment Santos grabbed his arm and pulled him away from the edge. Then more cops rushed out on to the roof to help.

'You saved his life,' Anna said beside him. 'That's got to feel awfully good.'

'Yeah, it does,' he admitted. Then he grinned. 'Funny thing happened later in the day, though— funny to me, at least. This man on Forty-Fourth is in the bathroom, working on his toupee, and his can of hairspray is defective, so for some reason he empties it into the toilet. When he's done, his wife goes in, sits on the toilet, and lights up a cigarette. A spark falls into the bowl and—*boom!*' He was laughing. 'I got called in to investigate the explosion and get the poor woman to the emergency room. Blew up half the bathroom.'

Anna couldn't help laughing, too. 'That poor woman. Maybe that will convince her to stop smoking.'

He took a swig of his soda, then grew serious. 'You wanna mix a little business with pleasure?'

'What does that mean?'

'I was walking past your garage today and this old man came up to me. Said he lived across the street and had a few complaints. I tried to tell him to call three-one-one, but he started rattling off his "few" complaints, which were definitely more than a few.'

'Like what?' Anna asked, not sure she wanted to know.

'Let's see. Loud radio music coming from the garage...'

'Not on my shift. I don't allow that and neither do Hal or Gerry.'

'OK, OK,' he said, placating her. 'Don't get defensive. I'm just telling you what he said.'

She waited to hear more.

He went on, 'Then there was the loud noise, of course, especially the beeping when the trucks back up. Guy says he never gets a good night's sleep. Then there's the stink—'

'What stink? Santos, that garage does not stink. Our trucks are clean and there's only garbage in the garage if a truck comes in before it goes out to the transfer station.'

He shrugged. 'Maybe he's got an extra-sensitive sense of smell.'

'Maybe.'

'Oh,' he said, remembering another one. 'He saw a rat.'

She shrugged. 'Welcome to New York City. You know, I don't think I want to hear any more about this. I should have known not to mix business with pleasure, as you put it.'

He gave one nod. 'Fair enough. By the way, our friend Mrs Dovner was outside. I said hello, but I don't think she remembered me.'

'Oh, she remembered you all right. She doesn't

forget anything. She's probably mad at you because you didn't stop me from speaking to Isaiah after she reported me.'

'How could I have stopped you?'

'I know, it's crazy. But I know her. She reports me to you; Isaiah shows up again anyway; then he gets himself killed in our courtyard. It's all our fault, you see.'

He took a long swig from the can. 'That makes absolutely no sense at all.'

'Doesn't matter.'

'Maybe if we figured out who killed the poor guy, she'd like us better,' he said.

'She couldn't care less who killed him.' She looked at him. 'Do you think you will? Figure out who killed him, I mean?'

'Doubt it. Highly unlikely.'

'Why is that?' she asked, not surprised but wanting him to explain.

'We canvassed all four buildings that look out on the lot. No one saw anything. Most people don't even use those windows. Not much of a view.'

'Anything else you can tell me?'

'We've got time of death now. Best guess is around three o'clock on Wednesday.'

Right around the time he asked to speak to her, she realized with a sharp pang.

'And that's it?' she asked after a moment. 'You

speak to the people in the four buildings, you figure out the time of death, and that's it?'

'What else would you like us to do?' he asked patiently.

She remembered her conversation with Will earlier in the day. 'Have you tried to figure out where he lived? Shelters, that kind of thing?'

'Anna, how could we possibly figure that out? Do you know how many shelters there are in this city?'

She gave him an angry look. 'Yes, of course. But how many are in this neighborhood, near here? What about food pantries, soup kitchens?'

He didn't answer, just looked down.

'I know,' she said. 'It's not just you. Of course the cops could take Isaiah's picture around to the shelters, soup kitchens, and food pantries in this area, find out if anyone knew him, if anyone had seen anyone arguing with him, that kind of thing. But no one wants to bother. He's just some dirty old homeless man.'

'Anna, that's not fair.'

'No, it's not fair, is it? Not fair to Isaiah. Who cares who killed the bum? No one cared about him when he was alive, why should anyone care about him now that he's dead? The police have a lot of bigger fish to fry, isn't that right?'

'Actually,' he said, 'we do.'

'There you are, then,' she said without rancor. She glanced at the clock on the kitchen wall: seven forty-five. 'Hey, you hungry?'

'Yeah,' he said, but didn't move, clearly thinking. At last he looked up at her. 'You're going to do this, aren't you?'

'Do what?' she asked, but she knew what he meant.

'Try to find out who killed Isaiah.'

'Yes,' she said softly. 'I know, you think I'm crazy.'

'No, that's not it. What will it accomplish, finding out?'

'It…' Her gaze wandered as she formed the words. 'It will bring Isaiah justice.'

'That's it?'

'Yes, that's it. Isn't that enough?'

'I supposed it is. Then I'd better give you this.' He rummaged in his pocket and brought out a slip of yellow paper.

'What is it?'

'I'm afraid you're right, Anna. Like you said, the cops aren't going to go around to the shelters and soup kitchens and whatnot with Isaiah's picture, trying to find somebody who knew him. Whether it's because they don't think it would do any good, or they don't care, or whatever the reason, they're

just not. I know that. But there is a place…a clue…
if someone wanted to follow it up.'

He held up the slip between two fingers and she
twisted around to read it. Written in pencil in his
firm handwriting were the words *House of Hope*.

'What is it?' she asked.

'A homeless shelter on West Forty-Fifth Street.
Isaiah sometimes slept there.'

'How do you know?'

'There's this other cop, guy named Margolin. He's a buddy of mine, we went through the
academy together. He and I were out on patrol
yesterday and we got to talking. Somehow the
conversation came around to Isaiah, and Margolin
knew about him. He was one of the cops called to
the scene after you found Isaiah's body. You were
inside with Roche and Rinaldi when he got there.
Anyway, when Margolin saw Isaiah, he recognized him. He'd seen him at House of Hope one
time when he had to go and break up a fight between Isaiah and some other guy.'

'So did Margolin go back to House of Hope, see
what he could find out about Isaiah?'

'Of course. He didn't come up with much…and
that may be because he really didn't try very hard.
For instance, no one could tell him who Isaiah had
been fighting with the previous time Margolin
was there—he hadn't taken down their names.' He

gave her a pointed look. 'Isaiah slept there from time to time—something we already knew—and never used his real last name. Always signed in as Isaiah Austin. We followed up on that. Far as we can tell, there's no such person. Not around here, anyway.'

'When you mentioned Isaiah's body, I realized I hadn't thought to ask—what happens to it?'

He shifted uneasily. 'For all intents and purposes, he's unidentified. The morgue will check fingerprints for a match in the missing-persons databases. If no match is found, they'll take dental X-rays, draw blood for DNA, and photograph the corpse. Whether it will turn up anything...'

'You'll let me know.'

He smiled. 'Yes, I'll let you know.'

'What happens if they can't identify him?'

He shifted again. 'Department of Health and Mental Hygiene issues a permit to transport the body to Hart Island.'

'Hart Island?'

'You know what it is, Anna. Potter's Field.'

Yes, she knew what it was. She stared unseeingly into the middle distance. 'How horribly sad.'

After a moment, Santos turned over the slip of paper. 'I wrote it down for you. The address for House of Hope. Figured you'd want it.'

'You're right, I do.' She tucked the paper into the pocket of her jeans.

'Anna?'

She turned to him, brows raised.

'Be careful.'

She smiled with pleasure, put her arms around his neck. 'That's what my brother, Will, said.'

'You promise?'

'Promise. Now you promise me something.'

He waited.

'That you'll bring me any more information like this.'

'I told you I would,' he said. 'But if there's anything else to tell you, I'll be surprised.'

SIX

ANNA WOULD NEVER have found House of Hope if she hadn't had the address. Its ornate white façade was that of the hotel that had once occupied the building. Crisp white lettering on a dark green awning that extended almost to the edge of the sidewalk read 'HOTEL DARLINGTON'. Matching awnings over the windows flanking the entrance bore an elaborate letter *D*.

The inside, however, bore no resemblance to a hotel. The spacious lobby had been completely cleared of any furniture. Occupying the left wall, the former reception counter displayed seemingly dozens of notices in Plexiglas stands. 'NO SMOKING! NO SEX! YOUR COOPERATION WITH THESE POLICIES BECOMES PART OF YOUR CONTRACT BETWEEN YOURSELF AND THIS SHELTER. FAILURE TO OBEY THESE POLICIES *WILL* RESULT IN YOUR BEING ASKED TO LEAVE THE SHELTER IMMEDIATELY.'

Anna approached the counter. No one sat behind it, but through a doorway in the back wall she saw a woman sitting at a metal desk, talking animatedly on the telephone. Sensing Anna's presence, she quickly ended her call and came out. She eyed Anna suspiciously. 'Can I help you?'

Anna smiled, but this had no effect on the woman, who looked about forty and had curly gray hair and pudgy, hangdog features. 'I'm Anna Winthrop. I spoke to you on the phone last night.'

The woman shrugged. 'That wasn't me. Must have been Rhonda. She's the director. I'm just a day monitor.'

'And your name is…?'

Another suspicious look. 'Sarah Thatcher,' she said at last. 'I'll call Rhonda for you.'

Sarah went back into her office and picked up the phone. Meanwhile, Anna turned and took a look around. Just as she was wondering where everyone was, a tall dark-skinned man wearing jeans and a T-shirt walked into the lobby pushing a rolling bucket and mop. He gave Anna a quick glance before sloshing soapy water on to the already clean white linoleum floor and getting to work with the mop.

'Ms Winthrop—' Sarah had returned to the counter. 'Rhonda will see you now. Her office is just down that hallway, fourth door on the left.' She indicated the door through which the man with the mop had just come.

Anna was glad to have a chance, however brief, to look around. She smiled her thanks to Sarah and went through the door into a wide corridor with doors along the left side. Through the first door she saw a large room filled with long conference tables and molded plastic chairs. At the far end of the room, a group of men sat in a circle. 'And I shouldn't have taken that first one,' came a low voice, followed by grunts of agreement. Inwardly Anna nodded. An AA meeting.

Moving on, she passed an empty locker room, then a small cafeteria in which a man and a woman worked filling warming trays behind the buffet line.

Waiting in the fourth doorway was a tall woman in her early fifties with delicate features and salt-and-pepper hair cut in an old-fashioned pageboy. She wore baggy jeans and an untucked navy blue shirt. Her smile struck Anna as being extraordinarily warm and completely sincere. 'Ms Winthrop.' She put out her hand. 'I'm Rhonda Barker. Come in.' She sat down behind a metal desk much like Sarah Thatcher's and indicated another chair for Anna.

'I appreciate your taking the time to see me,' Anna said, glancing around the small office. Taped to the wall behind Rhonda's desk was a poster showing an aerial view of a crowded stadium. Beneath it was printed in small letters: 'AND ALL THY CHILDREN BE TAUGHT OF THE LORD;

AND GREAT SHALL BE THE PEACE OF THY CHILDREN.
ISAIAH 54:13'.

Rhonda followed Anna's gaze and smiled.
'House of Hope is not affiliated with any church,
but I believe God does a lot of his work here.'

'I was just thinking how ironic it is that it's from
the Book of Isaiah, and that it's Isaiah I've come
to talk to you about.'

Rhonda said, 'The policeman I spoke with said
Isaiah was murdered.'

'That's right.'

'How did he die? And why are you here? I mean,
this is tragic news, but what does it have to do with
us?'

Anna decided to begin at the beginning. She
explained how she knew Isaiah, all the way up to
finding him gone when she was finished with her
call from Kelly. She paused, then finished, 'The
next day I found him in the courtyard behind my
building. He'd been murdered—his throat was
cut.'

Unconsciously, Rhonda clasped a hand to her
neck. 'How horrible.' She shook her head ruefully.
'There is a lot of violence among the homeless.
Perhaps you didn't know that.'

Anna remembered what Detective Rinaldi had
said about homeless killing homeless. 'I don't
think that's what we're talking about here. Isaiah

needed help. He was in trouble. That's why he came to me.'

Rhonda looked down at her desk blotter. 'I'm not disagreeing with you. Someone was probably after him to get something he had—alcohol, drugs…it could have been anything. And yes, I have seen one homeless person kill another for as little as a bottle of liquor or a pack of cigarettes.'

But Anna didn't buy it. 'When I came home, only Isaiah was there. There was no one else around. Who are you suggesting this other homeless person was? And where was he or she?'

'Hiding, maybe. Waiting until Isaiah was alone. Who knows?'

'No, I don't think so. Isaiah was in some sort of terrible trouble. He may very well have been running from someone, but it wasn't someone after a bottle of liquor or a pack of cigarettes.'

Rhonda gave her a helpless look. 'Perhaps you're right. But I'll ask you again, what does it have to do with us—or you, for that matter? Isn't this something for the police?'

'Is it?' Anna replied, her tone ironic. 'I don't believe they think so. What's a dead homeless man to them? Yes, they spoke to the people with windows overlooking the courtyard to see if anyone saw anything. No one did. They asked a few questions here. And that's that. What does it have to do with me? I believe I was the closest thing Isaiah had to a friend on this earth. He came to me for help. I let him down. I should have spoken to him when he asked me to, not taken a call from work first.'

Rhonda's eyes grew sad. 'Don't do that to yourself,' she said, echoing Will. 'You couldn't possibly have known. It's not your fault. But you do feel guilty, I see that. So you're trying to do what the police won't. And if you succeeded, what would you do? Nothing will bring that poor man back.'

Anna didn't answer right away. Finally she said, 'He'll have justice. You're right—that's all I can give him. But it's important.' She took a deep breath. 'I understand he stayed here. Did you ever see him fighting with anyone? Did he ever speak to you or to anyone here? Get close to anyone? I'm looking for any information I can get.'

Rhonda sat back in her chair. 'I actually got to know Isaiah pretty well. Or as well as one can expect to know these people.'

'These people?'

'That sounds awful, doesn't it? Have you had much to do with the homeless—other than Isaiah?'

'No...'

'I didn't think so. In many cases, mental illness is responsible for a person being homeless. Then there are addictions of various types. It's not easy to get close to an addict, a person whose main thought is where he's going to get his next drink or his next fix. These people will steal from us, from each other, do anything they need to do to get what they need. They aren't about to get close to anyone unless it will get them what they want, and in those cases they're faking it.

'As for mental illness, it's even worse. These are people who at one time would have been institutionalized. But thanks to President Reagan closing all the federal hospitals back in the eighties, these people are on the streets. But I didn't answer your question. I knew Isaiah pretty well because he came here a lot over the years. He knew he was safe here. The staff all liked him. He knew the rules and followed them…until the end, of course.'

'The end?'

'Yes, until the business with Maria.'

Anna frowned in puzzlement. 'Maria?'

'Maria Trujillo. I assumed you knew all about that.'

Staring, Anna remembered her conversations with detectives Roche and Rinaldi about Isaiah being a suspect in Maria's murder. 'I don't understand. Maria Trujillo was the woman on Forty-Third Street who was strangled. What does she have to do with the shelter?'

Rhonda nodded to herself. 'Then you don't

know that part of it.' She leaned back in her chair. 'Maria was a volunteer here, had been for some time. She helped us out, usually as a substitute when one of our people couldn't come in—kitchen monitor, transitional monitor, intake; wherever she was needed. She was also a generous donor. At any rate, she'd known Isaiah for some time.

'About a month ago, I noticed that things were different between Maria and Isaiah. Members of my staff noticed it, too.'

'Different? In what way?'

'It was a subtle thing, really. They were... closer. She seemed to take a special interest in him. Sometimes I'd see them sitting on the sofa in the common room just talking.'

'And there's something wrong with that?'

'Oh, absolutely. You have to understand. We are not these people's friends. A friendship between a resident and a staff member is completely forbidden. It's unprofessional and inappropriate. So I spoke to Maria. Told her to remember who she was.'

'And what did she say?'

'She actually got angry at me, said it was none of my business and that she and Isaiah weren't doing anyone any harm. I told her that it was most definitely my business, and that no harm may have been done yet, but that that was where they were heading.'

'What do you mean?'

'Obviously, Isaiah was playing her. He saw that for whatever reason, Maria had a soft spot for him, and he was going to take full advantage of the situation. But Maria denied that. She said she knew Isaiah as well as anyone could and that he wasn't like that. She said he was special.'

Anna knit her brows. 'Special?'

'Mm, that's what she said. When I asked her how he was special, she wouldn't answer.' Rhonda shook her head, remembering. 'Things just went from bad to worse. She clearly had no intention of listening to me. The intimate conversations continued. Then, another of our volunteers who was close to Maria told me something I couldn't believe at first.'

Anna sat up, waiting.

'She said Maria and Isaiah were lovers.'

Anna glared at her in shock.

Rhonda nodded vigorously. 'Needless to say, I couldn't believe my ears, either. But it was true. I know it was true because I confronted Maria and she admitted it. She told me again that I didn't understand, that Isaiah wasn't like the others, that he just needed someone to help him get back on his feet. She said I was behaving just like her daughter. Apparently, Maria had a daughter who disapproved of nearly everything her mother did.'

Anna remembered her conversation with Esperanza on the street. 'Did Maria tell you this time why she felt Isaiah was special?'

'No. I asked her again, of course, but she said that was something she'd promised Isaiah she wouldn't talk about. Not yet, at least. To this day I have no idea what she meant.

'Of course, I had to ask Maria to leave. What she was doing was a blatant flouting of our rules. And though I hated to do it, I told Isaiah he was no longer welcome here. It didn't matter, because I knew from the other volunteer that Isaiah was spending most of his nights at Maria's, but do you know—he actually cried when I told him. His eyes filled with tears and he said he understood. Then he thanked me for all we'd done for him over the years. I felt bad about it all, I really did. He was a sweet man and he may very well have been special, but I couldn't let that kind of thing go on here. House of Hope has only fifty-eight beds. I had to give Isaiah's bed to someone willing to follow the rules.'

Anna was still trying to get her mind around this new information. She remembered what Santos had said about the cop named Margolin. 'Do you know anything about a fight Isaiah had with another man?' Rhonda shook her head. 'Do you have any idea what was—wrong with Isaiah? I always assumed he had some form of mental illness, but I never knew what. Do you know?'

'Schizophrenia, I believe,' Rhonda replied lightly. 'But Ben Van Houten would know. He's the shelter case manager.'

'May I speak to him?'

'Let's find out,' Rhonda said, picking up the phone and punching out an extension. She got Ben on the third ring and they spoke briefly. 'You're in luck. Ben's got a few minutes between cases, but you'd better grab him before someone else does.'

At the door, Anna thanked the older woman.

'My pleasure,' Rhonda said. 'I think it's commendable what you're doing for Isaiah. In most cases, these people have no one who cares about them when they're alive, let alone when they're dead.'

'He has me,' Anna said sadly, and continued down the corridor to an office three doors down that Rhonda had indicated.

Ben Van Houten was an overweight man in his early thirties with closely cropped black hair and black wire-rimmed glasses. His clothes fit so tightly that they looked as if they might burst at any moment. He gave Anna a sweet smile—

a smile, it occurred to her, that must have served him well in his work.

Anna told him about Isaiah's death. His smile vanished, replaced by a frown of extreme distress. 'I'm truly sorry to hear this. I liked Isaiah a lot.' He shook his head. 'His life was a constant struggle.'

Anna tilted her head, waiting for him to explain.

'Isaiah was actually quite a serious case. Paranoid schizophrenic. The first time he came to us he was in a bad way. Hearing voices, mumbling—all the things these extreme cases do. But he was willing to let me take him right over to the clinic, and they put him on medication. It had an immediate positive effect.'

'Really?'

He nodded. 'These medications are amazing. The patient is suddenly quite normal again. There's only one problem. The patient has to keep taking the medication.'

'Why is that a problem?'

'Several reasons. First of all, there's a procedure for medication at this shelter—at all shelters. Residents have to turn in all prescription and over-the-counter medications at intake. Then it's their responsibility to request their medication and take it as it's prescribed. Here at House of Hope, residents can request their medication half an hour after meals: 7:45 a.m., 1 p.m., and 7 p.m. We'll also sometimes dispense at 10 p.m. This helps residents who work during the day and don't get back here until well after dinnertime.

'Anyway, as I'm sure you've guessed, residents more often than not either forget or just don't bother to request their meds. But there's another problem.' He shook his head, smiling sadly. 'I'm sure you've heard this before. Ironically, if the resident does take his medication faithfully and begins to feel better, he often then decides he doesn't need the medication anymore. I believe this is what happened with Isaiah.'

'What do you mean?'

'I spoke with the doctors at the clinic several times about his case. They had put him on Clozaril—that's the brand name for clozapine. It's a heavy antipsychotic—what we might call a tranquilizer or neuroleptic.'

Ben shrugged. 'He didn't take well to the medication at all. He kept coming to me complaining of side-effects—he was tired, dizzy… The worst side-effect, he said, was that his passion was gone. That's exactly how he put it. I told him it's true that these medications have a tranquilizing effect, but that the doctors felt Clozaril was the best medication for him and that the side-effects—which the doctors were trying to treat with additional medication—were nowhere near as bad as his schizophrenia symptoms. He was extremely reluctant. Not only did he not like the side-effects, but he also said he was doing better in his life and didn't need the medication anymore. As I said, that's the danger in these cases.'

The fact is, Anna, I'm doing really well now. I see a way out of this life.

'Did he say *how* he was doing better?'

He cleared his throat, clearly uncomfortably. 'I knew from Rhonda that he and one of our volunteers had been—having an inappropriate relationship. I assumed that's what he was talking about. I told him even if he felt better, was doing better, he had to keep taking his meds or he would relapse. I told him he would most likely be taking them for the rest of his life, but that if he did so faithfully, he might never have another schizophrenia symptom again. But I know he didn't listen.'

'How do you know that?'

'Because,' Ben said easily, 'I saw him exhibiting symptoms right here in the shelter. One day I was in the dining room and I saw him sitting at a table in the corner, facing the wall, saying, "No! No! No!" over and over again. Another time, during a session with me, he zombied out in the middle of a conversation and was clearly listening to whatever voices he had in his head. That's often the worst of it, you know—the voices.'

'What did you do?'

'What do you think I did? I told him I could see that he was relapsing and urged him to get back on his meds. But he told me again that he needed "his passion" and couldn't do that. He said his life was improving and that he didn't need the meds anymore.' Ben shook his head sorrowfully. 'He just didn't get it.'

'No,' Anna agreed, getting to her feet. 'Thank you for your time.'

Before he could reply, a woman with frizzy blonde hair appeared in the doorway, clearly for an appointment. Ben gave Anna a quick smile before ushering the woman into his office and quietly closing the door.

It was after two when Anna left the shelter. She waved goodbye to Sarah behind the front desk and emerged on to the street, the day bright under a sky filled with puffy cumulus clouds.

'Miss! Miss, wait!'

Anna stopped and turned. Sarah Thatcher stood under the shelter's green awning. Anna walked back to her.

'I just heard about Isaiah. That's horrible. He was a sweet man. Is it true you're trying to find out who killed him?'

'Yes.'

'Have you spoken to Janice Duffy?'

Anna shook her head.

'Janice is another of our volunteers. She and Maria Trujillo were friends. I just heard about what happened to Maria. Anyway, one day I overheard Janice and Maria arguing, and it must have had something to do with Isaiah because I heard them say his name several times. Maybe Janice could tell you something helpful.'

'Yes, maybe she could. How can I get in touch with her?'

'Here's her number,' Sarah said, handing Anna a half-sheet of paper. Then she shot an apprehensive look in the direction of the shelter. 'I remembered something else,' she said, and handed Anna a sealed white business-size envelope she'd had tucked under her arm.

'What is it?'

'Isaiah gave it to me ages ago to put in the safe in my office. That's what they're supposed to do with their valuables. What's in it, I've got no idea, but when I asked him if this really needed to be in the safe, he said, "Absolutely," and that it was something he would always treasure.'

Anna stood looking down at the envelope, on which someone—presumably Sarah—had written *Isaiah Austin* in pencil. An odd lightness growing in the pit of her stomach, Anna tore open the envelope. It contained a letter, typed on heavy white paper.

THE CITY OF NEW YORK
OFFICE OF THE MAYOR
NEW YORK, NY 10007
March 9, 1988
Mr Isaiah Parkhurst
92 Wainscott Stone Road
East Hampton, New York 11937

Dear Isaiah,
I would like to take this opportunity to personally thank you for donating your painting 'The World in Central Park' to this year's auction to benefit Let the Children Play. As you probably know, the winner of the painting was Mr Harvey Harcourt with a bid of $23,500.

Thanks to your generosity, the children of New York are closer to having a new injury-free playground in Riverside Park.

My very best to you.

Sincerely,
Robert Gould
Robert I. Gould
MAYOR

The two women looked up from the letter and stared at each other.

Why was the name Isaiah Parkhurst familiar to Anna?

'Painting?' Sarah said, frowning. *'Isaiah?'*

Anna gazed again at Mayor Gould's signature. 'It appears Isaiah was special indeed.'

SEVEN

ARRIVING HOME, Anna went straight to the laptop computer she kept on a small desk in the corner of her bedroom. A Google search for 'Harvey Harcourt' revealed that he was executive producer of the NBC World News. Then Anna typed in 'Isaiah Parkhurst'.

What came up amazed her. First, there was the one photograph of Isaiah himself. A handsome man in his mid-thirties, tall, slim, clean-shaven, with wavy black hair and a gleam in his hazel eyes. Barely, just barely, she was able to connect this image with that of the man who used to come for her empties.

Then there was the brief biographical material. An up-and-coming American artist best known for his eccentric cityscapes. Often compared to Keith Haring and Jean-Michel Basquiat.

Was this possible? How had this handsome young man with everything going for him become shuffling Isaiah?

Finally, there were the paintings. Two came up. The first was a wild, vividly colored depiction of

Fifth Avenue. Shoppers loaded down with bags and parcels crowded the sidewalks and marched in and out of Tiffany's, Harry Winston, and Saks. Policemen on horseback watched comical-looking five-card monty hustlers. The street itself teemed with cars, buses, taxis, bicycles, police on horseback, and impossibly long limousines. The pure joy of the painting made Anna laugh.

The second painting featured the boat pond in Central Park. Children lined the edge, all of them holding remote controls for the small, brightly colored sailboats that practically filled the pond. On the periphery, more children in strollers or holding parents' hands licked enormous ice-cream cones. Two dogs played Frisbee. And a smiling sun gazed down on it all.

Anna felt a wave of pleasure as she took in the minute details of these magical images.

On an impulse, she phoned her father at home. He answered on the third ring. 'This is a pleasant surprise.'

'Dad, you know a lot about American artists, right?'

'I should hope so. The Winthrop and Carnes corporate art collection was pretty much my responsibility.'

'That's what I thought. Have you ever heard of an artist named Isaiah Parkhurst?'

'Of course.'

'Really?'

'Really. We had two of his paintings in our collection. And I'll do that one better. I've met the man. A long time ago, of course.'

Anna sat up straight. 'You've met Isaiah?'

'Certainly. So have you.'

'Me?'

He laughed. 'You were only a girl at the time, of course. This was in the mid-eighties. Let's see…you would have been around six. Do you remember the exhibition we had to celebrate the acquisition of several important new works? Two of them were the paintings I just mentioned by Isaiah Parkhurst.'

She did remember, vaguely. A gala, black-tie affair held at the Winthrop & Carnes Park Avenue headquarters to which she, Will, Gloria, and Beth had accompanied their parents. But she didn't specifically remember meeting anyone. 'So what happened? When I met him, I mean?'

'Nothing much. He shook your hand, you smiled, that sort of thing. As I said, you were just a little girl.'

She wished she could remember.

'Why are you asking about him?'

'It's…a long story. I'll explain it the next time

I see you. Does Johnson and Johnson still have Isaiah's paintings in the corporate collection?'

'Oh, they sold the collection years ago.'

She said goodbye to her father and returned to the laptop, scrolling down. On the screen was a brief biography of Isaiah Parkhurst. The first paragraph seemed to jump out at her.

> Isaiah Parkhurst (April 9, 1950—October 28, 1997) was an artist of the naïve art movement whose work responded to the New York City street culture of the 1980s.

1997? But Isaiah had died only five days earlier.

She Googled 'Harvey Harcourt' again, but this time she grabbed a spiral notebook and began making notes.

ARRIVING AT WORK Monday morning, Anna had to jump out of the way when a collection truck came barreling out through the gate, barely missing her. The truck jerked to a halt, the door flew open, and Pierre jumped out.

'Anna, are you OK? I'm really sorry.'

'What happened?'

'Guess I had my mind on other things.'

'You didn't even stop before you pulled out on to the street.'

Tommy had hopped out of the other side of the cab and was watching.

'It won't happen again, Anna, I promise.'

Anna didn't say anything. She gave one nod and continued into the garage as the two young men got back into the truck. She would have to keep an eye on Pierre. If she saw him driving badly again, she would speak to Safety and Training, where he had been taught and might need to be taught further.

Waiting for her in her office was Izzy Martinson.

'We staked out the vacant lot on Fifty-First three times,' he told her, sliding her a cup of coffee he'd picked up for her at Dunkin' Donuts. 'No action. But I checked the lot again this morning and more debris had been dumped. And there was something there that hadn't been there before.' He opened a folder and brought out a stained, wrinkled sheet of paper covered with numbers written in pencil. At the top of the sheet was printed 'RAYBURN GENERAL CONTRACTORS, INC., 3367 60TH AVENUE, FLUSHING, NY 11368'. Beneath this were telephone and fax numbers.

'You'll follow up?' she asked.

'I already did. Guy named Sam Rayburn. He

was completely shocked—said he'd never dumped anything illegally in all his years in the construction business. Had no idea how this could have gotten in there.'

'What do you think?'

Setting down his coffee, Izzy scrunched up his eyes in doubt. 'I don't know, Anna. This guy's a small-time operation—bathroom remodels, turn your garage into a family room, that kind of thing. Most of the time he wouldn't have that much to dump. He let me see paperwork showing that he dumps all his stuff at a local transfer station out in Queens. It doesn't cost that much, relatively speaking. Why would he bring this stuff all the way into Manhattan? It doesn't make sense.'

'OK. So now what do we do?'

'Only one thing *to* do. Keep staking out the place until we actually see somebody doing it.'

'When's the next one?'

'Not sure yet.'

'Mind if I come along?'

'Not at all. I'll call you.'

After Izzy had left, Anna called Janice Duffy's number for the fourth time. This time, instead of an answering machine, a woman answered.

'Ms Duffy?'

'Yes?' She had a refined, fruity voice.

'My name is Anna Winthrop. I was given your

name by someone at House of Hope. I'm calling about Maria Trujillo and Isaiah Parkhurst.'

There was a moment's silence on the line. Then, 'Parkhurst? Was that his name?' Anna told her it was. 'And you're calling about him and Maria? What about them?'

How to explain?

'Are you aware of what happened to Isaiah?'

'Yes. It's just terrible.'

'Isaiah was a friend of mine. I'm looking for information that might suggest who killed him. I'm aware that Maria and Isaiah were...involved in a relationship, and I think there might be something helpful there. I was told at the shelter that you and Maria were friends.'

'I suppose you could say that. So you know about them. I'll be happy to speak with you, but I doubt I know anything helpful. When would you like to meet?'

'I could do it after work today if that's convenient for you. I finish at two.'

'You finish at two?' Janice asked, sounding puzzled. 'What do you do?'

'I'm a supervisor for the Sanitation Department. Would three work for you?'

'Yes. Why don't you come up to my place?' Janice gave Anna an address in the West Sixties. 'It's near Lincoln Center. I'll give the doorman your name.'

ACCORDING TO ANNA'S RESEARCH, Harvey Harcourt worked at NBC headquarters at 30 Rockefeller Plaza. During her lunch break, she called his office. His secretary, a Mrs Madge Fossella, was wary at first. Then Anna explained that she was looking for information about the Isaiah Parkhurst painting that Mr Harcourt won in a charity auction.

'Oh, good heavens, that was over twenty years ago,' Mrs Fossella exclaimed. 'How do you know about that?'

Anna decided to try the truth—always her preference. 'I knew Mr Parkhurst. I'm trying to find out more about his life.'

'Forgive me, deary, but you don't sound as if you're much more than—what?—thirty?'

'Twenty-nine.'

'So you knew him as a teenager?'

'Well, no—'

'Must have. He died in 1997. You would have been eighteen.'

'Actually,' Anna said, 'that's not true.'

There was a long silence. 'Deary, I think you're either confused or you've got your names mixed up. I knew Isaiah Parkhurst, too. Why do you need this information?'

Anna frowned, beginning to compose an explanation, then abruptly saying, 'Mrs Fossella, would it be possible for me to see you? I promise I won't take up much of your time. I can explain it all to you, I promise.'

'I guess we could do that.' Mrs Fossella sounded curious. 'When can you come up?'

'Anytime after two.'

'Come up at two-thirty. Give the guard my name.'

THE MAN BEHIND the massive security desk in the magnificent muraled lobby of 30 Rockefeller Plaza didn't have either Anna's or Mrs Fossella's name, but he called up to her and was satisfied that Anna was expected. 'Twenty-third floor.'

Madge Fossella was waiting for Anna in the reception area directly in front of the elevators. She was a tiny woman—five feet at most—with a sweet round face and light brown hair in a swirling bouffant.

'Sit,' she instructed Anna, indicating a sofa to the right of the reception desk, behind which a young man made a show of not listening. 'Now what's all this? Talk fast because Mr Harcourt could be back at any moment.'

Anna explained that Isaiah had actually died only days earlier and that he had been homeless.

'What!' Mrs Fossella squawked. 'That's not possible. Like I told you on the phone, he died in '97.'

They were getting nowhere on this point. 'What else can you tell me about him?'

Mrs Fossella's features softened into a beatific smile. 'Oh, he was a lovely man. Such a gentleman.'

'Who was, Madge?' came a man's voice from the elevator.

Mrs Fossella froze, eyes bulging. 'No one, Mr Harcourt,' she said, with forced offhandedness.

But Mr Harcourt approached them. He was of medium height, slim and dapper in a dark suit, with smartly cut silver hair. He smiled at Anna. 'Hello.'

She smiled back. 'Hello, Mr Harcourt. I'm Anna Winthrop. I hope you'll forgive my coming up here to speak with Mrs Fossella.'

'Of course,' he said, putting out his hand to her, and Anna sensed Mrs Fossella visibly relax. 'Winthrop... No relation to Jeff Winthrop, I suppose?'

'Actually, he's my father.'

His face lit up. 'Really! Haven't seen him in years. How's he doing?'

'Very well, thanks, Mr Harcourt.'

'What's he up to these days?'

'Golf, mostly,' she said with a laugh.

'I'm not surprised. He made a killing when he sold Winthrop and Carnes to Johnson and Johnson. But you know that. Give him my best, will you?'

'Definitely, Mr Harcourt.'

'Now,' he said, 'what can we do for you?'

'It's about Isaiah Parkhurst,' Mrs Fossella supplied.

Harcourt drew his head back in surprise. 'Haven't heard that name in years. What about him?'

The last thing Anna wanted to do was get into another argument over the time of Isaiah's death. 'You won a painting of Isaiah's at an auction for Let the Children Play.'

He thought for a moment, then his face brightened. 'Yes, of course. It was to help build something at Riverside Park for the children. One of those new injury-free playgrounds. I daresay by now it's probably ready to be replaced, if it hasn't been already.'

'Did you know Isaiah?'

'No, not really. Met him at the auction, and then he came up here to see how we'd hung the painting.'

'What was he like?'

Harcourt considered. 'A quiet man. "A man of few words" is how you'd have described him, I guess. A gentle soul.'

Madge shifted impatiently. 'Ms Winthrop says he died only days ago.'

He gave Anna a look that conveyed the ludicrousness of this idea. 'You must be confused. He died in 1997, everyone knows that.'

'How did he die?'

At this question, both Madge and Harcourt frowned, concentrating. Then Harcourt raised a finger. 'No one ever knew, isn't that right, Madge? He disappeared.'

'Disappeared?'

He nodded. 'After a while his wife had him declared dead.'

Anna turned to him sharply. 'His wife?'

'Mm. Laura…no, Lara, that's it.'

'Do you know her? Any idea how I could get in touch with her?'

'Not a clue. I suppose you could ask at the museum.'

'What museum?'

'Museum of the City of New York. That's where the painting is.'

'You mean it's not here?' She'd been about to ask to see it.

'Oh, good heavens, no,' he said with a laugh. 'It was never here. It hung in my home in the Berkshires. Then, a good twelve years ago, I sold it to the museum. At a considerable profit, I might add. They were overjoyed to get it.' He nodded firmly. 'Talk to the people there. If anyone knows anything about Isaiah Parkhurst, it's them. You can't go today, though. Closed on Mondays.'

JANICE DUFFY WAS A LARGE, effusive woman in her late fifties, with heavy features, stylishly cut frosted hair, and the kind of complexion that flushes easily. She showed Anna into a large, sunny apartment filled with expensive furniture and knickknacks.

'I'm a widow,' she said as they sat on facing loveseats, a cocktail table bearing coffee things between them. 'I think that's why Maria and I were first drawn to each other—we had that in common. Though I must correct something you said. Maria and I weren't friends, not in the usual sense.' Pouring coffee for Anna, she shook her head. 'I don't honestly know if it was possible to be friends with Maria.'

Anna asked her why.

'She was an extremely private person. She didn't like to let people in, if you know what I mean. Me—' she gave a grand, careless shrug '—my life's an open book. I blab to the whole world about my gorgeous daughters, my amazing grandbabies; anything anybody wants to know. But Maria only dropped a few bits of information in passing, and I even wondered if she felt she'd opened up too much.'

'What kind of information?' Anna asked, and sipped her coffee.

A large Siamese cat padded into the room. When Janice made a smooching sound and held out her hand, the cat came directly over and let her scratch its ears.

Janice turned back to Anna. 'I only found out she was a widow because one day I heard her consoling a resident at House of Hope who had just lost her husband. I didn't know Maria at that point because I had just started volunteering there. Maria told the woman she knew exactly how she felt, that the pain numbed over time, but that it could be a long time. I was standing nearby, helping another resident make up her bed and get her children sorted out, and I said, "Amen to that." Maria turned to me and smiled, and later she came up and introduced herself and we had a cup of tea together during our break. I told her I'd lost my Harold fifteen years earlier and still missed him terribly.'

'Did she tell you anything about herself?'

'That she had one daughter named Esperanza and that they didn't get along very well.'

'Did she say why?'

'She said Esperanza was extremely judgmental and that Maria was too old and too rich to have to justify her life to other people.'

'Rich?' Anna asked, though she'd heard this before.

'Oh, yes. Her husband was Juan Trujillo. Made an awful lot of money in the import/export business. Like my Harold, he died many years ago. He and Maria must have been very close, because she told me she was so shattered by his death that it was years before she could bring herself to deal with his things—clothes, belongings, collections. Apparently he was quite a collector of valuable objects.'

Anna nodded thoughtfully. 'Did she say anything else about Esperanza? For example, why Esperanza was judgmental of her?'

Janice narrowed her eyes, trying to remember. Finally she said, 'I think she was mainly talking about the whole Isaiah business.' When Anna raised her brows enquiringly, Janice went on, 'You've said you know about that, so I'm not giving away any secrets. Poor Maria's gone anyway. Esperanza said it was shameful and inappropriate—those were the words she used—for her mother, a volunteer at the shelter, a woman at a high socioeconomic level, to have any kind of personal relationship, let alone an affair, with a shelter resident.

'Esperanza also pointed out that the affair was completely against shelter rules and that if anyone found out, Maria would be terminated immediately. This was true, of course. Rhonda Barker, the shelter's director, did find out and told them both to leave.'

'How did you find out about Maria and Isaiah's relationship?'

'Quite by accident, really. One night Maria and I were both working in the dining room, serving. Isaiah came through the line and started to talk to her about something. She told him, "Not now," but I heard what he said: "They know about us, you know."

'Once most of the people in line had been served, Maria asked me if I would mind if she took a little break. I said I wouldn't mind at all. She went directly to where Isaiah was sitting and they started to talk softly. I watched them and I could see that they were getting upset.

'A little while later I passed her in the corridor and asked if everything was all right. She started to cry. I found out later Rhonda had just asked her to leave. Maria asked if she could talk to me for a few minutes. I said of course and we went into an empty meeting room. That's when she told me about her and Isaiah, that they were having an affair.'

'What did you say?'

'I was stunned, needless to say. I'd worked in a number of shelters and soup kitchens and had never heard of such a thing. I asked her how it could possibly have begun. She called me a snob and said it began how these things usually begin—with friendship. When I asked how *that* began, she said it was because she recognized Isaiah.'

'Recognized?'

'Mm. She said one night she'd seen him with a couple of other men, and they were all laughing. Isaiah had drawn a caricature of another resident with whom he didn't get along, a man named Lawrence. Maria said the likeness was uncanny and that Isaiah was clearly extremely talented. But she said she also found something about his drawing style familiar. It took her a few days, but she put two and two together and realized he was an artist she'd heard of because her husband had collected art, among other things. Now you tell me his last name was Parkhurst. Isaiah Parkhurst, then.' Janice shook her head. 'I'm afraid I'm hopeless when it comes to things like that. When I've got a choice between shopping and a museum, I'm afraid I always go for the shopping. Was Isaiah Parkhurst an artist of any note?'

'Yes, he was.'

'How interesting. Maria said that once she knew this about him, she would try to draw him out, get him to tell her about his life since his painting years, as she put it.'

'Did he tell her?'

'He probably did—how could they have become lovers without his telling her something about his life?—but she never told me any of it.' Janice shook her head in wonder. 'How had the poor man sunk so low?'

'That's something I intend to try to find out.' Anna set down her coffee cup. 'Is there anything else you can remember about Maria? Anything she told you, that you might have noticed?'

Janice's gaze wandered as she gave this some thought. 'No, not really. As I said, she was a private person.'

Anna rose and thanked her. 'I appreciate your time.'

'Not at all,' Janice said, rising too. She regarded Anna's spruce-green shirt and trousers. 'You work for the Sanitation Department, you said?'

'Yes, that's right. Manhattan Central Thirteen Garage. I'm a section supervisor.'

'How interesting—that you're a woman, I mean.'

'Oh, there are many women in the department.'

'Ignorant me. That's how you met Isaiah, then—you found him sleeping or something in your territory?'

'In my section. He came to my block once or twice a week for cans and bottles. Sometimes he slept in the courtyard of my building. I didn't know him well, but I thought he was a gentle man. Special.'

EIGHT

AT TUESDAY'S MORNING roll call, Pierre was absent. Anna checked to see if he'd called in. He hadn't. Tommy waited until six-thirty, and when Pierre still hadn't shown up, left on his route alone, none too happy about it.

At seven-twenty, Anna glanced out her office window and saw Pierre crossing the garage. Instead of his green uniform T-shirt, he wore a plain white undershirt. She decided to go out and speak to him as soon as she finished entering some data on her computer.

He came to her first. 'Hey, Anna, sorry 'bout being late.'

'Come in, sit down.'

He sat in the chair next to her desk and gave her his big, handsome smile, but she could tell he was uneasy.

'What's going on?' she asked, keeping her tone light.

'Ah, just some stuff at home. My dad—you know he lives with me, right? He's not doing so good these days. Cancer. He was in a lot of pain this morning and he needed me.'

'I understand that, Pierre, but you should have called in.'

He hung his head. 'Yeah, I know, Anna. Guess I forgot, with all that was going on.'

She gave him a sympathetic smile. She didn't know much about him—just that he was originally from Jamaica and had family in the city. She'd never had any reason to doubt he was a good man. 'Next time, please remember to call. Tommy had to go out without you. If he'd known you weren't going to be much longer, he could have waited. As soon as we're done here, you can catch up with him.'

Pierre gave her a smile, but this one was completely forced. 'Don't know if Tommy wanted to wait anyway.'

'What are you talking about?'

'No big deal. I just don't think he likes me.'

'Why not?'

'Because I'm not Garry. I never met the man, but from what I've heard, I don't think anybody could fill his shoes.'

She waved the idea away. 'Don't be ridiculous. Garry's a great guy and he's doing a wonderful thing for our country, but he's no better than you. Tommy just needs more time to get used to you. He and Garry were partners for several years.'

They stood. 'Good luck with your dad,' she said.

'Thanks, Anna,' he said, heading out the door.

'Tommy—'

He turned.

'No more T-shirts. Uniform only.'

He looked down at his shirt as if he hadn't realized he was wearing it. He probably hadn't.

'Uniform only,' he said. 'Got it.'

'WHY, OF COURSE it's here!' Rhea Feinblum said, her voice echoing faintly in the Museum of the City of New York's white marble rotunda. She gave Anna a smile full of wonder. 'Everyone knows that.' The petite, fifty-ish woman with a blonde buzz cut looked Anna up and down. 'Are you a journalist?'

Anna laughed. 'No. Actually, I work for the city.'

'Oh?'

'Yes. The Sanitation Department.'

Rhea looked puzzled. 'I don't...'

'That has nothing to do with why I'm here. You see, I knew Isaiah Parkhurst, though I had no idea he'd been an artist. I found out one of his paintings is on display here and just wanted to see it.'

From across the rotunda came a man's voice. 'Just a moment.'

Both Anna and Rhea turned. At the foot of the floating marble staircase, next to a pedestal bearing an enormous flower arrangement in blues and reds, stood a man who was even smaller than Rhea. Everything about him was tiny, from his feet in shiny black shoes to his blue blazer to his facial features, which at this moment were scrunched up suspiciously. He walked with small fast steps to where Anna and Rhea stood.

'Who are you?' he demanded.

Anna noticed that Rhea had frozen, her gaze fixed on this man, clearly someone of authority. If Anna hadn't wanted something out of this visit, she'd have given his rudeness right back to him, but under the circumstances... 'My name is Anna Winthrop,' she said, smiling sweetly and putting out her hand. 'I'm grateful to Ms Feinblum for agreeing to show me the painting I've come to see.'

Rhea piped up, 'You see, Mr Abernathy, Ms Winthrop knew the artist. Isaiah Parkhurst.'

Mr Abernathy gave Anna a speculative look. 'Really? How old are you, twenty-five?'

'Twenty-nine, actually.'

'Isaiah passed away in 1997. Which would have made you eighteen. How did you know him?'

Anna decided a stretching of the truth was in order. 'He was a friend of my father's. Perhaps you've heard of him. Jeff Winthrop...Winthrop and Carnes?'

'Of course I've heard of Jeff Winthrop. You say he was your father?'

'Still is.'

'And Isaiah and he were friends? Your father is a lot older.'

'Yes, he was a sort of patron to Isaiah.'

Abernathy considered this, finally gave a small nod, and fixed a new look of disgust on Rhea. 'You don't have to show her the painting. It's hanging in the "New York in Art" exhibit for all to see.' He turned to Anna. 'Be our guest.' Then he turned back to Rhea. 'I believe you have work to do.'

Rhea opened her mouth but must have thought better of it because she shot Anna an apologetic look and scurried away. Abernathy didn't bother to look at Anna as he himself turned and went off in the opposite direction.

Left standing alone in the middle of the floor, Anna consulted a brochure she'd grabbed on entering the museum. Scanning the table of contents, she found an entry for 'New York in Art: Painters' Visions of the Greatest City in the World'. Following a map in the brochure, she found her way to the exhibit, walking behind a young couple who had appeared from another exhibit.

Ahead of her, the young woman let out a small gasp of delight. Anna stepped around the couple,

Isaiah's painting came into view, and she gasped as well.

The painting was the focal point of the large exhibit hall. That wasn't difficult, since the painting was easily fifteen feet square and occupied an entire wall. It was, Anna realized, one of the largest paintings she had ever seen. A panoramic view of Central Park, it resembled the painting she had seen on her computer, but was far more ambitious.

Vivid grass green was the predominant color, representing the park and extending to a horizon nearly at the top of the picture where the famous old Dakota apartment building could just be made out. Across the green, children ran, dogs jumped, policemen galloped.

If you looked closer, you saw the painting's wit. A long row of children in private-school uniforms marched along a path, their teacher leading the way. All the children carried paper cotton-candy cones, and they had all lost their cotton candy, which lay in a fluffy pink row behind them, being lapped up by a row of dogs in matching red collars.

At the boat pond, children as well as grown-ups avidly worked their remote controls. The surface of the pond itself was so full of toy sailboats that no water could be seen. At the edge of the pond, partly hidden by a massive tree, a full-size sailboat could be seen, ridiculously out of place, dwarfing its remote-control cousins.

The longer she looked, the more of these eccentric details Anna found. A fur-wrapped matron strolling through the zoo, her French poodle lagging behind to lock gazes with a bear in a cage. Skaters on the Wollman and Lasker rinks, though it was clearly the height of summer.

'Isn't it fabulous?' the young woman said.

'Amazing,' Anna agreed, shaking her head in wonder and catching, out of the corner of her eye, Mr Abernathy standing at the edge of the room in front of a red velvet curtain, watching her, his expression dark.

She looked at him in puzzlement and he walked quickly over to her. 'May I have a word with you?' he asked.

'Yes, of course,' she replied, and he turned and led her back to where he'd been standing. She waited.

He looked at her again with those slitted eyes. 'Isaiah Parkhurst wasn't really a friend of your father's, was he?' It was more a statement than a question.

'No,' she admitted. 'He was a friend of mine.'

'How did you know him? Is he still alive?'

'No, he died a little over a week ago.'

He nodded. 'I was afraid of that. Now tell me, how did you know him?'

She paused, seeking the words to explain. 'I didn't know him well, not well at all, really,' she said at last. 'He was just a poor homeless man who came by once or twice a week for my cans and bottles.'

He looked deeply saddened. 'Homeless. Cans and bottles.'

'Yes. He would trade them in for the deposits.'

'I knew what you meant. And this was how you knew him? Where did he live? Did he ever tell you anything about himself?'

'Sometimes he lived at a shelter, but I'm afraid I don't know any more than that.' She wouldn't mention Maria. 'He was a quiet man, private. I could tell he didn't want to tell me anything about himself. I could also tell he was different some-how...special. I can't explain how I knew that. Sometimes he slept in the courtyard of my apart-ment building. That's where I found him dead. He'd been murdered. Someone had cut his throat.'

'How horrible. Who would have done such a thing?'

'I have no idea. That's why I'm here. To try to find out.'

'Surely that's up to the police.'

'You'd think so,' she said bitterly. 'But they don't

appear to want to know very badly. So I'm doing it. I believe that as little as I knew him, I may have been the only one he had.'

Mr Abernathy turned slightly, examining the hem of the velvet curtain. 'It wasn't always that way,' he said quietly. 'Isaiah was the toast of Manhattan. Young, handsome…he had everything going for him. I should know. He lived with my wife and me for four years when he was just getting started. You see, Isaiah and I went to college together. Harvard. We were roommates, in fact. I could see he was enormously talented, but he came from nothing, had no money at all. So after graduation Louise and I took him in, became his patrons, you might say. Up until he met Lara, of course.'

'His wife.'

'Yes. She was extremely beautiful and witty and charming and he fell immediately under her spell. She was the daughter of Jonah Stanton and enormously wealthy. They married, she became his life, and then there was a child—'

'A child?'

'Yes, but I don't know what became of it, don't even know if it was a boy or a girl. That's because I never saw Isaiah again after he left our home. He was furious with me, you see.'

Anna waited for him to explain.

'I didn't like Lara and I told him so. I told him I thought she was only interested in his celebrity. That insulted him, of course, but I didn't mean it that way. It was just that he was the talk of New York and quite a trophy, if you know what I mean. He wouldn't listen. He said it could just as easily be said that he only wanted Lara for her money. He was right, of course. He moved out of our house immediately. I never saw him again. No, that's not quite true,' he corrected himself. 'I did see him, once, though he didn't see me.

'It was about a year and a half ago. I was here, working in my office at the end of the day. There was a blizzard, and I glanced out my window to check on the snow before I started home. When I looked out the window, I saw a dark figure standing on the sidewalk on the other side of Fifth Avenue. It was a man, I could see that, and he was gazing up at the museum. There was something about the way he was standing, the way he craned his neck. I knew it was Isaiah. I looked more closely and couldn't believe how he had changed. That handsome young man had turned into a stooped old man…a tramp!

'I knew he was there for me, looking for me, but that he was afraid to come into the museum. So he was waiting for me to come out.'

'And did you?'

He shook his head, looking down. 'No, and I'll regret it for the rest of my life. You see, I told myself that if I went to him and saw him like that, he would be ashamed. I told myself I was sparing him humiliation. But that's ridiculous, of course. Isaiah needed me. Deep down, I knew that.

'The truth was that I couldn't face what Isaiah had become, couldn't let the memory of him as a young man shatter. So I left the museum by a back door and slipped down a side street, telling myself I'd been mistaken, that it hadn't been Isaiah after all. But I was lying to myself. I'd reached Madison Avenue and walked two blocks south when I regretted what I'd done and hurried back to Fifth Avenue to find him. But he was gone. I'd lost my chance. And so, you see, I've always regretted what I did. If I'd done the right thing, he'd probably be alive today.

'And that's all I know. I've never been in touch with Lara, of course, because Isaiah told her what I'd said about her and she snubbed me instantly. I didn't blame her. But that meant once Isaiah went missing, I had no way of finding him, of even knowing what had happened to him. When he'd been missing five years, I read in the newspaper that Lara had had him declared dead. But I wondered about that. I don't know why, but I wondered if that was really true. And when I saw him standing in the snow across the street from the museum, I wasn't really surprised he was alive.'

Puzzled, Anna asked, 'Why did you feel he was still alive?'

He shook his head. 'I don't know if I can explain it. It's just that when I knew Isaiah, he was so *alive*. There was a magical energy in him. I felt that if he had disappeared, it wasn't because he was dead, but that he needed to change his life somehow...though I never expected that he would be reduced to a homeless beggar.'

'Did it occur to you that his mental illness may have played a role in his disappearance?'

'So you know about that. I was never sure exactly what was wrong with Isaiah, and even as close as we were, he never talked about his problems.'

'He was schizophrenic.'

'I'm not surprised. I suspected that was his problem.' He raised his head, his gaze meeting hers. 'It's a wonderful thing you're doing. You're being the friend to him I never was. Find out who did that to him. Get justice for Isaiah.'

'I intend to try,' she said with a gentle smile.

'Go see her. But don't mention my name.'

'Her?'

'Lara.'

'She's still alive?'

'Of course,' he said. 'Richer than ever and very much alive. Lives in the same ridiculously large mansion in East Hampton.' He gave a sour sneer. 'Where else would she be?'

Leaving the Georgian-style mansion that housed the museum, Anna gazed across Fifth Avenue into the Central Park Conservatory Gardens, lush with summer foliage. She tried to imagine Isaiah—the Isaiah she'd known—standing in the snow on the sidewalk across the street, gazing up expectantly at the museum. Oddly, though, the image she conjured was of an entirely different Isaiah—young, handsome, and standing next to his rich, beautiful wife.

NINE

On Wednesday, Anna took the day off work, and headed out of the city.

By eleven o'clock she was sitting in traffic on Main Street in affluent East Hampton on Long Island. She glanced to each side. The shade-dappled sidewalks teemed with people—talking, laughing, carrying designer shopping bags, popping in and out of shops.

Behind a riot of flowers, red-white-and-blue bunting decorated the white-railed porch of Ralph Lauren's Polo Country Store in anticipation of the Independence Day festivities on Friday. On the other side of the street, the window of Hampton Cards & Gifts displayed an array of red, white, and blue vases bursting with red, white, and blue wildflowers.

Suddenly, unaccountably, traffic moved. Anna advanced half a block, spotted a café, and pulled into a just-vacated parking spot. She'd grab a sandwich before her meeting with Lara Parkhurst.

Inside the café, at a table against the window,

she munched on her lamb-on-focaccia sandwich and watched the steady stream of people pass by.

She was no stranger to East Hampton, though she hadn't been there in years. Her father had spent much of his youth here. When Anna was eight years old, her parents had bought a 'summer home' on Georgica Pond. Anna remembered long, lazy afternoons at the beach and playing on the vast sunny lawn. After two years, her mother had tired of the house, declaring it 'too much bother', so she and Anna's father sold it, at a tidy profit. Anna could only imagine what the house was worth today.

She hadn't been surprised to learn from Mr Abernathy that this was where Lara Parkhurst lived. East Hampton had long been known as an artist colony. Anna's paternal grandfather had spoken of knowing Jackson Pollock and Willem de Kooning 'in passing' in the forties. With a smile, Anna realized that today's Hamptons celebrities were of quite another kind—people with 'newer' money, much of it from Hollywood.

Leaving the café, she continued driving down Main Street, took a left on to Sayres Path, and quickly bore right on to Wainscott Stone Road, on which Lara Parkhurst's house was located. She found number 92 on the right, the drive nearly hidden between two mammoth rhododendrons.

It was actually a road in itself, dark beneath old maples that met overhead. Thick woods lined both sides of the drive, which suddenly turned sharply on itself. As Anna negotiated this turn, her cell phone rang on the console beside her. She grabbed it.

'Anna, it's Gloria.'

Anna had wondered when she would call. 'Hi,' she said coolly. She pulled the car to the side of the drive and put it in park.

'Where are you?'

'Why?'

'*Why?* Just wondering. Can't a person ask where her sister is?'

'I'm in East Hampton, actually. Visiting a friend.'

'Ooh, mysterious.'

'Not that kind of friend.'

'Oh.' Gloria sounded disappointed. 'Listen, Anna, I want to apologize for what I said at Mom and Dad's. You know I adore you, sis.' Anna didn't respond. 'You do know that, right?' A note of mild desperation had crept into Gloria's voice.

Part of Anna wanted to keep silent, not let Gloria off the hook that easy, but a bigger part of her couldn't do that. 'Yes, I do know that, Gloria, but you've got to respect me, respect my choices.'

'I do respect your choices. I just think you

should consider more of them. Now. I never got to tell you this on Saturday. Another resident at the hospital—his name is Ian—has a sister who's a big exec at Citigroup. Ian told her about you, how you studied finance at U. Penn and everything, and this woman—her name is Pam Young—wants to talk to you.'

Anna let out a deep sigh. There really was no stopping Gloria. She would go far. Perhaps if Anna talked to this woman and then said no, Gloria would leave her alone, at least for a while.

'All right, I'll call her.'

'You will?'

'What's her number?'

Gloria gave it to her and Anna jotted it down on a pad she kept on the console.

Someone banged hard on her window. She jumped, turned.

Staring in at her was the thin face of a man, scowling darkly. He motioned for her to roll down the window.

'Gloria, I've got to go—emergency,' Anna said, flipped the phone shut, and opened the window.

'You know this is private property.' It was a statement, not a question.

'I know that. I—'

'Service entrance in the back.'

'Actually, I'm here to see Mrs Parkhurst.'

'Oh, yeah? Looks more like you were catching up on your phone calls.'

She gave him an icy look. 'I had an emergency call. Who are you?'

'Caretaker.'

She glanced around and saw a white golf cart parked right behind her.

Now he brought out a phone of his own. 'Let's check your story. Name?'

She frowned. 'Anna Winthrop.'

In a moment he was speaking into the phone, his back to her. Turning around, he said grudgingly, 'Drive up to the house, park in front, ring the bell.'

'Gee, I think I could have figured all that out for myself, thanks very much.'

'From New York City, are you?'

'Yes, how did you know?'

'Big mouth. All the women in New York City have big mouths.'

She was a hairsbreadth away from showing him just how big her mouth was, then thought better of it. Rolling up her window, she pulled back on to the drive and followed it until the woods opened up to an expanse of perfect green lawn and a massive Cape Cod–style mansion, its shingles weathered a pale gray-brown beneath multiple gables.

Visible behind the house was the sparkling blue water of the lagoon called Georgica Pond.

As the caretaker had implied, the drive looped around to the front of the house. She parked there, climbed a few steps to the wide, railed porch, and rang the bell.

Almost instantly the door was opened by a tall, gaunt woman who could have been the caretaker's sister, right down to the dark scowl. *American Gothic*. The woman waited.

'I'm Anna Winthrop. I have an appointment with Mrs Parkhurst.' She forced a little smile.

'No,' the woman said in a surprisingly deep voice, 'you have an appointment with me.'

'But Mrs Parkhurst agreed—'

'I know what Mrs Parkhurst agreed to. You're to speak with me first. If I feel everything is in order, you will then speak to her.'

'And who are you?'

'Mrs Parkhurst's household manager,' the woman replied, stepping aside so that Anna could enter.

This woman without a name led Anna across a large bright foyer into a small room at the side. In it was a desk, a bookcase, and two chairs. The woman sat in the chair behind the desk and Anna took the other.

'Now,' the woman said, 'what is it you want, exactly, from Mrs Parkhurst?'

'What do I want? I told her, but now I'll tell you. I want to speak to her about her husband. I knew him, you see. He…died recently.'

The woman regarded her suspiciously. 'That's what Mrs Parkhurst said you told her.' She leaned forward on the desk and said calmly, 'I don't know what kind of gambit you've got going, but it would have been quite difficult to have known Mr Parkhurst recently, since he died in 1997.'

'But he didn't—that's the point. He—' How could she explain this without launching into the whole long story?

'It's all right, Phyllis. I'll speak to her.'

They both turned. In the doorway stood a woman who looked to be in her mid- to late-fifties. She was dark and slim with attractively cut black hair and smoky green eyes. Movie star features. A beautiful woman. She held herself up on crutches and there was a cast on her right leg.

Phyllis jumped up. 'Mrs Parkhurst, you shouldn't be walking around. Here, sit down.'

'Don't mind if I do.' Mrs Parkhurst clumped over to the chair and fell into it with a sigh. Phyllis had taken her crutches and leaned them against the wall near the desk.

'Had a little accident,' Mrs Parkhurst told Anna.

'The railing on my bedroom balcony came loose.' Then her face grew stony. 'Phyllis, you can go.'

Obediently, Phyllis left the room, shutting the door behind her.

'Ordinarily I wouldn't have anything to do with someone like you,' Mrs Parkhurst said without preamble.

'"Someone like me"?'

'Mm. Journalist. Book author. Blackmailer— whatever you are. But your story got the better of me, I'll give you that. You said you knew Isaiah until recently. That's a neat trick, since he died eleven years ago.'

'But you see, Mrs Parkhurst, he didn't. That's why I'm here. I knew him. He…'

And she launched into the whole story… About Isaiah being homeless…coming by for her cans and bottles…telling her things had gotten better for him. Then how only a week ago she'd found him behind her building, his throat cut…how the police didn't seem to care…and her visit to House of Hope and what she'd learned there, ending with the extraordinary letter from Robert Gould.

As she listened, Mrs Parkhurst's eyes filled with tears. She found tissues in the desk and wiped her nose. 'And what is it you do, Ms Winthrop?'

'I—I'm a section supervisor at a sanitation garage in Manhattan.'

Mrs Parkhurst let out a little laugh of surprise. 'You've got gumption, if nothing else. Take the day off, did you?'

'No, I came out after my shift was over.'

Mrs Parkhurst sat for a moment, motionless. Then she picked up a phone on the desk and spoke into it. 'Tea in the foyer office,' she said, and put it back down. 'Winthrop...Any relation to Tildy Winthrop?'

'She's my mother. Do you know her?'

'Your family had a house here, oh, twenty years ago. I knew your mother, but not well. She's a few years older than I am. And after a couple of years she decided she didn't like East Hampton.'

The door opened and a uniformed maid entered bearing a tea tray, which she placed on the desk. Mrs Parkhurst, not looking up, poured Anna a cup and handed it to her as the maid retreated.

'Do you know anything about Isaiah's life with me?' Mrs Parkhurst asked.

Anna shook her head.

'We were so happy at the beginning,' Mrs Parkhurst said quietly. 'He was the talk of the town, *the* artist everyone had his eye on. And I...I was Lara Biddle Stanton, beautiful young debutante.' She said these words with irony.

She sipped her tea. 'I didn't know the truth about Isaiah until we were married. He was a very sick man. He knew it, of course, but had kept it from me. I don't know if he thought he could hide it forever, or if he thought I wouldn't marry him if I knew—he may have been right—I don't know. But he did hide it, and that was a very bad thing to do. It didn't take me long to see he wasn't well.'

'Was he medicated?'

'Medicated?' She laughed. 'Depends on how you define that. Did he *have* medication? Of course. Did he take it? Sometimes. Said it took away his passion, made it impossible for him to create his paintings. I can see how it would have. Then again, that medication was his only salvation, and it killed me that he couldn't see that.'

'He simply stopped taking it?'

'No, it wasn't as cut and dried as that. He would take it, get better, then believe he didn't need it anymore and not take it, which made him get worse…and on and on. It was the classic syndrome. The point is, when he was bad, he was very bad. Hearing voices, obeying what he heard them telling him to do…' Pain darkened her face and she looked away.

Anna waited, hoping she would elaborate. As if hearing her thoughts, Mrs Parkhurst turned back to her and said, 'We had a child, did you know that? I mention this because some of the things Isaiah did when he wasn't on his medication put our child in danger. For example, one morning, I took Austin—that's our son's name—to do some shopping downtown. We were gone for a few hours. When we got back, Isaiah had poured paint, gallons and gallons of it, all over Austin's room, all over his furniture, his clothing, everything. And Isaiah sat in a corner of the room, covered with paint himself, crying. I had the hospital come for him—the first of several times I had to do that.'

She put down her teacup and looked up brightly, her next words at odds with her expression. 'It got worse. He got into drugs. All of his artist friends were into drugs, and Isaiah, poor impressionable, weak Isaiah, he did it, too. As you can imagine, everything fell apart—our marriage, everything. He would be gone for days, then return and trash his studio. Once he tried to throw Austin in the pond. I couldn't have it, of course. I should have done it far sooner than I did, but I finally worked up the courage to give him an ultimatum: either check into the hospital long-term and get the help you need, or leave. He left.'

She took a deep breath. 'That was seventeen years ago now. Amazingly, he was at the height of his success. It seemed the worse he got, the richer and more famous he got. But his personal life wasn't working and that was all that mattered to me.'

'Did you ever see him after he left?'

'Exactly three times over the next year. Two weeks after I threw him out, he appeared at the front door and begged me to take him back. He swore he would take his medication and give up the drugs. Only problem was, he was drunk. I had him escorted off the grounds.

'He must have been angry with me after that, because I read a few comments he'd made about me, comments that suggested I'd been the problem. He said I was controlling, that I discouraged him from pursuing his art—none of it true, of course. The second time I saw him was at a party here in East Hampton. A friend of mine thought it would be a good idea to get us together, hoping we would patch things up.' She shook her head, baffled.

'He did approach me at the party, but he was strangely formal. He actually shook my hand. I rushed out crying.'

'And the third time?'

'The third time, I made the move. I'd heard from mutual friends that Isaiah had taken studio space in New York City, near the gallery that exhibited his work, and I don't know what possessed me but I decided to go and try to work things out. I told myself it was for Austin's sake but the truth was, I missed him terribly, if you can believe that. I went to the studio and rang the bell. When he opened the door, he was crazed. I'd never seen him that way. He looked as if he hadn't taken his medication in ages, and he was clearly on some drug or drugs. I said hello and he stared at me. He didn't know who I was.' Another tear ran down her cheek. 'I ran out crying. After that, I promised myself I would never run out crying again.'

'And that was that?'

'Not quite. As Austin entered his teens, it bothered me no end that he didn't have a father. I could see it troubled Austin, too. I thought perhaps after all this time, Isaiah might have gotten the help he needed. I hadn't heard anything about him in a while. So I hired a private detective to try to find him.'

She tapped the table once. 'No luck. According to this gentleman, Isaiah had vanished from the face of the earth. He and I came to the conclusion that Isaiah was dead. It was a relief, in a way. In 1997, when Isaiah had been missing for five years, I had him declared legally dead. And that was the end of it, I thought...until today.'

Now the tears came at full force. Mrs Parkhurst put her face in her hands and sobbed.

Wishing she could comfort the older woman with an embrace, Anna waited.

'I never stopped loving him, do you know that? Crazy, isn't it? I just kept thinking about the Isaiah I knew when he was well—handsome, vibrant, funny—and wanted to get him back somehow, recapture those happy times.' Mrs Parkhurst's gaze wandered, unseeing.

Gently Anna asked, 'You mentioned the gallery that showed Isaiah's work. Can you tell me its name?'

'Of course. It's the Bentley Gallery. East Seventy-Seventh Street, just off Fifth. But what could they tell you?'

'Probably nothing. But isn't it possible that Isaiah had contact with them longer than he had contact with you?'

'The detective told me it wasn't long after I went to Isaiah's studio that he disappeared, so no.' Mrs Parkhurst shrugged and shook her head, finished with the whole business. 'But suit yourself.' Then her features softened. 'Forgive me. Here you are, trying to find out what happened to my husband, and I'm being rude. Here,' she said, jotting something on a slip of paper and handing it to Anna, 'take my number. Let me know if you ever find out who did this to Isaiah.'

'Of course I will,' Anna replied, taking her

own card from her pocket and handing it to Mrs Parkhurst. 'If you happen to think of anything you think might be helpful, please call me.'

'All right. You'll excuse me if I don't see you out.' Mrs Parkhurst gestured toward the crutches leaning against the wall.

'Of course.' Anna rose. 'One more question before I go, if you don't mind.' Mrs Parkhurst waited. 'How can I get in touch with your son?'

'I was waiting for you to ask me that. I can give you his address, but I doubt he'll talk to you. He never talks about his father.'

'But I'd like to try. How old is he now?'

'Twenty-five.'

'And the address…?'

'I know what you're thinking. That Isaiah might have been in touch with Austin after he was in touch with me.' Mrs Parkhurst gave her head a quick shake. 'Austin would have told me. No, from the day I threw Isaiah out, Austin never saw him again. But here you go.' She jotted something on a piece of paper and handed it to Anna. 'I'll give Austin a call and let him know I've spoken with you.'

'Thank you, Mrs Parkhurst,' Anna said, shaking her hand. 'And…I'm sorry.'

TEN

As soon as Anna reached New York, she headed for the Upper East Side and the address Lara Parkhurst had given her for Austin. Finding it—268 East Sixty-First Street, between Second and Third avenues—she frowned, wondering if Mrs Parkhurst had made a mistake. It was the address of a brick townhouse covered in scaffolding. Eight steps between wrought-iron railings led up to double front doors, one of which bore a discreet sign in violet letters etched into stainless steel: 'ORCHID'.

Continuing around the block, she found a parking spot at a meter on Sixtieth Street. As she opened the car door to get out, her cell phone rang. It was Santos. 'This is a nice surprise,' she said.

'Thanks. Listen, I've got the drug-screen results on Isaiah for you.'

She felt her heart race. She slipped back into the car and shut the door. 'Why are you whispering?'

'You know why. Remember what we talked about.'

'Yes, yes. Now tell me.'

'Nothing. No alcohol, no drugs, nothing.'

'Interesting.'

'Maybe. Just keep in mind that just because he wasn't on anything when he was killed doesn't mean his murder wasn't drug-related.'

'Of course. But it makes it less likely, doesn't it?'

'Not in my book. To me it makes it more likely, not less.'

'Then we're reading different books,' she said lightly. 'Thanks, Santos. I'll see you soon, OK?'

'Wait, there's more.'

'What?'

He lowered his voice again. 'Some information about Maria.' Anna waited. 'Seems she'd had intercourse shortly before her death, though there were no signs of rape—no bruises, abrasions, lacerations. The DNA from the semen found in Maria matched Isaiah's DNA. Both of their DNA was on the sheets.'

'Not a surprise. They were lovers.'

'Without a doubt. Isaiah's fingerprints were found in the brownstone. It doesn't look good, Anna—I mean, about whether he killed Maria. Not good at all.'

'Just because Maria had sex with Isaiah shortly before she died doesn't mean he killed her.'

'All right, I'll give you that.' But Santos didn't sound as if he believed it at all.

'Were any other fingerprints found in the brownstone?'

'One other person's, but we're pretty sure it's the cleaning lady. We're checking. Oh—one more thing. Maria had a bad cold. Her night table was covered with over-the-counter decongestants, cough syrup, et cetera. She was supposed to have been on a trip to Cape Cod the night she was killed, but apparently she was forced to postpone the trip because of her cold.'

'Cape Cod?'

'Mm. Someone else was going with her, but from the hotel reservation papers we've found, we can't tell who. Maybe the daughter.'

Closing her phone, Anna got out of the car and walked back to the townhouse. Now a man in stained white painter's pants stood at the top of the stairs, smoking a cigarette and gazing out at traffic.

'Excuse me, I'm looking for Austin Parkhurst,' Anna said to him, sure he would tell her she had the wrong address.

But he tilted his head toward the building. 'In there,' he said, looking her up and down. He positioned himself so that Anna had to pass within inches of him and his smoke to get to the front door. She ignored him, knocking.

'Just go in,' he said, practically in her ear.

She pushed the door open and stopped, stunned at what she saw.

She stood in an atrium as tall as the building it-self—five floors. Each of these floors looked out on this atrium, sliced and suspended and without railings of any kind. Men worked on each of these floors. The sounds of hammers and power saws came loudly down to her.

She was about to go looking for Austin when a man in his mid-twenties with dark blond hair entered the atrium from a door on the right. His resemblance to Isaiah was striking—the deep-set hazel eyes, the handsome patrician features. Crossing the floor, he saw her and his face regis-tered puzzlement. He came toward her.

'Help you?' he asked, hollering above the noise.

'Mr Parkhurst,' she yelled back, 'my name is Anna Winthrop. I'm here to speak to you about your father.'

He gave her a strange look. 'Let's step outside.'

When they emerged on to the front landing, the painter was just finishing his cigarette. He practi-cally snapped to attention when he saw Austin.

'I thought I told you no smoking on my job.'

'Won't happen again, chief.'

'You bet it won't happen again, because you're fired.'

The painter's mouth dropped and his eyes widened in amazement. 'Hey, give a guy a break, huh?'

'Beat it.'

The painter's brows met. 'Give me my paycheck and I might.'

Suddenly Austin grabbed the other man by his shirt collar and the back of his pants and threw him down the stairs. The man rolled several times before he was able to stop himself on the second step and get up. When he did, blood was running profusely from cuts on his cheek and chin. 'What are you, crazy?' he screamed.

Austin just glared at him. The painter looked around for help, got none, and limped away. Anna was seriously considering following him when Austin calmly turned to her. 'Now what was it you said?'

'I'm Anna Winthrop. I'd like to speak to you about your father.'

'That's what I thought you said. You've got the wrong guy, miss. My father's been dead for eleven years.'

'Obviously your mother hasn't called you.'

'My mother? Lady, what are you talking about?'

'Is there somewhere we can talk? Somewhere quiet?'

He thought for a moment, then led her back into the townhouse, across the atrium, and out a door at the back to a little brick courtyard surrounded by trees. 'OK, it's quiet here. Now what was it you said about my mother?'

'I've just been to see her. It's about your father. He hasn't been dead eleven years. That's why I'm here. He died a little over a week ago…was murdered, actually.'

He regarded her under lowered brows. 'My father, you're talking about.'

'Yes. Isaiah Parkhurst.'

'And who the heck are you?'

'I told you, my name is Anna Winthrop. I work for the New York Sanitation Department, but that has nothing to do with why I'm here, nothing to do with your father. I live on West Forty-Third Street and your father would come by once or twice a week to collect my empty cans and bottles.'

He was staring at her. 'Just what are you saying? That my father was a bum?'

'He was homeless, if that's what you mean.'

'That's exactly what I mean.' He gazed down at the bricks of the patio, then shook his head firmly. 'No, that's not possible. My father is long dead.'

So she told him everything she had told his

mother. When she was finished, he looked at her coldly. 'And just supposing I believed you, why is it you care so much who killed him? What does it matter?'

'I considered him my friend. The police don't seem to care. As far as I know, they've stopped working on the case. I think your father deserves better than that. I think he deserves justice.'

He smiled sourly. 'That's very democratic of you, Miss Winthrop. I hope you enjoy playing detective. Just keep me out of it.'

She looked searchingly into his eyes. 'You really don't care?'

'Nope. I really don't. You see, my father didn't care about me. That's why he left one day seventeen years ago and I never saw him again. It's funny—for years I worried he *would* reappear and try to start a relationship. Now that I know that can't happen, I'm glad. Now,' he said briskly, 'I'm very busy trying to get my club ready to open within the next century.'

She gazed back at the building. 'This is an amazing place. I'll certainly come here when it opens.'

'Will you? Oh, good.'

'You don't have to be rude.'

'I know.' He stared at her.

Clearly, the meeting was over. She turned and

went back through the door into the atrium. She heard him enter behind her and suddenly shout, 'Jimmy, I told you not to put it there!' A door slammed.

At the front door, Anna glanced back over her shoulder. He was gone. She paused, looked around again, and instead of going out, turned right and crossed the foyer to an archway into what looked as if it would be a coatroom when construction was complete. Beyond it was a narrow hallway. Starting down it, she suddenly smelled food—vinegar and cold cuts. Soon she came to a small office in which a wizened little man in a brimmed cap sat munching a hero sandwich. 'Help you?'

Before she could think of what to say, he spoke again. 'I was just out in the back—you didn't see me—and heard Austin yellin' at ya. Sweet kid, ain't he?'

She nodded, warming to him. He might be helpful. 'Are you helping with this renovation?'

'Helping?' He smiled endearingly while giving an exaggerated shrug. 'Don't know if you could call it that.' He laughed. 'Just kidding. Yeah, my boys are helping. Austin—better call him Mr Parkhurst, that's what he tells us—he wants this place to be a "mosaic masterpiece", that's what he said. And that's me.'

'You?'

'Yeah. We're the tile guys.'

'Ah.'

'What about you?'

'I…' She hated to lie, but '…I'm a designer. Helping with the décor.'

'I see. Then you got your work cut out for you, too. Easy he ain't, but I guess you figured that out already.'

'Definitely. Tell me—' she glanced around, making sure they were alone '—who's backing this place? I mean, all this renovation—it must be costing Austin a fortune.'

'You better believe it.'

'Then you know who's behind it?'

'No.'

Her shoulders slumped.

'But Billy would.'

'Billy?'

'Billy Harris. Manager of this place till two days ago. That's when Austin fired him—no, lemme correct that. Nearly killed him.'

Her eyes widened questioningly.

'They was arguing about something—don't know what—way up on the fourth floor. I don't know if you noticed, but those floors ain't got no railings yet. Anyways, Austin got so mad he grabbed Billy and nearly threw him off. Good

thing one of my guys was right there and grabbed Billy before he went over.'

'I'd like to speak to this Billy,' Anna said.

'Yeah?' He frowned, took another big bite of his sandwich. The smell was making her hungry. 'Why?'

'I've got to be careful about who I work with. If what you're saying about Austin is true, I may have to rethink this project.'

'Oh, it's true, all right. But Billy could tell you more. You want I should call him?'

'You have his number?'

'No.' He picked up a sheet of paper from the counter between them. 'But it's right here.'

She looked at the paper. On it was a handwritten list of names and phone numbers. With a thick, grout-crusted index finger the old man pointed to *Billy Harris* about a quarter of the way down. Anna found paper and pen in her purse and wrote down the number. 'Thanks,' she said, giving the man a sweet smile.

'You're more than welcome. Take some advice from me and turn this job down. Life's too short.' He tipped his hat, then hunkered down to take another huge bite of his sandwich.

AFTER STOPPING AT the nearest Blimpie's for a hero sandwich of her own, Anna called Billy Harris.

He answered on the first ring. His voice was deep, emotionless.

'Mr Harris?'

'Who is this?'

'You don't know me. My name is Anna Winthrop. I wonder if you could spare me a few moments?'

'For what?'

'I need to ask you some questions about Austin Parkhurst.'

There was a long silence. 'Who are you, one of his lawyers?'

'No. Actually, I'm making enquiries about Mr Parkhurst's father.' She would explain later—if he agreed to see her.

'Where are you now?'

'Fifty-Ninth and Third.'

'You'd be in luck if I weren't so drunk. I'm on Sixty-Fourth between Third and Lex.' He gave her the building number. 'Come tomorrow morning. Early, before I start drinking again.'

SHE WAS OFF THE NEXT DAY. She left her apartment early and walked to the Upper East Side, reaching Billy Harris's apartment building around nine. Despite the fancy address, it was a nondescript building just off Lexington on Sixty-Fourth Street, between a florist's and a Korean grocer. In the tiny vestibule, she buzzed his apartment and the door immediately clicked open.

A garlic-scented elevator took her to the sixth floor. Billy Harris was waiting for her at the end of the corridor. As soon as he saw her, he turned and went into his apartment. She followed him into a living room bare of furniture except for a card table and two folding metal chairs. He was tall, a good-looking man—dark brown hair in a flattering short cut, brown eyes, straight nose. He wore gray sweats and in his left hand held a bottle of Grey Goose by the neck. He put out the other hand to Anna.

'Thanks for agreeing to speak with me.'

'Pleasure.' He indicated one of the chairs and she sat in it. He took the other, setting down the bottle on the table. 'You like vodka?'

'No—thank you.' She saw no glasses anyway.

He gave a mirthless laugh. 'I won't say I'm disappointed. More for me.'

She didn't know what to say, how to begin.

He took a swig from the bottle and leaned back in his chair, legs wide apart. 'So, how do you know Austin?'

'I don't, actually. As I said on the phone, I knew his father.'

'Right, you said that.' He frowned. 'You in the restaurant business?'

'No. I work for the Sanitation Department.'

'The *New York* Sanitation Department?'

She nodded.

'You collect garbage?'

She smiled. 'I used to. I'm a supervisor now.'

'Good for you.' His tone was sincere. 'The world is changing, isn't it?'

It occurred to her that he would be surprised to hear how many women worked for the Sanitation Department, but she wasn't here to talk about that.

'So how'd you know Austin's dad? He work for Sanitation, too?'

'No. I knew him at home. I mean, he used to come by for my cans and bottles.'

Billy sat up straight. 'Wait. Are you telling me Austin's father is a bum?'

'Was. I mean—he was homeless, if that's what you mean.'

'Oh, yeah, sorry. "Bum" isn't politically correct, is it? But get outta here! *Austin*'s father?'

'It's true. I didn't know him all that well, but he was a sweet man. Troubled.'

'How so?'

'He was schizophrenic.'

'Ah,' Billy said.

'Isaiah—that was his name—was once a famous artist. Quite successful. But because of his illness and drug addiction, his life apparently spiraled downward. A little over a week ago I found him dead in the courtyard behind my apartment building. Murdered.'

Billy's dark brows rose. 'Murdered? How?'

'Someone cut his throat.'

'Whoa. That's rough. But why?'

'That's what I'm trying to find out. And who, of course.'

His eyes narrowed. 'But why you? You're with Sanitation, not the police.'

She explained that she considered Isaiah her friend, and that the police didn't seem much interested in pursuing his case.

He took another slug of vodka. 'I'm not surprised. You sure I can't get you something? I got Dr Pepper in the fridge.'

'No, thank you.'

He nodded, then sat back and looked around the room thoughtfully. Suddenly his brows came together and he looked at her. 'Wait a second. I just remembered something. When I first went to work for Austin, we were having lunch one day and we got to talking about how we grew up. And I could have sworn he said his dad had died years before.'

'That's what he thought. You see, Isaiah and Austin's mother separated when Austin was nine. His mother saw Isaiah three times after that but never again. He seemed to have vanished. So after five years, Lara—that's Austin's mother—had Isaiah declared dead. And that's what everyone thought, that he was dead. But he wasn't. I don't know how long it was before he was on the streets, but that's where he ended up.'

'I see. And you're investigating his murder. But what could Austin tell you? Or his mother, for that matter? They both thought he was dead.'

'I know that now. I just thought they might be able to tell me something that could lead me...'

He was shaking his head, a knowing look on his face. 'You're not making any sense. They wouldn't be able to tell you anything about the Isaiah *you* knew. You're trying to put this guy together, find out exactly who he was—am I correct?'

She supposed he was. Was that wrong?

'What is this,' he said, 'some kind of obsession for you or something?'

'No, of course not. But isn't it possible Isaiah might have been in touch with them?'

'They told you he wasn't. They thought he was dead. You just said so yourself.'

'What if one of them is lying? Austin, specifi-cally.'

He frowned. 'Why would he lie?'

'Think about it.' She herself hadn't thought about this until now, but it made sense. 'We don't know the financial ramifications.'

'Ramifications?'

'Yes. Where does Austin's money come from?'

'From his mother, of course. His dreams keep getting bigger, and she keeps funding them. He's got the whole thing planned, told me all about it. One day he intends to make his biggest dream come true: an entire restaurant/entertainment complex. Restaurants, nightclubs, theaters... But for that to happen, he needs more than an investment from his mother. He needs her to die. Which may not happen for a while. You met her. I don't think she's even sixty.'

'And from what I understand, she's worth millions. She inherited them from her father.'

'That's right,' he said.

'Tell me...where would Lara's money go if Isaiah were still alive?'

He gave this some thought. 'To Isaiah, I guess. From what Austin told me, it was her lawyers and money guys who pressured her to have him declared dead. But she never stopped hoping he would come back.' He leaned forward, nodding. 'I get you. It would change things for Austin, wouldn't it?'

'Yes, it would. Considerably.'

'So what are you saying?' he said with a laugh. 'That Austin killed his own father?'

When she didn't laugh along with him, his expression turned serious. 'I wouldn't put it past him. The man's an animal. You met him.'

'Yes, I did. He nearly killed a man for going outside for a smoke.'

He nodded. 'Nearly killed me, too. Know what for?'

She waited.

'I told him I thought it was crazy what he was doing with those floors just hanging there, no railing or anything.'

'You mean he wasn't going to put anything there?'

'That's just it. The plan was to put in railings for the inspections, then replace them with low walls of glass. He said it would be dramatic. Meaning dangerous. And it was. He nearly threw me off.' He rolled his eyes. 'Thinks he's the club king of New York. As if he would ever have gotten away with that.'

But she was still thinking about falling. 'Lara fell...' she said slowly.

'Hm?'

'She was on crutches when I saw her yesterday. Had her leg in a cast. Said the railing on her balcony broke.'

Their gazes met meaningfully. He said, 'With Isaiah definitely dead, killing Lara would just about do it, wouldn't it?'

'Exactly what I'm thinking.'

As she left Billy Harris's building, Anna was already thinking about when she could get back to East Hampton.

BUT WHEN ANNA CALLED Lara, she refused to see her. 'I told you everything there is to tell. In fact, I probably told you more than I should have.'

Anna decided not to argue this point. 'It was just your accident I wanted to ask you about.'

There was a brief pause on the line. 'My accident? What does that have to do with Isaiah?'

How to explain *that?* 'If I could just meet with you, I could tell you.'

'No, sorry, I'm afraid not. It's sweet what you're doing, trying to find who did this to poor Isaiah, but I've said all there is to say. It's all just too painful. Please understand.' And she hung up.

For the next hour or so, Anna puttered around her apartment, tidying, dusting a little, running the vacuum—and asking herself how she could find out more about what had happened to Lara.

The deep rumble of a truck came from the street and she stepped to the window and looked out. A sanitation collection truck was making its way between the parked cars on either side of the street. Behind the truck, Jay Rapchuck grabbed bags from trash cans and threw them in. Then he turned and she saw that it was Winston, not Jay. The Bobbsey Twins. Jay sat at the wheel, gazing out boredly at the buildings. Directly below there was a crashing of trash cans as Winston grabbed two garbage bags in each hand. Holding them high, he squeezed between two cars, then threw the bags into the truck's hopper. They landed with a dull thump. Winston called out to Jay, who drove the truck forward a few yards, the hydraulics letting out a high-pitched whine.

Anna turned from the window, deciding to put all thoughts of Jay and Winston out of her head. She made herself a cup of coffee and sat at the kitchen table.

Ten minutes later, she had an idea. Hurrying into her bedroom, she quickly changed into black trousers and a pale blue cotton blouse. Back in the kitchen, she grabbed her purse and was nearly to the door when her phone rang.

'So what happened when you talked to Pam Young?'

Anna let out an exasperated sigh. She'd completely forgotten. 'I haven't called her yet.'

'I know,' Gloria said. 'I just spoke to her.'

'Then why— Oh, never mind.'

'Anna,' Gloria said in a scolding tone, 'these jobs don't stay open for long. Not only that, but

'For one thing, you're so young. He died before you were, what, fifteen?'

She gave him a coy smile. 'Eighteen. He died in 1997, if I'm not mistaken.'

'You are correct.'

'Daddy loves his work. That's how I know about him.'

'Daddy?'

'Jeff Winthrop. Winthrop and Carnes? He's retired in Greenwich now.'

At this, the slightest frown appeared on Kavanaugh's face and quickly vanished. Then a gleam of avarice appeared in his eyes. 'And do you collect Parkhurst?'

'Oh yes, I have several of his pieces. Gifts from Daddy. But now that I've moved into my new place, I've got more walls to cover!' She gave an airy laugh.

'Indeed,' he said, sharing the laugh. 'And where is your new place, if you don't mind my asking?'

'Riverview Terrace,' she replied, naming a street in posh Sutton Place.

The gleam in Kavanaugh's eye intensified. 'Well, you've come to the right place, as they say. We do have some excellent Parkhurst pieces.'

'Wonderful,' she cooed, and cast her gaze about, as if looking for them.

'Oh, they're not out here. Not now,' he added quickly.

She wrinkled her brow. 'Why not?'

'We're having them reframed.'

Another man appeared in the doorway. He could have been Kavanaugh's twin except that he had no mustache and he was a good thirty pounds heavier. He, too, wore a dark, well-tailored suit.

'What are we having reframed?' he said, smiling, as he glided across the room to where Anna and Kavanaugh were standing. 'Neal, please introduce me to this lovely young lady.'

'Miss Winthrop,' Kavanaugh said, 'this is my partner, Bert Meltzer. Bert—Anna Winthrop.'

She shook his hand. His grip, in contrast to Kavanaugh's, was firm to the point of painful.

'Our Parkhurst pieces,' Kavanaugh said, answering the other man's question. 'Miss Winthrop collects him.' The most fleeting of looks passed between them.

'Ah,' Meltzer said. 'We would be delighted to arrange for you to see them.'

She lowered her brows in puzzlement. 'Can't I see them now?'

'Oh, no, no,' Kavanaugh said with a laugh. 'They're not here. We have a storage facility where they're kept.'

'I thought you said they were out for reframing?'

Both men looked at her shrewdly. 'They are,' Meltzer answered smoothly. 'At the storage facility. If you would like to make an appointment, we can have them brought here for you to see.'

'All right. How soon can I do that?'

'Tomorrow is a holiday, but if you're available we can arrange it for you.' When she nodded, Meltzer said, 'Shall we say eleven o'clock? That will give us enough time to transport the paintings.'

'Perfect,' Anna said, shaking hands with each of them. 'Till tomorrow, then.'

She could feel their eyes on her as she went out the door to the street.

ON HER WAY HOME she stopped at the Food Emporium and picked up some fresh fish for dinner. Then she walked to Mr Carlucci's for some fruit.

He was busy with a customer when she entered the small, tightly packed store. When he was finished, she called to him, 'Hey, Mr Carlucci, you got anything that isn't rotten today?' She laughed, expecting him to laugh along with her as he always did, but his face was grave as he came over to her.

'Anna, I only just heard about Maria Trujillo. Horrible.'

'Yes. Did you know her?'

'Sure, she came into the shop all the time. For years. First with her husband, then without him after he died. Have you heard whether the police have any idea who did it?'

'No,' she said, remembering her promise to Santos. Besides, there wasn't anything to tell anyway.

'Poor woman,' he said. 'She never took that trip to Cape Cod.'

Anna looked at him. 'What trip?'

He smiled sadly. 'About three weeks ago she came in for some vegetables and we got to talking. I asked her if she was going to be taking a vacation this summer—you know, just idle chatter—and she told me she was going to Cape Cod. Come to think of it, she'd planned to leave the night she was killed. Never made it, poor soul.' He shook his head. 'I teased her and said, "With someone special?" She smiled and said yes, that it was someone very special. I wonder who it was... I'll tell you one thing for sure. It wouldn't have been that monster of a daughter, Esperanza.' He shuddered.

'What do you mean? You've met her?'

'Sure, a number of times. Until a few years ago, she lived in that townhouse with her mother. Then she bought her own place a couple of blocks away. You should have seen her face when I was talking with her mother about the Cape Cod trip. Could have turned you to stone.'

'Wait a minute. Are you saying Esperanza was

with Maria? But you just said this was only two weeks ago.'

'Right. So?'

I hadn't spoken to her in over a year...

'Nothing. What can you tell me about Esperanza?'

He nibbled the inside of his cheek, thinking. 'She's a doctor, I know that, but I don't know what kind. She and her mother never got along. In my experience, as kids get older, they get along better with their parents. But with this girl it was the opposite.'

'What do you mean?'

'There wasn't a time Maria and Esperanza came in that Esperanza wasn't harping at her mother about something. And you know how it is—we shopkeepers are invisible. That's why people talk on their cell phones while we're ringing them up. But when you're invisible,' he said, a twinkle in his eye, 'you hear things.'

She raised an eyebrow, waiting.

'For instance,' he said with relish, 'there was the time Mr Henderson from Forty-Sixth Street called his mistress and had a fight with her on his cell phone while I was ringing up his pineapple and chives.'

'No,' she said, 'I want to know what you overheard between Maria and Esperanza.'

'Oh. Well, there was the time many years ago Esperanza didn't like the private school she was attending because it wasn't where the "quality kids" went. Spoiled rotten, that one.'

'What else?'

'Oh, there was the time not long ago she was shouting at her mother about being a bleeding heart and a sucker. I couldn't figure out what that was about. And, like I said, there was the time a couple of weeks ago when Maria told me she was going to Cape Cod. When they were on their way out I heard Maria say, "I'm the mother and you're the daughter. This is my life and I'll live it the way I want to." And Esperanza said, "You won't live it the way you want to when it affects me. It's humiliating." I heard Maria say the name Isaiah. And then they were too far away for me to hear any more.'

The door to the back of the shop opened and plump Mrs Carlucci huffed out. 'Gianni Carlucci,' she said, planting herself in front of him, 'I can hear every word you're saying. Shame on you, gossiping like that about a dead woman.' She turned to Anna and gave her a completely blank look that spoke volumes.

'You're right, Mrs Carlucci, I'm sorry.'

Mrs Carlucci gave a small, indifferent shrug and plodded away toward a display of pears.

Mr Carlucci turned to Anna and mouthed the word, 'Sorry.'

She gave him a wink and left the store. It wasn't until she reached her apartment that she realized she'd forgotten to buy fruit.

TWELVE

A LITTLE AFTER eight o'clock that night, Anna walked out of the Waldorf-Astoria Hotel on to Park Avenue. A golden dusk had settled over Manhattan, and a faint breeze stirred the air. Deciding to walk to House of Hope, she started west on Forty-Ninth Street. She needed time to think, anyway.

Her drinks date with Pam Young had not gone well. Which was to say, it had gone altogether too well. The two women had hit it off instantly. When Pam described the job in question—a middle-level management position—Anna found herself more interested in it than she'd ever imagined she'd be. Pam thought Anna was well qualified, given her education in finance as well as her current management position at the Sanitation Department. And Citigroup was looking for 'fresh blood'— people from other fields who brought new perspectives. At the end, Anna heard herself agreeing to call Citigroup Human Resources as she jotted down the number.

What had she done? she asked herself as she

waited for the walk sign at Fifth Avenue. She liked her job. Was she just giving in to Gloria? Her own recent doubts about her suitability to the Sanitation Department weren't helping, she was sure.

She'd think more about this later, she told herself, picking up her pace.

When she entered House of Hope, the lobby was filled with men and women waiting in a line that snaked back and forth before reaching two tables at the back of the room. The sound of people talking and laughing was deafening.

Anna found Sarah Thatcher behind the front desk. When Sarah saw Anna, her eyes widened. 'Did you find anything out about that letter?'

'I did, actually. It seems Isaiah was indeed an artist. Quite a famous one, in fact.'

Sarah made a *tsking* noise and shook her head. 'Hard to believe. How on earth did he ever end up here?'

'It's a long story,' Anna said. 'One I'm still putting together. You can help me. I'm looking for people who knew Isaiah, talked to him. Friends, people who stayed here at the same time that Isaiah did, that sort of thing.'

Sarah looked doubtful. 'It's not so easy to find someone who stayed here when Isaiah did. Every night we get a different crowd. And many of these people move around. Besides which, even if they want to spend the night here, it's first come, first serve—' she indicated the long line behind Anna '—and we have only so many beds.'

'Friends, then.'

'Friends...' Sarah knitted her brows. 'Don't know if I can help you there, either. Would an enemy do?'

'An enemy?'

'Mm. There's this guy by the name of Lawrence—not sure about his last name—who used to make fun of Isaiah.' Sarah shook her head. 'Crafty old coot. Did it enough to make Isaiah mad, but never enough to get himself kicked out of here. Except for one time, that is. Isaiah drew a picture of Lawrence that Lawrence didn't like very much. They got into a fight and we had to call the police to break them up. We warned them both that if it ever happened again, they couldn't come back here. Lawrence is here a lot.'

'Any idea where I can I find him?'

'He's in line right over there.' Sarah pointed.

Anna turned around to look.

'See that really tall guy in the jeans and red sweatshirt?' Sarah said. 'That's Lawrence.'

Anna thanked her and made her way toward him. At first he didn't notice her. When he did, he threw a look over his shoulder, as if she were after someone else. When she kept coming toward him, he put a finger to his chest as if to say, Me?

'Hi.' Anna put out her hand. 'I'm Anna Winthrop. Could I talk to you for a minute?'

She was drawing curious looks from the people nearby. Lawrence looked embarrassed.

'Lady, I don't know who you think I am, but there ain't nothing I can do for you.'

'That's not true,' Anna said with a reassuring little smile. 'I understand you knew Isaiah Parkhurst. I'm looking for information about him.'

'Heard he died.'

'Yes, he did.'

'You think I killed him or something?' Lawrence asked, and his chest heaved up and down a few times in quiet laughter. When Anna didn't laugh along with him, he grew serious again. 'What is it you think I can tell you?'

'Let's go somewhere we can talk.'

Lawrence pointed to the people around him. 'Lady, I get outta this line and I ain't got no place to sleep tonight. So we can either talk here or maybe you got some better idea.'

'I'll wait until you're finished with intake. How's that?'

'Suit yourself,' he said with a deep shrug.

Anna returned to Sarah Thatcher's counter.

'When he's finished with intake, would it be all right if he and I had a talk somewhere?'

'Don't see why not. You can talk to him while he eats dinner.'

After Lawrence had been signed in, he approached Anna. 'I'm all yours.'

She smiled. 'I'll sit with you at dinner, if you don't mind.'

'Never been known to mind havin' a pretty lady for company.'

She followed him into the noisy, crowded dining room and waited for him at an unoccupied table while he got his food. While she was waiting, a dark-skinned woman in a purple-and-yellow turban set down her tray and sat down, flashing Anna a toothless smile. 'Not eating?'

Anna smiled back and shook her head. 'Just went for drinks and ate the whole dish of nuts.'

'Must be nice,' the woman said wistfully, taking her seat. When Anna looked puzzled, the woman went on, 'Going for drinks. Never done that before.'

Lawrence had arrived at the table. 'Stop feeling sorry for yourself, Verbena.'

'Just sayin', is all,' Verbena said, and busied herself with her meal.

Lawrence shook his head. 'If people did more

doin' and less feelin' sorry for theirselves, they might be better off.'

But Verbena ignored him. He didn't seem surprised. 'Now,' he said, looking up at Anna, 'what can I do you for—Miss Winthrop, was it?'

'Please call me Anna. As I told you, I'm looking for information about Isaiah Parkhurst.'

'What kind of information?'

'Information that will help me find out who killed him.'

They both looked at her. Clearly Verbena had also heard about Isaiah's murder.

Finally, Lawrence spoke. 'Parkhurst, you said. Never knew his last name. I gotta warn you, he and I didn't get along too good.'

'What do you mean?' Anna asked, remembering what Sarah had said.

'Took hisself real serious, Isaiah did. No sense of humor.'

'You mean when you made fun of him?'

'Made fun of him?' Lawrence waved away the idea. 'I was just havin' some fun, is all.'

'What, exactly, did you make fun of?'

'Oh, he used to put on airs. Told me all kinds of foolish things.'

'Like what?'

'Like that he was once a famous artist.'

'He was. Quite famous, in fact. His work hangs in museums.'

Shaking her head, Verbena speared a piece of chicken with her fork. Lawrence looked dumbstruck. 'But how can that be?'

'You should know better than that. Did you always live here?'

'No,' he agreed slowly. 'I had a wife and kids… an apartment. But I wasn't no famous artist,' he pointed out. 'I was just a regular workin' stiff, tryin' to get by.'

'Isaiah was mentally ill. You must know that.'

'Yeah, I thought that was why he said those things about being an artist.'

'No, he was telling the truth. But he was also schizophrenic. That's what caused most of his problems.'

Lawrence put down his knife and fork and looked down at the table, drawing in a deep breath. 'Wish I could take it all back. Poor soul. But those things he said—they was just so hard to believe.'

'What did he say, exactly?' Anna asked, and Verbena looked up from her food, waiting for his answer.

'Oh, that his paintings were worth a lot of money now, that art collectors had some of them and others were in museums, like you just said. And he went on about some mural he'd just painted.'

'Mural?' Anna asked, sitting up a little straighter.

'Mm. Wanted to take me to see it, prove it to me. I told him he was full of it and pushed him away.' Lawrence shook his head ruefully. 'Man, I shoulda kept that cartoon he drew o' me.'

'Where did he say this mural was?' Anna asked.

Lawrence thought for a moment. Then his eyes lit up. 'The Rat Cave, that was it.'

Hearing this, Verbena gave him a skeptical look. 'You crazy? Nothing at the Rat Cave but bag ladies and bums—and rats.'

'Yup,' Lawrence insisted, 'that's what he said— the Rat Cave. Said he'd just finished his mural. That he painted it with some woman.'

'Oh?' Anna said.

Lawrence nodded. 'Said she was a talented artist "in her own right", that's how he put it. I told him he was puttin' on airs again, talkin' like that.'

'Where is this Rat Cave?' Anna asked.

Verbena said, 'Oh, you don't wanna go there.'

'She's right,' Lawrence said. 'It's not a place for you, miss, if you don't mind my sayin'.'

'Why not?'

'It's dangerous. Not a nice class of people there. Mean and stubborn. The cops clear them all out, and once the cops are gone, everybody pours right back in.'

Now Anna knew what he was talking about. 'So it's a homeless encampment.'

'That's right,' Verbena said.

'Where is it?'

Lawrence blinked. 'My, you're a stubborn one yourself. Looks like you're gonna go there no matter what we say. Let's see now. Under the Manhattan Bridge, ain't that right, Verbena?'

Verbena thought about it and nodded. 'Mm-hm.'

'Can you give me the exact address?' Anna asked.

Lawrence and Verbena burst out laughing.

'There ain't no "exact address",' Lawrence said, and Anna could see what his teasing would have been like. 'Only way you're gonna find it is if I take you there. Which I'll be happy to do.'

'No, I couldn't ask—'

He put up a hand. 'It's something I'd like to do, miss. You think it might help you find out who killed Isaiah?'

She gave a little shrug. 'I don't know. I hope so. I won't know unless I try, will I?'

'That's for sure. How 'bout this. You be waitin' outside this place tomorrow morning—say, seven o'clock?—and I'll take you to the Rat Cave. That a deal?'

She gave him a warm smile. 'Deal.'

SHE ENJOYED THE WALK back to her apartment. The air, though still now, was cool and fresh. It felt more like early fall than mid-summer.

Someone had left the front door of her building ajar. She knew that for some time something had been wrong with the door. It didn't fully close on its own. She would have to speak to Mr Vickery, a distasteful thought.

As she entered the building, cooking smells reached her from Mrs Dovner's apartment. Liver and onions, she thought. This wasn't the first time the older woman had filled the foyer with mouth-watering aromas. Too bad she was so crazy, Anna thought. If they were friends—a bizarre notion—Anna might get a home-cooked meal once in a while. Though Anna was a good cook, she seldom took the time to prepare anything but simple fare for herself.

She started up the stairs, then abruptly stopped, hand on the railing, and listened. She had definitely heard it: a strange, high-pitched sound, like someone crying. Where was it coming from? She strained to hear it more clearly. It was nearby... downstairs, at the back of the first-floor hallway, in the shadows beneath the stairs.

She walked back down and made her way slowly around to the back. Silence now.

'Hello?' she called out softly.

No answer. Still silent. She waited, straining to hear.

There it was again, a quiet whimpering. A

child? She walked farther toward the back, peering into the darkness.

An arm shot out and roughly grabbed her, swinging her violently around so that she was facing away from whoever it was. The arm, clothed in some rough black material, clamped her neck so tightly she could only breathe in a thin thread of air...couldn't scream.

A face, also covered in some rough black material because it scratched against her cheek, came close to hers. From the corner of her eye she saw a mouth outlined by a hole. A ski mask. His foul breath reached her before his words: 'What is it with you, baby? Like to play private eye?' The voice was low, gravelly—clearly disguised.

She made no effort to answer, but she wouldn't have been able to anyway because now his arm clamped her neck even tighter, lifting her on to her toes. 'You know what happens to little girls who play dangerous games?' the man asked. After a beat, he answered his own question. 'They die. Be smart. Let it go.'

And with that, he let *her* go, dropped her. She gasped for breath, falling to her knees. Footsteps sounded softly on the hallway floor, followed by the rattling of the front door as he let himself out.

She was shaking badly, her breath coming in

short bursts. She concentrated, pulling herself together, deciding what to do.

A soft creaking sound came from the front of the hallway. She froze. He hadn't really left. He'd only pulled the door open and let it slam to make it sound as if he had. He was waiting for her...

Another creak...

She remained motionless, her mind working frantically. Did she have anything on her to fight him with? A metal ballpoint pen was the best she could come up with. Stealthily she slid her hand into her pocket and brought out the weapon.

A long black shadow grew across the floor in front of her.

She raised her arm, brandishing the pen, and jumped out into the light.

Mrs Dovner screamed. Anna screamed. Then the two women stood gaping at each other, breathing hard.

'You scared the blazes out of me,' Mrs Dovner cried. 'What are you doing under there?'

'Mrs Dovner, I'm sorry. I...I was just attacked.'

'Attacked!' Mrs Dovner cast her gaze about the hallway, eyes bright. 'Who attacked you?'

'I don't know. A man. He was wearing a mask. He was waiting for me under the stairs.'

Mrs Dovner hugged herself. 'That's what I heard, then.' Then her face grew angry. 'So now, thanks to you, men are waiting under the stairs to attack us.'

Anna couldn't believe her ears. 'You selfish woman. You haven't even asked me if I'm all right.'

'Well…are you?' Mrs Dovner asked in a little voice, embarrassed. 'You look fine.'

'I am fine,' Anna told her, heading up the stairs, and hollered down, 'no thanks to you!'

She ran the rest of the way up to her apartment and let herself in, closing the door behind her.

She frowned. In the living room, a lamp at the end of her sofa was on. She never left the lights on. She turned sharply. The door to her bedroom, nearly closed, had begun to swing slowly inward.

She screamed. She spun around, rushing to the apartment door and worked madly at the knob.

'Anna!'

She turned back around. In her bedroom doorway stood Gloria, in a beaded black cocktail dress and scarlet heels.

Anna blew out her breath. 'What are you doing here?'

'That's a nice welcome. I had a charity event tonight at the W Hotel. It's right near here. I thought for sure I told you about it at Mom and Dad's, said I'd drop by.'

'How did you get in?'

'I still have a key from when I slept over last year when my floors were being refinished. What are you so jumpy about?

'I was just attacked downstairs.'

'What?'

Anna nodded. 'I heard this noise under the stairs—it sounded like a child crying—and when I went to look, a man grabbed me.'

'How horrible!' Gloria hurried over to her sister and put her arm tightly around her shoulders. 'Come on, sit down.' She led her over to the sofa. 'Are you all right? Did he hurt you?'

'No, but he said something.'

'What?'

'Something about me playing private eye, how little girls who play dangerous games die.'

Gloria sat down beside her. 'Strange…' Then her eyes widened and she looked at Anna. 'Will told me about how you're trying to find out who killed that homeless man. Is that what this guy meant?'

'I don't know. I suppose it could be.'

'What else could it be about?' Gloria looked at Anna shrewdly. 'You know who it was, don't you?' It was a statement, not a question.

'I think I do.'

'Who?'

'It's complicated. Well, actually, it's not. It's Isaiah's son.'

'His son?'

Anna nodded. 'He's a monster. And he had good reason to want his father dead. The last thing he wants is someone nosing around.'

'Then stop nosing around,' Gloria said, hands outstretched, as if this were the easy answer.

'No. I have no intention of stopping. This only proves that what I'm doing is the right thing to do…and that I'm on the right track.'

'Even if you die?'

'Oh, Gloria, don't be so dramatic. I'm not going to die.' Anna fervently hoped this was true.

'We've got to call the police.'

'No.'

'No? Don't you want them to do something about this animal?'

'No, I don't—at least, not yet. That would spoil my investigation.'

'Oh, for pity's sake, Anna, who do you think you are, Nancy Drew? This isn't a game. Obviously you're on to something—this creep knows it—and he clearly intends to stop you if you get any closer to the truth.'

'Then I'd better be more careful, hadn't I?'

Gloria looked at her, speechless. She grabbed the phone and jabbed out 911.

'No!' Anna grabbed the phone and switched it off. 'I told you, no police. I'll call Santos. He's a cop.'

Gloria rolled her eyes. 'He's a beat cop. He's also your boyfriend.'

'It's as close as we're going to get,' Anna replied, and dialed Santos's number.

He was there in twenty minutes. When she opened the door, he quickly took her into his arms for a hug. He wore jeans and a faded brown sweatshirt. She put her head against his chest and inhaled his cologne—the same peppery cologne he'd worn when he came to talk to her about Isaiah.

'What's going on?' he asked softly. He noticed Gloria standing a few feet away. 'Oh, hello.'

Anna turned around. Gloria was practically salivating.

'Well, hello,' she said in a voice that had suddenly gone smoky and low.

'Gloria—Santos. Santos—Gloria, *my sister who's getting married a week from Saturday.*'

While Gloria filled Santos in on what had happened, Anna made coffee. When she came back to the living room, Gloria and Santos were sitting together on the sofa—a little too close for Anna's liking. Anna set the tray bearing the coffee things on the cocktail table and jammed herself into the space between them.

'Anna,' Gloria said, annoyed. 'What are you doing?'

'Sitting between two of my favorite people,' Anna said, giving them each a sweet smile.

'I'm glad you're in such a bubbly mood,' Santos said, not smiling at all. 'Do you realize what could have happened to you?'

'Yes, Santos, I do,' she said in a tone she had once used when her father scolded her when she was a teen.

Gloria leaned forward to speak to Santos around Anna. 'But that's just the problem. She doesn't really know or believe that something much worse could have happened to her. And do you know why? Because this life she leads—this world of garbage and trucks and—and—who knows what—has numbed her to violence.'

Anna looked at her in amazement. 'Gloria, give it a rest, would you, please? I do know what could have happened to me. I was the one attacked, remember?'

'Then why won't you agree to stop?' Santos asked.

She looked at him with hurt in her eyes. 'Traitor.'

'I'm not kidding, Anna,' he said. 'Obviously, you're right. There's more to Isaiah's murder than

it appeared. But if you keep doing what you're doing, you're going to end up right—'

'—and dead,' Gloria finished for him.

'Stereo!' Anna exclaimed, wondering how they would react if they found out about her plans to visit the Rat Cave in the morning.

They both turned away from her in exasperation. Then Santos, ever the cop, turned back to Anna.

'What can you remember about this guy? What was he wearing?'

'I don't know. All I saw was his sleeve, which was made of some kind of scratchy black material—wool, probably—and his face, which was covered by a ski mask. I did see his mouth.'

'What did it look like?' Gloria asked.

'A mouth.'

'What about his voice?' Santos asked. 'What was that like?'

'Low, gravelly, scary. Definitely disguised. Oh—he had terrible breath. So I guess we know he has bad dental hygiene.'

Santos just shook his head. 'Tall? Short? Fat, thin, what?'

She shrugged. 'He lifted me off my feet, so he must be taller than I am—which isn't very helpful—and he was strong. But I didn't get a good look at him.'

Gloria and Santos left about an hour later. Santos had agreed to walk Gloria to Eighth Avenue and help her get a cab to take her to her apartment on the Upper East Side.

Once they were gone, Anna's apartment was blissfully quiet. She was pleased. She had managed to get through the evening without calling the police—not officially, at least—which she was convinced would have been a wrong move. Thinking about her talk with Lawrence at House of Hope, she busied herself taking the coffee tray back into the kitchen.

The phone rang. Santos, she thought, making sure she was all right. She grabbed it. 'I promise I won't leave the apartment again tonight.'

'What?'

A man's deep voice. Not Santos.

'Who is this?'

'Who do you think it is?'

A shiver ran through her. Part of her wanted to hang up, but the part of her that didn't won. 'You sniveling coward,' she sneered, 'hiding under the stairs. Wearing a mask. What's the matter, afraid of me?'

There was a brief silence on the line. Then, 'Lady, what are you, nuts?'

'Then who is this? Say your name.'

'You know who it is, but I'll say it, sure. Aus-

tin Parkhurst. I don't know what you're talking about—stairs and masks. But I'll tell *you* something. You ever pull a stunt like the one you pulled at my mother's house and I'll have you in court so fast your head will spin. "From the insurance company"! What you did was not only wrong, it was illegal.'

'Illegal? And what do you call murder?'

'Murder! I'll say it again. I don't know what you're talking about.'

'I find that surprising, since you've done it once and are trying to do it again. I heard all about your mother's "accident".'

He didn't respond.

'How did you get my number?' she demanded.

'Don't worry about it. Just remember what I said. Stay away from me, stay away from my mother. You want to find out what happened to dear old Dad, be my guest, no skin off my nose. But keep my mother and me out of it.' And with a sharp crack, the line went dead.

Lost in thought, she stood at the kitchen sink, washing the coffee mugs and placing them on the rack to dry. The apartment seemed too quiet now. Had she locked the door behind Gloria and Santos? She hurried to the door and found it locked, bolted, and chained. On her way back to the kitchen she glanced at the phone in the living room and almost grabbed it to call Santos. Then she thought better of it. If he called her, fine, she'd listen to more of his lectures. It would be nice to hear his voice.

But she wouldn't call him. That would be like admitting he was right.

THIRTEEN

THE CITY WAS QUIET the next morning, as it always was on holidays. When Anna pulled up in front of House of Hope at seven, Lawrence was waiting for her outside. Seeing her, he smiled broadly, and she noticed for the first time that he had beautiful white teeth.

'Can't remember the last time I got picked up by a pretty young lady,' he said, getting in.

She took Broadway downtown to Canal Street, where she got on the Manhattan Bridge. When they were over the East River, Lawrence looked back at the towering skyline of lower Manhattan, then forward at Brooklyn, and let out a low whistle. 'Magnificent. Hard to believe there's a place like the Rat Cave somewhere down there.'

'Is it that bad?'

'You'll see,' he said, and instructed her to get off the bridge.

'Dumbo,' she said, as the ramp off the bridge circled through a small urban park.

'Beg your pardon?'

'*D*own *U*nder the *M*anhattan *B*ridge *O*verpass. Quite a chic neighborhood these days.'

'Not all of it.'

Once they had left the bridge, she looked to him for instructions.

'This here Jay Street?' he asked.

She found a street sign and nodded.

'Then keep going. You can get to it from Jay Street. It's right where the BQE goes under the bridge,' he said, referring to the Brooklyn—Queens Expressway.

She went a little farther and he suddenly sat up straight. 'Whoa. This is it. It's right through there.'

She parked at a meter and they walked back, reaching a point where the sidewalk ran alongside one of the bridge's stanchions. Beyond the stanchion, the Brooklyn—Queens Expressway ducked under the bridge.

'Where?' she asked.

She followed him off the sidewalk and around the stanchion. Here, running parallel to the stanchion, was a thick concrete wall. Between this wall and the stanchion ran a narrow path, littered with dented beer cans and cigarette butts. The path ran for only about a dozen feet before disappearing into the shadows. Lawrence pointed.

'In there?' she asked.

By way of response, he started down the path. She followed close behind.

At first all she could see was blackness, though the air felt cool and dank, as if they were in a large space. Gradually her eyes adjusted to the dark and she drew in her breath at what she saw.

Beneath the soaring crisscrossed expanses of the Manhattan Bridge and the Expressway, in the hazy dimness, lay a veritable city, a sea of boxes and makeshift tents and shelters. Near some of them, people moved about, talking to each other or just walking aimlessly.

She marveled at the sheer size of this place. It reminded her of cartoons she had seen as a child in which the inside of a small tepee was impossibly larger than it was outside, as if it were another dimension. That's what this place felt like: another dimension, a shadowy other world.

Places like this didn't exist anymore—not officially, at least. A couple of years earlier, the mayor had instituted an aggressive push to reduce the number of people living on the city's streets. Homeless men and women were being pressured to leave makeshift dwellings like this in favor of supportive housing, treatment programs, or shelters. Anna had even heard the city was erecting barriers in these places to keep people from getting back in. Clearly, they'd missed a spot.

'You see what I mean, miss?' Lawrence said, breaking into her thoughts.

She turned to him. 'They're just people.'

Without speaking, he pointed casually to a spot six feet from where they stood. Seven rats the size of cats were feeding on the carcass of a dead animal. She turned away.

'Heh-heh. Never seen rats before, I bet.'

'Actually,' she said, turning to him, 'I see them all the time. I just don't like them.'

His brows lowered in curiosity. 'What kind of work you in, that you see rats all the time?'

'I'm a sanitation supervisor.'

He laughed. 'Get outta here.'

'No,' she said, smiling, 'I really am.'

He shook his head in wonder. 'That how you knew Isaiah?'

'No. He used to come to where I live for cans and bottles.'

'We've all done that at one time or another,' he said. 'Now, let's see about this mural he told me about.'

She would have had no idea where to begin, but Lawrence simply walked up to the nearest of the cave's occupants. A man in tan sweats who looked as if he was in his early thirties sat cross-legged outside an elaborate structure consisting of a refrigerator box connected to a tent made of ragged blankets attached to a large sheet of rotting plywood. Munching dry breakfast cereal from a large box marked 'Family Size', he looked up at Lawrence, squinted, and scratched his full beard.

'Mornin',' Lawrence said. The other man nodded once, warily. 'Wonder if you can help us out. We're looking for a mural we understand is here?'

'A what?' The cereal box was empty and he tossed it aside.

'A mural. Big painting on the wall. You know about it?'

The young man laughed sourly. 'What are you, crazy? There ain't no paintings in here. It's the Rat Cave.'

'I know what it is,' Lawrence responded, clearly irritated, and started to turn away when a woman popped up several tents away.

'I know what you're talking about,' she said. Nearly as wide as she was tall, she wore a loose-fitting muumuu in garish shades of green and orange. She stepped over several people and approached Anna and Lawrence. 'It's here all right.'

'Where?' Anna asked.

The woman didn't respond, instead looking them both up and down.

Lawrence turned to Anna. 'She wants something.'

'Oh. Yes, of course,' Anna said, opening her

bag. The heavy woman peered in with interest. Anna looked a question at Lawrence.

'Give her a few bucks.'

Anna complied.

The woman tucked the bills into a pocket of her dress. 'Follow me.' She started toward the far end of the cave, walking with an odd gait, her legs too far apart. Anna now noticed that on her feet she wore heavy black boots trimmed in fake fur.

Anna couldn't help gazing around her with interest at the various shelter configurations to each side of them. It was like a small busy city, not unlike pictures she had seen in books of squatter cities in Asia or Africa.

She didn't realize she had slowed down until the woman and Lawrence turned and looked back at her. She quickened her pace. The woman led them around one of the Expressway's massive concrete supports to a smaller area, also filled with tents and shelters. Abruptly the woman stopped, turned, and pointed.

Anna and Lawrence turned as well and were taken aback at what they saw. The mural occupied this entire side of the road support. Here some sunlight managed to find its way in, illuminating the brightly-colored scene.

It was Isaiah's work, no question about it, but different from the pieces Anna had seen. For one thing, it was painted in a looser style, the brush-work more free, the objects in it not as neat and tidy. The subject matter was different as well. This was Isaiah's impression of a squatter city like the one all around them: a vast expanse of tents and boxes, their inhabitants going about the business of their lives—eating, laughing, sleeping, making love, even playing a game of basketball on a small city court at the mural's edge.

Something moved at the bottom of the paint-ing and Anna jumped. An old woman, wrapped in a blue tarp, sat up against the wall and smiled a toothless smile. 'Nice, eh?'

Anna and Lawrence nodded. The heavy woman who brought them there had wandered away.

'What can you tell us about this?' Anna asked.

'What, this?' the woman said, looking upward to indicate the mural behind her. 'He painted most of it.'

'Who?' Lawrence asked.

'Isaiah,' the woman answered impatiently. 'Who do you think?'

From the corner of her eye, Anna spotted a rat making its way toward them. She forced her-self not to react, focusing her attention on the old woman. 'When did he paint this?'

'When?' the woman repeated, as if time were a new concept. She simply shrugged.

'You say he painted most of it. Who else worked on it?'

'The girl, who else?'

'What girl?' Lawrence asked.

'Sleeping Beauty.'

Anna and Lawrence looked at each other. 'Who's that?' Anna asked.

'You know...no, not Sleeping Beauty, a different story. Goldilocks, that's it! Goldilocks!'

Anna drew in a deep breath and let it out in disappointment. Clearly they would get no information of any value from this woman.

'No—Goldie!' the woman went on. 'Goldie, that's her name. The girl.'

'Goldie? Who's that?' Lawrence asked.

'Just a girl. Pretty little thing.'

'Any idea where we can find her?'

'Right over there,' the woman said, pointing to the area's far wall.

Anna looked and saw only a mass of crumpled newspapers. 'There's no one there.'

'Not now, there isn't. But that's her spot when she's here.'

Lawrence nodded. 'Is she here every night?'

'Pretty much. So's Isaiah...at least he used to be. Don't know where he is these days. But that's his spot, too.'

Lawrence said to Anna, 'We should come back

at night.' He turned to the old woman. 'You're sure that's where she sleeps when she's here?'

The old woman let out a wheezing laugh. 'I oughtta know. I'm here most all the time.' Her eyes, a rheumy gray, met Anna's, and she smiled warmly. 'This is my home.'

LAWRENCE OFFERED TO accompany Anna to the Rat Cave again that evening, but when Anna realized that by doing so he would forfeit a bed at House of Hope, she gratefully declined. There was no reason she couldn't go there alone, despite whatever Santos and Gloria might have had to say on the subject.

She dropped Lawrence off in front of the shelter, then drove back to the parking garage and left her car there. She walked toward Times Square by way of side streets in her section, making note of several places where plastic trash cans lay haphazardly on the sidewalk, sometimes blocking it. She would speak to her crew about throwing the cans from the truck.

Reaching Times Square, she smiled and cast her gaze about, looking for some new and outrageous billboard. Tourists moved all around her, yet even here, the Center of the World, the streets were quieter than usual. No doubt many people had already left the city.

Crossing to the west side of Broadway, she passed in front of the Marriott Marquis Hotel, then the long window of the Times Square Bookstore. Half of the displays advertised upcoming author book-signing events—a hip-hop artist who had written his life story…a lifestyle guru pushing her new decorating bible…an old-time actor who'd written a thinly veiled roman à clef about his many lovers…a young graffiti writer-turned-artist who had produced a coffee table book showcasing his work…

She stopped, moved closer to the window to look at this book more closely. On its jacket was a painting, in vivid, childlike colors, of a busy New York street scene. If Anna hadn't known better, she would have said it was Isaiah's mural at the Rat Cave.

She entered the store. An attendant standing near the revolving doors asked her if she was interested in anything in particular.

'Yes,' she said, looking back at the window, 'I'd like to know more about that book.'

He stepped over to the display. 'This one?' he said, pointing to the Hollywood tell-all.

'No, the one next to it.'

'Ah,' he said, smiling. 'Bonz.' He pronounced it 'Bones'.

'I beg your pardon?'

'Bonz. That's the artist's name. If you'd like to buy the book, we have a whole stack of them over here. And the artist himself will be here on Saturday to sign if you'd like an autographed copy.'

'Maybe,' she said pensively, taking a copy of the book from the stack. 'Thank you.' Lost in thought, she wandered over to the checkout line.

FOURTEEN

WHEN SHE GOT HOME, Anna placed the book on her kitchen table to look at later. She had time now only to change and get over to the Bentley Gallery. She took a cab, arriving at the stately townhouse a couple of minutes before eleven.

Immediately she sensed a subtle change in Neal Kavanaugh and Bert Meltzer, a cautious coolness.

'Ah, yes, Miss Winthrop, good to see you,' Kavanaugh said, though he didn't take the hand Anna offered. What was going on?

'And you,' she responded graciously as Meltzer appeared from another room of the gallery. 'I'm eager to see your Parkhurst pieces.'

'Are you?' Meltzer asked.

She looked at him oddly. 'Of course I am. That's why we made this appointment.'

Kavanaugh put his fingertips together as he formed his next words. 'We…did some checking.'

'Checking?'

'Yes,' Meltzer said. 'Is it possible that you—' he pursed his lips distastefully, as if he'd eaten something bad '—are a…sanitation worker?'

So that was it.

'And may I ask why you found it necessary to check on me?'

'We have to be careful,' Kavanaugh said, without explaining why. 'The fact remains that you are not what you represented yourself to be.'

'And what did I represent myself to be?' she asked, feeling her face flush.

'Certainly not a civil servant,' Meltzer said.

'I am a Sanitation Department supervisor,' she said defensively.

'Splitting hairs, aren't we? I hardly think your salary allows for purchases like this.' He vaguely indicated the gallery around them.

'But I am the daughter of Jeff Winthrop,' she said. 'He's worth three quarters of a billion dollars—not that it's any of your business. Doesn't that count for anything?' Why was she selling herself to them? she wondered, then quickly answered herself: for Isaiah.

'Perhaps,' Kavanaugh said. 'No doubt you have a trust fund. But you definitely don't have a new place on Riverview Terrace.'

'My, you did check carefully, didn't you? I still don't understand why. I'm sorry. I thought you wouldn't take me seriously. But money is money. And if you need to wait until my check clears— if I buy anything, that is—then that's up to you.'

She looked from one man to the other. 'Are you going to show me the pieces, or not?'

Their gazes met. Meltzer gave a tiny nod.

'Very well,' Kavanaugh said. 'This way, please.'

She followed him through a door at the back of the room into a private viewing room of curved white walls with a single white chair in the center of the room. It faced one of Isaiah's paintings which had been hung on the wall. This one depicted a beach scene: children building impossibly complex sandcastles, a dog running off with a little girl's swimsuit, rows of sun-worshippers on brightly colored towels. In the sky, an airplane towed a banner that read *'Eat at Joe's'*.

She couldn't help smiling. 'It's wonderful.'

They both agreed.

'It's called *Surf's Up,*' Meltzer said.

She gazed at the painting a moment more, then dropped her gaze. 'It makes me sad to think of what Isaiah's life could have been like.'

'I don't understand,' Meltzer said. 'You didn't know him.'

'No, of course not. But I've researched his life. Don't you research artists whose work you love? Maybe if Isaiah had received more help, things would have turned out differently.'

'Help?'

'Yes. There was certainly plenty of money.'

'Money wasn't the issue,' Kavanaugh said. 'At least not at the beginning.'

She gave him a questioning look.

'He knew he could get any help he needed,' Kavanaugh went on. 'The problem was he didn't think he needed help. He didn't like taking his medication because it killed him artistically. And when he didn't take it, he grew worse and worse, until he wasn't in any state to even think about medication.'

Anna regarded the painting. 'What did you mean when you said "not at the beginning" just now?'

Kavanaugh moved uncomfortably in his suit. 'In the beginning, money wasn't an issue because Lara was wealthy and Isaiah was making a fortune of his own selling his art. Then he went downhill, left Lara, and his life swirled out of control. No money anymore. But he needed it now—needed it badly—because he'd gotten into drugs. Cocaine, specifically.'

'But surely his art was still selling. He would have made money that way.'

Meltzer shook his head. 'It was ironic. He stopped taking his medication because he felt it stifled his talent, yet when he wasn't medicated he was just too ill, mentally, to paint—to do anything, for that matter. So he wasn't producing paintings.

Nor, as I said, did he have Lara's money. So no, there wasn't much money anymore.'

'And a strange thing began to happen,' Kavanaugh said. 'He was gone from the scene. The art world is extremely fickle and has a short memory.'

She nodded, understanding. 'People were losing interest in his work.'

'Exactly. Isaiah couldn't accept that, he didn't think it was possible. He would come here at least once a week, badgering us. Had we sold anything? Were we pricing his paintings too high? He thought so. We didn't. We knew lowering his prices would be the kiss of death. He threatened to move to another gallery, but he never did.'

'How sad,' Anna said.

'Indeed,' Meltzer agreed softly.

Kavanaugh looked up brightly. 'But back to the painting. That's why we're here, isn't it? What do you think?'

'It's amazing, of course—all of his paintings are. But I thought you said you had several pieces?'

Neither man responded directly. 'This is the piece we are selling,' Meltzer said firmly.

'How much?' Anna asked.

'Two hundred fifty thousand.'

'I'll have to think about it,' she said, and turned to go.

'Uh, Miss Winthrop—' Kavanaugh said, a few steps behind her.

She turned.

'Whatever you decide, we ask that you keep all of this confidential.'

'Confidential? Why?'

'The Bentley Gallery sells to some of the wealthiest and most important people in the world for their private collections. Our clients value their privacy. For that reason, we never disclose details of our transactions.'

She gave a little laugh. 'That's your prerogative, of course. But whether I disclose the details of my own purchases is my business.'

Kavanaugh did not looked pleased, but he gave her a tiny smile and inclined his head. 'As you wish.'

Before leaving, she promised to get back in touch with her decision.

AT EIGHT O'CLOCK THAT NIGHT, she left her car at a meter on Jay Street and walked to the place where she and Lawrence had entered the Rat Cave. Behind the stanchion, a young man in a tattered shirt and jeans was urinating against the concrete wall. He glanced over at her but otherwise took no notice. She waited until he had finished before heading down the path into the encampment.

It seemed even more crowded than the first time she had been there. It was difficult to find a place to step among the tents and shelters. Eyes followed her every step of the way, but she kept her gaze straight ahead, walking purposefully until she reached the mural. With no light shining down from above, she could barely make it out. She scanned the lower edge of the wall. The old woman who had told her about Goldie wasn't there.

'You just missed her.'

Anna spun around. The old woman was coming toward her, wrapped in a blue tarp, limping slightly.

'Goldie?' Anna asked.

'Yep. I told her you were lookin' for her, but she said she didn't want nothing to do with you.'

'Why? Who does she think I am?'

'You're one o' them Outreach people, ain't you?'

'No. I should have told you who I was when I was here last time. My name is Anna Winthrop. Isaiah was a friend of mine. I'm trying—' Suddenly it occurred to her that this woman probably didn't know what had happened to Isaiah. 'Have you heard about Isaiah?'

The old woman sank down against the wall beneath the mural. 'He said he was leavin' here, that he wouldn't be back. Said he was "returning to

the land o' the living". Didn't say what he meant.
I figured that's what he did.'

'I'm sorry,' Anna said. 'Actually, Isaiah is dead.'

The woman let out a low whistle. 'Then he ain't
in the land o' the livin', that much I know.' She
looked searchingly at Anna. 'What happened to
him?'

'He was murdered.'

Another low whistle. 'Shame, that is. Sweet
man. So you was his friend, you say?'

Anna nodded. 'Could you tell Goldie that? All
I want to do is speak to her.'

'Sure, I'll tell her,' the old woman replied, and
cast her gaze this way and that among the shadows. Anna knew Goldie must be nearby. But she
wouldn't try to find her—not now.

'And that I'll be back Monday night,' Anna said,
raising her voice.

'Got it. And let me give you a little tip,' the old
woman said. 'When you come back, why don't
you bring her a little something?'

'Good idea.'

'MOVE OVER,' ANNA SAID, gave Santos a shove, and
burst into giggles. He joined in. They were sharing her desk chair, eyes trained on the screen of
the laptop. Santos, sitting on the right, controlled
the mouse.

They were at the website for Bonz, the graffiti artist. Scrawled across the top of the main page, in small letters, were the words: 'Dedicated to the memory of Tie One'.

'Who's that?' Santos asked.

'I already checked. He was a graffiti artist in San Francisco. Real name Jonathan Lim. Died in 1998, aged nineteen. He was climbing the fire escape of a building he intended to paint and a man who lived in the building confronted him and shot him. He's a martyr in the graffiti world.'

Santos nodded solemnly. 'OK, where to?' he asked, moving the cursor around the screen.

'Click on Bonz's bio.'

Santos complied, and the photograph of a homely young man, painfully thin, with multiple piercings in both eyebrows, appeared on the screen. His biography was actually a series of facts about him. From them, Anna and Santos were able to gather that he had once been an outlaw like any other graffiti writer, except that somehow he had infiltrated the art world and become the darling of the social set. His work hung in museums in the United States and Europe, and he designed murals for corporations and the homes of wealthy private collectors. His first book, the self-titled *Bonz,* had just hit bookstores; a series of Japanese manga-style comic books about a graffiti writer's hard life on the streets was soon to be released; and there was a Broadway musical about his life in the works.

'Oh, brother.' Santos shook his head, clicking on a page displaying some of the artist's work. 'What a bunch of baloney. It doesn't even give his real name. What kind of a name is Bonz?'

'I looked that up, too,' Anna said. 'It has several meanings. If you say something is Bonz, you're saying it's absolutely awesome. As in, "Those shoes are bonz." It can also mean "to be in a rush", as in, "I gotta bonz to class." Or it can mean "to do well at", as in, "I bonzed my driving test." So we've got "awesome", "in a hurry", and "do well". I'd say that's a pretty good name for a graffiti writer.'

Santos was studying the screen. 'Look at this stuff. We haul these guys in on vandalism charges.' He scrolled down. 'Weird—all of his paintings look different, like they were all done by different people.'

'Keep scrolling,' Anna said, and stopped him when he reached a painting depicting an urban scene entitled *Mean Streets*. 'Now watch this.'

She reduced the size of the window displaying this painting, then clicked on an icon that opened a window displaying a picture she'd taken the previous night of the mural at the Rat Cave.

Santos frowned, bewildered. 'It's the same picture.'

Anna nodded. 'Amazingly close, isn't it?'

'What do you mean?'

'I mean this one—' she pointed to Isaiah's work '—isn't by Bonz. It's by Isaiah.' She told him about going to see the mural at the Rat Cave. 'And no lectures,' she warned him.

'I'm not lecturing,' he said. 'I just hope you weren't alone.'

'Of course not.' He didn't have to know that when she'd gone there the previous night, she had indeed been alone. 'So, what do you think of this?' She indicated both pictures on the screen.

'I think they're too close for it to be a coincidence. You think Bonz knew Isaiah?'

'It's certainly possible. Remember, Bonz comes from the streets. He knows that world.'

'So he could have stolen the picture from Isaiah. But would it really have been stealing? I mean, I'd have to check on the laws about this, but the mural is illegal to begin with—it was painted on city property without permission. But aside from that, it's public. Who really owns it?'

'I'm not concerned with that. What I'm thinking is that if this Bonz character, this boy genius who's the toast of New York, did get the "inspira-

Now, you *do* want to have fun.'

She gave him an arch look. 'I'm compensating for Gloria's wedding. It's a week from tomorrow, you know.'

'What do you mean, compensating?'

'That will definitely *not* be fun. You're an angel to come with me.'

'How do you know it won't be fun? I'm looking forward to it, actually.'

'Poor thing, so innocent.' She shook her head pityingly. 'Wait. Just wait.'

tion" for his painting from Isaiah's,
wouldn't want anyone to know it.'

He looked at her meaningfully. 'Yo

'That it would be worth killing Isaia
bet. This kid's made millions and will n
more. A plagiarism scandal would be
for his career.'

'So what do you intend to do?'

'I intend to speak to this Bonz, and I i
speak to Goldie, the woman who helpec
paint the mural. I want to find out if the
any connection between the two men.'

'And how do you propose to get in to se
kid? It says here he works in a studio on the
house floor of a converted cardboard factor
Dumbo. You think you can just breeze in?'

'No,' she said thoughtfully, 'if I got in, it wo
have to be some other way. But I've got a be
ter idea. He's autographing his book at the Time

FIFTEEN

THE LINE OF PEOPLE waiting for Bonz to sign their books already stretched from the rear of the store to the front and was doubling back again. In the distance Anna could just make him out, sitting behind a table stacked with books, a small group of men and women hovering around him.

Hoping to get out of the store quickly since she was on her lunch hour, she joined the line behind a young man whose long, coal-black hair stuck straight out from his head in long, hard-looking spikes—sort of a goth Statue of Liberty. He wore pale orange makeup around his eyes that made him look ill, blue lipstick, and a black shirt with cut-outs to show his nipples, which each sported three silver rings. He turned and gave her a sweet smile. 'This is exciting, isn't it?'

'Totally,' she replied. 'How long have you been a fan?'

'Forever. Since he first started writing in New York. Man, he was fearless.'

She glanced again at Bonz sitting behind the table. He looked anything but fearless, as a woman who must have weighed at least 300 pounds leaned over the table so that her face was inches from his. She said something, he uttered a few words, and then he moved his chair back.

The goth Statue of Liberty man, who had also witnessed this exchange, laughed. 'The ladies love him.'

Anna frowned, trying to figure it all out. The line crept forward.

'People,' said a store employee who had appeared beside the line, 'I need to ask you to stand close to those bookcases, OK? A lot of people are here to meet Bonz and we need to keep everything safe and orderly.'

Obediently, everyone shifted toward the right wall.

It was another half hour before the man in front of Anna had his turn. 'Good luck,' he breathed to her before hurrying up to the table and shaking Bonz's hand. He gushed something before Bonz signed his book and he was hustled on by one of the author's retainers.

'All right, miss,' the same retainer called to Anna. She nodded and stepped up to the table.

She now saw a possible reason why the man in front of her was such a Bonz fan: they looked very much alike. Bonz's hair was the same artificial blue-black. She didn't know about his nipples, but his eyebrows, each of which had had three rings in his website photo, now each had at least ten. Anna hurt just looking at them. He was even homelier in person than in his photo—his eyes small and squinty, his nose an odd flat shape, his lips a bit too large.

He looked exhausted and the event had barely begun. Giving Anna a glazed look, he said nothing, waiting for her to speak.

'Great to meet you,' she said, putting out her hand. When he took it, his grip was nonexistent. He simply let her hold his hand. She let it drop.

The young woman who had told her to step up, officious-looking in a black pantsuit and heels, grabbed a book from the nearest stack and handed it to Anna. 'How would you like it inscribed?' she asked, speaking for Bonz.

'For Anna,' she replied, handing the book to Bonz.

Without a smile, he took the book, opened it to the title page, and with a Sharpie pen scrawled *For Anna—Best wishes, Bonz*. Then he closed the book and handed it back to her.

'You can take it to the register right over there,' the young woman instructed her, then shifted her gaze to the next person in line.

'Um, not yet,' Anna said.

Bonz and the woman stared at her.

She opened her purse and brought out prints of

the photographs she had taken of the mural at the Rat Cave. 'First I have something to show you.'

The young woman started around the table. 'No, I'm sorry, he can only sign copies of his book.'

Anna ignored her. 'I don't want these signed,' she said, laying out six photographs of Isaiah's mural on the table in front of Bonz.

He looked down at them, his gaze traveling from one to the next. After a few moments, he looked up at Anna, then at the young woman. 'Call security,' he said.

The woman looked surprised but immediately raised her arm and snapped her fingers. Almost instantly a very large man with a flat-top hair-cut and no neck appeared at the end of the table. 'Problem?'

'Get her out of here,' Bonz said.

As the security man started toward her, Anna pointed to the photos. 'Didn't think anyone would find out about it, did you?'

The security man took her firmly by the upper arm and began propelling her out of the store. Under other circumstances she would have been mortified, but she felt nothing but pleasure as she was shoved toward the revolving door.

The look on Bonz's face told her everything she had wanted to know.

'YOU *WHAT?*' CAME SANTOS'S VOICE from her cell phone. She was walking along Forty-Third Street, half a block from the garage.

'I got thrown out.'

'That's what I thought you said. Why?'

'Why do you think? Because he saw my photos of Isaiah's mural and wanted me to disappear. I'm sure those pictures already have.'

'OK, so you've established that Bonz may have stolen the design from Isaiah—'

She stopped in her tracks. 'May have! You saw those pictures on my computer. Of course he did.'

'So you think Bonz is a suspect in Isaiah's murder. He kills Isaiah so he can't come after him for stealing his work.'

'Right, a good possibility, I think, especially after meeting this character. Now let's think logically—work backwards—for a moment. If Bonz did kill Isaiah, it's possible the two men met at some point. And if they met…and someone saw them meet…then that's an important connection I would need to know about.'

'And how would you establish this connection?'

The answer was, At the Rat Cave, but she wouldn't say that. 'Oops, gotta run,' she chirped, and snapped her phone shut, a preoccupied smile on her face.

AT THE OFFICE she found two voicemail messages. The first was from Izzy Martinson. He would be staking out the illegal dumping site on West Fifty-First and would come by for her at the garage at eight that night.

The second message was from Pam Young at Citigroup, urging her to call back as soon as she could. Anna punched out her number, which she'd scrawled on her desk blotter.

'Anna, have you called Human Resources yet?'

'No, not yet,' Anna replied, embarrassed.

'I didn't think so,' Pam said thoughtfully. 'You're not sure about this, are you?'

'No, I guess I'm not.'

There was a brief silence. 'OK,' Pam said finally, all business. 'Here's where we are. Your sister is a good friend of my brother Ian, so I want to help here. And I'm an excellent judge of character. I know you're right for this position, even if you don't. What have you got to lose by going after it? They haven't offered it to you yet. If they do, which I think is a good possibility, you can decide then what you want to do.'

It made good sense, she supposed. Then why did this whole business give her a sick feeling in the pit of her stomach?

'All right,' she told Pam. 'I'll do it first thing Monday. Thanks.'

'Good girl,' Pam said, and hung up.

LATER THAT DAY, the mysterious woman on West Fifty-First Street called again.

'Do you know who it is yet?' she asked in her breathy voice.

'No, ma'am, we don't. Have you seen him again?'

'Yes.'

'You have? Did you get any more information this time?'

'Yes. It was dark but I saw some lettering on the side of the truck. I could make out two words—"Flushing", like maybe Flushing, Queens? And also the name "Rayburn". Do you think that might help?'

'Possibly,' Anna said, her eyes narrowing suspiciously. 'If you'll put this information on an Illegal Dumping Tip Form—'

'Why?' The woman sounded irritated. 'What difference does it make if I put it on a form? I've just told you—isn't that enough?'

'Ma'am, it's more official if—'

But Anna realized the woman had hung up. When she looked up, Allen Schiff was standing in her doorway, looking down on her with a kind expression.

'What's up, chief?' she asked.

'You got time for a drink?'

Uh-oh. 'Yeah, sure.' She glanced at the clock

on her desk: 2:35. 'I'm just wrapping up. Meet you out front in ten minutes?'

'Sounds great. We can go to Harley's.'

She quickly gathered up her things. Something was definitely on his mind. Ten minutes later they were at a small table in the dark bar, ordering beers.

'So,' Allen said, setting down his glass on a coaster and grabbing some peanuts from a bowl on the table, 'how are things?'

She liked Allen, but he was old-fashioned about a lot of things, like the way he treated women with kid gloves. She smiled. 'Things are great for *me*. But *you've* obviously got something on your mind.'

He sat back and laughed, his double chin shaking. 'You're just like my older daughter, Jessica. I can't put anything over on her, either.'

She waited.

'All right,' he said, looking straight at her. 'Do you know a gentleman by the name of Austin Parkhurst?'

So that was it. A dark feeling came over her. 'You know I do. He called, didn't he?' It was a statement, not a question.

'Yeah, 'fraid so. But I want to hear your version of things before I tell you his.'

'That's good, Allen,' she said, setting her own drink down, 'because as far as I can tell, I've done nothing wrong. I went to see him at a bar he's got under construction to ask him some questions about his father.'

'Aren't you leaving a few things out? Like, that his father was a homeless person who got murdered in your backyard?'

'Does it matter? I don't mean to be rude, but what has this got to do with you?'

His face grew serious. 'It's got a lot to do with me when you show up there under the auspices of the Sanitation Department of New York.'

Her jaw dropped. 'Is that what he said I did?'

Allen said nothing.

'Well, I didn't. Yes, I told him I worked for Sanitation, but I never said what I wanted to talk to him about had anything to do with the department. In fact, I told him it didn't. Allen, the guy is a major jerk. He's angry that I confronted him— that I stuck my nose into his business—and he's trying to get back at me.' *Or he knows I'm on to him and wants me off his tail.*

Allen put out his hands. 'OK, I believe you. I just had to put it out there. And I felt you ought to know he called.'

'Thanks. I appreciate it.'

'Not a problem.' He snarfed some more nuts. 'So,' he said with exquisite nonchalance, 'how's it all going?'

She looked at him again. 'You mean my job?'

'Yeah, sure, if that's what you want to talk about.'

'Oh, Allen,' she said, bursting into laughter, 'you're wonderful. Tiptoeing around me because I'm a girl. But I'm really very strong, you know.' She flexed a muscle. 'One of New York's Strongest.'

'All right,' he conceded. 'How do *you* think your job is going?'

'I think it's going really well, since you asked. I've got a good rapport with my crew—for the most part—and they're performing well. Though you'd be the best judge of that.'

'For the most part,' he said thoughtfully, 'your section is achieving its productivity goals. There's room for improvement—always is—and we can accomplish that with some rerouting, changing some people around. But it's your rapport with your crew, as you put it, that I'm not so sure about.'

'And why is that?' she asked, surprised.

'To begin with, Jay Rapchuck and Winston Avery seem to be giving you problems.'

'I won't say they're easy.' She sipped her beer. 'They just need to accept that their supervisor is a woman.'

'If you don't mind my saying so, Anna, that's something they should have accepted long ago.

It's something you should have forced them to accept, rather than waiting for it to happen. Now I wonder...'

'What, that it's too late?'

'Well,' he said, looking at her, 'yes.'

'Listen, Allen. Every supervisor's got a joker or two on his or her crew—it's the nature of the beast. Jay and Winston have given me some problems, I'll admit that, but I think I've dealt with them effectively. And if the problems don't stop, I'll ask to have them transferred.'

'That's what I want to hear. Take a hard line with them.'

'Be tough, you mean?'

'Yes.'

'That's what this is about, isn't it? You're not sure I'm tough enough for this job.'

'I just don't want it to become a girls' club, Anna.'

'A girls' club? What are you talking about?'

'I've noticed that sometimes you have Kelly and Brianna in your office.'

'Yes, that's right, for coffee in the mornings once in a while. Is that a problem?'

'No, not per se, of course not. But you don't want to create the perception that you're favoring them.'

'I'll take that under advisement,' she said, tiring of this conversation. 'Any other feedback?'

'No, not feedback, but a few questions. Like how are things going with that kid Pierre?'

She smiled. 'He's a sweet kid. Got some problems at home. And filling Garry's shoes was a tall order. But he's doing well, under the circumstances.'

'Drives like a maniac. You keep an eye on that and don't be afraid to send him back for more training if that's what he needs. He getting along OK with Tommy?'

'Anyone would get along with Tommy—or should I say Tommy would get along with anyone. He's a true pro, never a problem. I doubt I'll ever have any problems with him.'

'Third-generation Sanitation Department, that kid, and it shows, doesn't it?'

She nodded. 'Who else?'

'Just one more.'

'Let me guess. Bill Hogan.'

He nodded reluctantly. 'How's he doing?'

'With his drinking, you mean? To be honest, not well. Which is why I told him he had to get back in touch with Medical Services to set up counseling.'

'Good, good. And what about you, Anna?'

'Me?'

'Are you happy?'

'Yes,' she said, looking at him oddly, 'of course.' She remembered her last conversation with Pam Young.

'What I mean is, now that you've been in Sanitation—what, four years?—what do you think? Is it the right place for you?'

She concentrated hard, searching for the right words. 'I don't know if I can explain this, but I find this work enormously satisfying. Every day, New York City generates twenty-five thousand tons of garbage that has to be gotten rid of—more garbage than any other city on earth. Garbage isn't something people usually like to talk about—it's something they like to see quietly disappear. But that doesn't make it any less important. Without the Sanitation Department, this city would grind to a stop. So we're doing an incredible thing, and I'm a small part of that.' She looked at him. 'Does that make any sense?'

He grinned. 'It makes a lot of sense, Anna. In fact, it was what I was hoping you'd say.' He looked at his watch. 'Better get going. Marie's holding dinner, I'm sure.'

Back out on the street, he gave her that fatherly grin. 'Don't be a stranger, Anna. If you've got a problem, let me help. That's what I'm here for.' He headed back to the garage to get his car.

Walking home, Anna wondered how much she had reduced Allen's concerns.

AT HOME SHE MADE HERSELF a light dinner, then returned to the garage, arriving a few minutes before eight. She waited on the sidewalk outside the gate, admiring a golden glow that had settled over the buildings across the street in the summer dusk. After a few moments, Izzy Martinson drove up in his red GMC Jimmy. In the front passenger seat was a thin, red-haired man in his early thirties whom Izzy introduced as his partner, Aubrey Quinn.

Anna climbed into the backseat and they headed west. She told them about the call she'd received that afternoon from the mysterious woman, about her mentioning seeing the words 'Flushing' and 'Rayburn' on the side of the truck.

Aubrey wrinkled his brow. 'Something doesn't sound right there.'

Izzy agreed. 'If this dumping bothers her so much, why isn't she willing to fill out a form?'

Anna said, 'From her first call it was clear she was afraid the dumper would find out she was the one who turned him in and go after her.'

Izzy shook his head. 'Still doesn't sound right. I don't buy it.' He drove up Eighth Avenue, took a right on to Fifty-Second Street, then down Broadway a block so that he could turn on to West Fifty-First. He parked just off Broadway, on the north side, as far from the vacant lot as possible, though they could still see it clearly. When he killed the engine, a deep quiet descended over them. Aubrey handed out cups of coffee and they sat, waiting, as the darkness deepened.

Half an hour passed in which only a few sedans passed along the short block on their way elsewhere. About forty-five minutes after that, they heard a deep rumbling and a dump truck appeared behind them, grinding along the street. They sat up straight, scrutinizing the truck for details—license plate number, color—taking quick notes… until it passed the vacant lot and kept going. They relaxed, lapsing once again into watchful silence in the blackness of the SUV.

The narrow street was almost completely dark when the woman appeared. They couldn't make out much about her except that she was small and thin, youngish, though they couldn't be sure, that she had a small dog on a leash, and that she was pushing a shopping cart with a cloth of some kind over its mounded top.

Izzy slowly straightened up in his seat. 'What the…?'

The woman had stopped at the vacant lot. She turned slowly and looked down the short stretch of the street behind her, her gaze traveling over the dark vehicle in which Anna and the two men sat. After a moment, the woman moved away from the cart toward a lamppost and appeared to be fiddling with something on it.

'What's she doing?' Aubrey whispered.

Izzy said, 'I think…yeah, she's tying the leash to the lamppost.'

They watched. Now the woman was removing the cloth from the top of the shopping cart. She dropped the cloth on the sidewalk beside her. Then she rolled the cart into the lot, visibly struggling on the uneven ground.

Abruptly, she stopped, moved around to the side of the cart, and with a great effort, pushed it over. They heard the crash from where they sat. Out of the overturned cart spilled a small mountain of debris.

'That's it,' Izzy said, moving quickly in his seat. 'Let's go,' he said to Aubrey, and the two men shot out of the SUV and ran along the sidewalk to where the woman stood pulling the remaining debris from the cart.

Anna got out and watched from beside the SUV. When Izzy grabbed the woman's arm and turned her around, she let out a cry that was half shock, half despair. She said something to the two men; they responded, and then Anna heard a soft metallic clink as they put her in handcuffs. After a few moments they began walking back toward Anna, the woman between the two men.

She was a pretty little thing, late twenties maybe, with long dark-brown hair and big, soulful eyes. She saw Anna and gave her a sullen look. 'I don't know what this is all about. I was just walking Bruiser.' Then she remembered she'd left him tied to the lamppost. 'Bruiser! You can't leave him there.'

'I'll do it,' Anna said, and hurried along the sidewalk to where the dog sat patiently waiting. The sweet-looking little Pekingese was happy to see her, an excited white ball of fluff. 'Come on, Bruiser,' she said, and led him by the leash to the SUV. She got in beside the woman. Bruiser crawled into his mistress's lap.

'Did you call for backup?' Anna asked Izzy and Aubrey.

Aubrey looked at her. 'You gotta be kidding.'

'You're making a terrible mistake,' the woman said. 'Why are you doing this to me?'

'Ma'am,' Izzy said patiently, 'like I told you, you're under arrest for illegal dumping.'

'Illegal dumping! What are you talking about? What did I dump?'

Quinn rolled his eyes. 'Ma'am, give it up, OK? Those weren't groceries in that cart and you know it. What I'd like to know is why,' he added, clearly not expecting an answer, but he must have said the magic words because the woman burst into tears.

'He's a monster! Left me for that girl and didn't give me a dime. Making all that money on his building jobs. So I thought I'd make his life difficult, let him see what it was like.' Izzy turned a corner. 'Where are you taking me?'

'The police station, ma'am. Do you want to tell us your name now?'

She burst into fresh tears. 'Rita. Rita Rayburn. Oh, Bruiser,' she wept, burying her face in his fur, 'what are we going to do?'

SIXTEEN

By Monday morning, news of the illegal dumper's capture had somehow reached the garage. 'Way to go, Anna,' Allen Schiff called to her from his office doorway.

She smiled, shaking her head.

A little before ten o'clock, she got into her department car and drove over to the office of Dr Sheldon Warner at 424 Park Avenue.

It was a typical Park Avenue luxury apartment building: about twenty stories in tan brick, with a wide awning over the entrance. As soon as she pulled up, a uniformed doorman emerged from the lobby and approached the car.

'Good morning,' she said, getting out.

'Morning, ma'am,' he said, looking with bewilderment at the words 'Sanitation Department' on the side of her car. 'Is there something we can help you with?'

'Official business.' She opened the back door and hauled out one of the blood-soaked clear-plastic bags that Art and Terrence had brought back to the garage.

The doorman looked at it in horror. 'What is that?'

She ignored him. 'I'm here to see Dr Warner. What suite?'

'You can't just go in there,' he said, running after her into the lobby. 'I'll call the police.'

She turned to him. 'Maybe you should. I'll probably have to have Dr Warner arrested soon.'

He closed his mouth, quiet for the moment. Then he said, 'Suite One A.'

Carrying the bag, Anna crossed the lobby and headed down a corridor to a door bearing a stylized figure of a nude woman. Above it were the words 'WARNER PLASTIC SURGERY CENTER, SHELDON M. WARNER, M.D.'

She entered a serene oasis of soft carpet, even softer lighting, and an enormous saltwater aquarium that formed the waiting room's back wall. To the left, a beautiful young woman sat at a tiny desk. Seeing the plastic bag, she rose in horror. 'What—'

'I'm here to see Dr Warner.'

'Do—do you have an appointment?' The woman's eyes were fixed on the bag.

'No, but I think he'd better see me. My name is Anna Winthrop and I'm a supervisor at the Sanitation Department—Manhattan Central District Thirteen.'

'What is it about?' the woman asked, lowering her voice to a whisper. All around the waiting room, women had looked up and were watching the scene with interest.

Anna lowered her voice, too. 'I'll tell the doctor.'

The woman hesitated. Then, 'All right. Um, would you wait over here with that?' She indicated a small room behind her desk.

'All right,' Anna said pleasantly, 'if you'll get the doctor for me.'

'I am, I am,' the woman said, and hurried away.

Anna set the bag on the floor and peered out the doorway of the small room into the waiting room. At least a dozen women, each one more beautiful than the last. Tight, flawless skin, perfect, perky breasts...

'This way, please.' The young woman had returned. Anna followed her into a corridor behind the waiting room. At the end of the corridor was an open door, and through the doorway Anna saw a tall, silver-haired man in a white doctor's coat standing behind a desk.

'What is this all about?' he demanded as she walked into the room and dropped the bag on to his desk.

He recoiled in horror. 'What are you doing? Who are you?'

'You know who I am, Dr Warner. I told your receptionist here. You've been mixing your red-bag waste in with your regular solid waste that we've been taking away for you as part of the ProFee Program.'

'That's ridiculous,' he sputtered. 'We have a company that takes our medical waste.'

'Yes, I'm sure you do. Though I doubt they're getting much of it.'

'That's preposterous. We do participate in the ProFee Program, but we give them only our regular garbage. Now get out of here! And take this—' he regarded the bag with horror '—monstrosity with you.'

'No,' she said pleasantly, 'that's yours. I wanted you to have it back. And I have a couple of other things for you.' She took a filled-out summons from her pocket and placed it on his desk. Then from the same pocket she took an empty pill tube and set it down beside the summons.

Dr Warner stared down at the pill tube. 'So it's ours. That doesn't mean it was in the garbage.'

'It does when three people have witnessed it being removed from the bags, along with about a dozen more.' She shook her head. 'Shame on you. Endangering public health just to save a few bucks. Now it's going to cost you a few. The fines go up to fifty thousand dollars a day, not to mention the civil penalty of up to ten thousand dollars. You'll need to do a lot of face-lifts to earn that back.'

He opened his mouth to protest but she cut him off again. 'If you've got a problem with this, don't call the Sanitation Department. We have no jurisdiction over the resolution of summonses. You can contest the summons by contacting the Environmental Control Board. Oh—and you can request to have me present at your hearing.' She smiled sweetly. 'I'll be more than happy to attend.'

AT THE END OF THE DAY, Anna closed her office door and called the Human Resources Department at Citigroup. The man who answered knew who she was. 'Of course, Ms Winthrop, let's get something set up for you right away.'

And he did. Anna was to report to his office at four o'clock the following Monday.

Putting down the phone, she was overcome by a dizzying sense of guilt. But who did she feel guilty about betraying? The New York Sanitation Department…or herself?

BENEATH ISAIAH'S MURAL, the old woman in the blue tarp smiled, then turned her head in the direction of the space's darker recesses. Anna discerned the outline of a person—a woman, it looked like—

standing perfectly still. A thin shaft of moonlight glinted on something metallic, and as the figure emerged from the shadows and opened its mouth to speak, Anna saw a golden front tooth.

'You wanted to see me?' the young woman said.

What first struck Anna was how pretty she was—soft, feminine features, full lips, flawless light-brown skin. She wore denim overalls on top of a red gingham blouse, and a pink scarf around her head, a few wisps of hair sticking out. She couldn't have been more than twenty years old.

Anna put out her hand. 'I'm Anna Winthrop. I wanted to speak to you about Isaiah.'

The young woman took Anna's hand, though hesitantly. 'You brought me something?'

'Oh—' Anna searched in her pocket '—yes, of course.' She brought out a wad of bills, fifty dollars, and handed it to the woman, who counted it and tucked it into a pocket of her overalls.

'Name's Goldie.' She pointed to the gold tooth.

'I appreciate your willingness to see me. Is there somewhere we can go to talk?'

'Coffee shop just around the corner.'

'Sounds good,' Anna said, and followed Goldie around the stanchion, through the city of tents and shelters, and on to Jay Street. Just around the corner on Prospect Street was a tiny restaurant called The Two Bridges, after the Manhattan and Brooklyn bridges nearby. The shop window, featuring a neon coffee cup complete with steam, cast a welcoming golden glow over the sidewalk below. Inside, Anna and Goldie took a booth.

'I'm sorry I made you come back to see me and all,' Goldie said, taking a menu from the waitress. 'I just had to make sure you weren't one of those Outreach people.'

'I understand. It sounds like they do more harm than good.'

Goldie put down her menu and leaned forward slightly. 'Oh, no, it's not like that. Don't get me wrong—I got nothin' against those people. It's just that to them, I'm one more bag lady in training who needs to be taken off the street for a night. To me, I'm a person—a person who's had some rough times and wants to get off the streets—permanent. And the only person who's gonna make that happen is me.' She lowered her gaze, pain crossing her face. 'Learned that the hard way.'

'Where are you from?' Anna asked gently.

'New York City…in a roundabout way. I was born here, but when I was two my grandma took me away from my mom. My mom had a bad drug problem. One day she wasn't watching me and I almost fell out a window. Grandma got me outta there and took care of me herself. I loved that lady. But she died when I was six.'

Goldie picked up her fork and twiddled it nervously between her fingers. 'I had no family once she was gone. So I had to go to a foster home, this rich family up in Westchester. Big house, trees, grass...' She knitted her brows. 'I shoulda known it was too good to last. My foster dad, there was something wrong with his leg and he couldn't work, so he was home almost all the time. When I was nine he started doing bad things to me. It's funny, but I don't remember most of the stuff he did. Guess I blocked it out.

'My foster mom abused me in her own way. Nothing I did was right. She was always yellin' at me. If something went wrong in that house, I got blamed.

'School was just as bad. All these rich kids made fun of me because I was in a foster home. The teachers were no better. I tried to talk to them about what my foster dad was doin' to me, but they wouldn't listen. They just thought I was a troublemaker and a bother.

'Then an amazing thing happened. When I was eleven, I went back home to my mother. She'd gotten herself cleaned up and wanted me back. I kind of had to get to know her again, on account of not seein' her for so long, but once I did we were as happy as we could be.' Goldie sighed. 'Then Jed came along.'

'Jed?'

'This guy my mother was seeing. Great big dude with a mustache. He moved in with us, said he planned to marry my mom, though I never saw any sign of that happening.'

'Did he…hurt you?'

Goldie nodded. 'One Saturday when my mother was at some house-cleaning job, he took me into his bedroom and—well, you can figure out the rest. He told me if I told anyone he would kill my mother. He showed me the gun he would do it with, too. So it kept happening. Finally I couldn't stand it anymore and I told my mother what Jed was doing. And you know what? She started screamin' at *me*. She didn't want to believe it, or else she did believe it but she didn't want to lose Jed. She told me if I didn't like living there I could leave.

'So I left. Twelve years old and I walked right out of there. When I finally got tired, I sat down on some steps. After a while this big white limousine pulled up right in front of me, like a fairy tale, and this young guy got out. He was handsome, and he was dressed real nice. He asked me to come for a ride, so I did. Worst decision I ever made. There was this girl in the car, a beautiful girl in fancy clothes, high heels. She and the guy—his name was Lee—they were sharing a bottle of something and they asked me if I wanted some. Heck, I didn't know what it was, so I said, "Sure!" and started drinkin'. I got drunk, so drunk I didn't even care when Lee took me into his apartment and he and four other guys took turns with me.'

Goldie started to cry.

'I went to work for Lee. I had nowhere else to go. Besides, he was payin' me well, gave me a nice place to live, paid for me to get my tooth done, said it would be my "trademark". He also got me lots of drugs. After a while it was like I was in a dream all the time. Go out on the street, bring back some guy, take care of him, get high, go back out on the street…and give my money to Lee…

'Then one day I heard screaming coming from an apartment down the hall from the one I shared with another girl. She and I were terrified. We had no idea what was goin' on, until the next day another girl tells us this really young girl named Tonia was givin' Lee a bad time and he beat her up so bad she died.

'The girl I shared the apartment with—she was too scared to even move, but I said, "That's it, I'm outta here." And I snuck out. I went as far away as I could, as fast as I could. I had no money—Lee never let us keep any, that's how he controlled us, along with the drugs—and I didn't know anybody, so the first night I slept on a bench in a little park on the West Side. During the day all I got was looks of disgust from the people who walked by, so I got off the streets. I ended up at the Rotunda at Riverside Park, right on the Hudson River at Seventy-Ninth Street. You ever been there?'

Anna had seen the Rotunda, a great vaulted structure with a fountain, tiled arcade, and wide stairs on which an entire homeless community slept in mild weather.

'These people—homeless people—they weren't like anybody else I ever met. They didn't care who I was—they just wanted to help me. They got me some food and some clothes, made sure I had a safe place to sleep. They helped me get off the drugs.

'I met Isaiah there. One morning I woke up and here's this guy lyin' on the step above me, smiling the sweetest smile I'd ever seen.' Goldie's gaze wandered. 'I think I fell in love with him in that moment.

'And,' she went on, sitting up straight and collecting herself, 'I've been on the streets ever since. Not always exactly *on* the streets,' she amended, without explaining. She looked down, fishing in the pockets of her overalls and finally bringing out a cell phone. 'See this? Isaiah gave it to me. He said, "Goldie, you'll never get off the streets without a job, and you'll never get a job if you can't get calls for interviews.'" She smiled. 'That's not entirely true, of course, but you see what he meant. And he brought out this cell phone and gave it to me.'

'Is it...expensive to keep up?' Anna asked.

Goldie gave her an arch smile, the gold tooth shining. 'You're a practical thinker like me. I said, "How am I ever going to pay a phone bill? And where would they send the bills even if I could?" And you know what he said? "Goldie, I've paid ahead on your phone account. Not so much that it won't ever run out, but enough that you should be happily employed before it does. And by that time you'll be able to pay your own phone bill."'

Anna sat studying this young woman. 'Goldie,' she said, 'how old are you?'

'Eighteen.'

The waitress had returned, filling their cups with coffee and then taking their orders. Goldie ordered apple pie à la mode, Anna a toasted corn muffin.

Anna watched Goldie put sugar and cream into her coffee and take a big sip. When Goldie put down the cup, there was a smile on her lips but tears in her eyes. Without thinking, Anna reached out and placed her hand on Goldie's.

Goldie looked at her, sniffed. 'I loved Isaiah, you know. Guess that's why I'm crying. 'Cause he didn't love me back—at least not the way I loved him. He was kind to me and all—gave me this phone, helped me in any way he could—but he said I was like a daughter to him. I told him I understood, but it hurt real deep. He was smart—he knew how I felt—and he told me he'd found a lady—old, like himself, he said—' she laughed through her tears '—somebody more…appropriate. He said she was a wonderful woman who'd *saved* him. That's how he put it, saved him. And when he gave me the phone, he said it was because of this woman that he could help me.'

'Meaning she gave him the money for the phone.'

''Course. He didn't have that kind of money. He didn't have *any* kind of money.'

Their orders arrived. Anna broke off a piece of muffin, popped it into her mouth, and took a sip of hot coffee.

Goldie smiled brightly. 'But now that he's with this woman, he's got plenty o' money, right?'

Then she didn't know.

Anna placed her hand back over Goldie's and looked into her eyes. Goldie knew immediately what Anna was going to say. She burst into fresh tears, putting down her coffee cup so that it rattled in the saucer, and burying her face in her hands.

'He's gone, isn't he?'

'Yes. He was killed…murdered.'

Goldie's expression suggested that this was incomprehensible to her. 'Who'd want to kill Isaiah?'

'I don't know. No, let me rephrase that. Several people might have wanted to kill him. I'm trying to figure out which one actually did it.'

'Why? How did you know him?'

'I didn't know him well, really. He came by for my cans and bottles every week and I got to know him just a little bit. He seemed a very private person.'

'Mm, that he was. Cans and bottles…' Goldie said, shaking her head. 'Him and his shopping cart.' She looked again at Anna. 'How…did it happen?'

'One day he came by, but not for cans and bottles. He wanted to speak to me. He looked terrible, desperate. Something was definitely wrong. I got a call from work and went inside for a moment. When I came out, he was gone. From what I've pieced together, while I was inside, a man approached Isaiah and forced him into the alley beside my building and into the courtyard. And he…cut his throat.'

Goldie shut her eyes tight, but not tight enough to keep new tears in. 'Poor Isaiah,' she said in a squeaky voice. She opened her eyes. 'And let me guess. The cops couldn't give a rat's patoot, right?'

Anna gave a wan smile. 'Let's just say I don't have much confidence they'll ever solve the case. So I'm trying to do it. He needed me and I wasn't there for him. I want justice for this man.'

'Don't go beatin' yourself up because you went inside, because you know what? If whoever did that to him hadn't gotten him then, he woulda gotten him some other time, some other way.'

'You're probably right. Anyway, that's what I'm doing.'

Goldie nodded. 'Being his friend. I'm his friend, too. I wanna help you in any way I can.'

'Good,' Anna said, sitting up straight and wiping her hands on her napkin. 'Then tell me what you can about that amazing mural.'

With a sad smile, Goldie put down her empty coffee cup. 'Could we walk for a little while? I need some air.'

'Of course.' Anna paid the check and followed Goldie out into the balmy night.

'You asked about the mural.' Goldie's head was down, her hands deep in her pockets as she walked. 'Isaiah and I were both at the Rat Cave. I woke up one morning and he was gone. Few minutes later, he shows up with paint and brushes and says he's going to paint the wall. And he starts in.' She shook her head, remembering. 'It was one of the most beautiful things I ever saw—all those happy people in bright colors. I asked Isaiah what he was doing and we got to talking. He said this wasn't the first painting he'd done. He'd done them all over the city in places just like the Rat Cave, and he intended to keep doing them. I watched him for a while. Then I told him that when I was a little girl, I won an art contest at school. And you know what he did? He handed me the paintbrush he was using and said, "Then it's about time, isn't it?"'

Goldie paused. 'I started out slow at first—I was afraid I'd make a mistake, you know? Then I started painting—picking up where Isaiah left off and then making up stuff of my own. I couldn't remember when I'd had so much fun. And all of a sudden I remembered how much I used to love to draw and paint when I was a little girl, how it would take me somewhere else, somewhere safe and happy. That's how I felt painting the mural with Isaiah. I started laughing and then I was crying. Strangest thing…

'After that, Isaiah kept coming back to work some more on the painting—the mural, he always called it. He'd walk into the Rat Cave with that rusty shopping cart of his, and it would be full of paint cans and brushes. Said the paint stores had thrown 'em away. He and I must have worked on it for weeks, on and off.'

The street had grown quieter, only the occasional car passing.

'Goldie,' Anna said, 'did anyone else look at the mural?'

Goldie looked at her in puzzlement. 'Of course. You saw how many people live in that place.'

'No, what I mean is, anyone besides the people living there.'

'Oh, OK, I see where you're goin' with this. Yes, matter of fact there was someone. That was a bad night. Let's sit for a while,' Goldie said, dropping on to a bench on the sidewalk.

Anna sat down beside her. 'A bad night? How?'

'It was the night Isaiah and I finished the mural, come to think of it. We were so happy. We were standing there, admiring our work, when this group of young guys comes in. One of the guys—he was the leader, I could see that—he went up to Isaiah and the two of them talked quietly for a few minutes. I couldn't hear what they were saying. While they were talking, the other guys, there were three of them, they stood watching.

'Isaiah raised his voice and I saw the other guys start to run over, but the leader guy put up his hand and they stopped. Then they all left. Just before he was out of sight, the leader yelled back, "Think about it, old man."'

'Did Isaiah tell you what it was all about?'

'Only a little. I could tell he was upset and that he didn't want to get me upset. He made a fake laugh and said, "He wanted me to sign a contract. How can I sign a contract? I don't exist!"'

'Did he explain what he meant?'

'No, that was all he ever said about it.'

'Did the young man ever come back?'

Goldie shrugged. 'Not that I ever saw.' She fished in her pockets for a pack of cigarettes and matches, lit up, and blew smoke straight ahead of her. 'You don't mind, do you?'

Anna shook her head. 'What did this young man look like?'

'Nothing much to speak of. Skinny little guy. Black hair. Oh, and he had all these rings in his eyebrows. I hate that.'

Now it was Anna who searched in her purse. She brought out a photograph of Bonz, cut from the jacket of his book. 'Is this the man?'

Goldie nodded animatedly. 'Yeah, that's him.' She frowned. 'Who is he?'

'His name is Bonz.'

'*That's* Bonz?'

'Then you've heard of him?'

'Girl, anyone who lives on the streets has heard of Bonz. He's famous.'

'For what?'

'For graffiti. His stuff is all over town.' Goldie

laughed. 'I heard he's a famous *artiste* now. What would he want with Isaiah?'

This time Anna brought out a picture of Bonz's *Mean Streets,* also torn from his book.

Goldie looked at it and wrinkled her brow. 'That's our mural.'

'It is, but it isn't. It's actually a painting by Bonz.'

Goldie's eyes widened in understanding. 'Now I see. You think that's what he wanted Isaiah to sign a contract about?'

'Most likely. My guess is that it was all-encompassing, giving Bonz rights to all of Isaiah's mural work.'

'But Isaiah wouldn't sign.'

'Right. So did Bonz go to plan B?'

'Meaning getting rid of Isaiah?' Goldie stubbed out her cigarette on the side of the bench's concrete support. 'I saw the little creep. I wouldn't put it past him.' She lit another cigarette. 'Man, the idea that he would *kill* somebody over something like that…'

'"Something like that" represents millions of dollars to Bonz. People have killed for a lot less.'

'So he's what you would call a suspect.'

'Yes—one of them.'

'There's more?'

'Goldie,' Anna said, turning to her, 'did you know Isaiah had a son?'

Goldie nodded sadly. 'Austin.'

'How did you know. Did Isaiah tell you?'

'Just that he had a son named Austin, nothing about him. I don't really know anything about Isaiah's past. Anyway, one day about a month ago Isaiah and I were walking down the street and all of a sudden he goes up to this pay phone and says he's calling his son.'

'Did he reach him?'

'Yeah. I heard Isaiah tell Austin he was sorry about the past but that he loved him, that he was working on getting well, and...that his life was better now that he had someone special in it.' Her voice broke.

'What did Isaiah want from Austin?'

'Just to see him. He begged him.'

'Did Austin agree?'

'Oh, he agreed, all right. Said he would meet Isaiah the next day at some diner somewhere on West Forty-Fifth.'

'And did they meet?'

Goldie gave a little shrug. 'I asked Isaiah that, and for some reason he wouldn't answer me. All he said was, "I suppose I deserve a broken heart." I figured they hadn't met. Now Austin will never have his chance.'

They sat quietly for a few moments. Then Anna spoke.

'Goldie, can you think of anyone—besides Bonz—who might have wanted to hurt Isaiah?'

Goldie nibbled the inside of her cheek, thinking. She looked up. 'There is somebody, now that you mention it. This guy named Pete.'

'Yes?'

'Crazy fool. He really liked me, see, and he thought me and Isaiah were an item. So he was jealous. Picked a fight with Isaiah, punched him in the mouth, made him bleed.'

'Didn't Isaiah tell him that you and he weren't… romantically involved?'

'That's cute,' Goldie said. '"Romantically involved". No. You see, Isaiah, he was a gentleman, and he told me a gentleman doesn't discuss a lady's private business.

'Pete kept comin' on to me, you know? Seemed like every time I turned around, there was Pete. Then one night I was asleep over there—' she pointed in the general direction of the Rat Cave '—and suddenly I felt somebody on top of me, pullin' at my pants. It was Pete. I started to scream, but suddenly Pete wasn't on top of me anymore. Isaiah had him by the scruff o' the neck. He punched his lights out. Pete was hurt bad. Finally he crawled away. He said Isaiah would be sorry.

Isaiah told me later he hated to hurt anyone, even scum like Pete, but he had no choice.'

'Did you ever see Pete again?'

'Oh, yeah,' Goldie said matter-of-factly. 'Only now he kept his distance, just made faces, wiggled his eyebrows, pointed to his private parts—you get the picture. He didn't dare come near me.' She met Anna's gaze. 'He hated Isaiah. I used to think he was just waitin' to make his move, to get back at Isaiah for hurtin' him like that. Once Isaiah told me Pete followed him all the way from Brooklyn to the South Bronx. Isaiah gave him the slip. I haven't seen Pete in a while. Maybe *he* killed Isaiah.'

'Maybe. Does this Pete live in the Ra—over there?'

'No,' Goldie replied with a laugh, 'not since the night Isaiah beat him up. He moved, but not to a very nice address.'

'What do you mean?'

Goldie's expression grew serious. 'You ever heard of the Catacombs?'

Anna shook her head.

'It's a place under Grand Central where people live. A lot of people.'

'You mean underground?'

'Yeah. That's where Pete lives—least, last time I heard.'

'I think I should talk to him.'

Goldie snorted doubtfully. 'You mean *we*. You're not goin' there alone. You got no idea what it's like.'

'Will you take me there?'

'Sure. When do you wanna go?'

'Could you take me tomorrow night?'

'Uh, let me check my social calendar. Yeah, sure. How 'bout you meet me in front of Grand Central—say, ten o'clock?'

'So late?'

'Later the better. More chance of finding him. No knowin' where he'll be in the daytime.'

They traded cell phone numbers in case anything came up. Then they walked back to the stanchion on Jay Street. Before heading down the path, Goldie turned to Anna and said, 'Wait a second.' She pulled the money Anna had given her from her pocket and held it out. 'I don't want this.'

'I don't understand. Can't you use it?'

Goldie let out a laugh. '"Course I could use it. But I'm not gonna take it. Wouldn't be right.' She walked toward the darkness, then abruptly stopped and turned around again. 'Wear dark clothes. And bring two flashlights. Big ones. And that fifty bucks. You'll need it.'

SEVENTEEN

ON FORTY-SECOND STREET, Anna neared Grand Central Terminal, having walked from her apartment. It was a few minutes after ten o'clock. At first she saw no sign of Goldie and wondered if she had decided not to show. Then she spotted her, waiting in the deep shadows beneath the Park Avenue overpass, where the street split to circumvent the station.

Seeing Anna, Goldie smiled. She looked Anna up and down, taking in her black shirt and jeans and nodding approvingly. She herself wore the same overalls she had worn the previous day, but with a deep purple T-shirt underneath. 'Less chance we'll be spotted. You bring the flashlights?'

Anna opened her large shoulder bag and Goldie peered inside. 'OK, then we're ready. You're sure you want to do this?'

'Of course. Why not?'

Goldie had to laugh. 'Why not? Because some of the people down there are like animals, that's why. Ain't you never heard of the mole people?'

Anna scoffed. 'Silliness. They're just people, Goldie. You should know better than that.'

'Mm, just people,' Goldie repeated, starting toward the station's front entrance, 'but being down there does something to 'em. Some people say they eat rats. Some people say they even eat each other.'

'Oh, for goodness' sake!' Anna followed her down the ramp on to the cavernous main concourse, filled with bustling crowds even at this late hour.

Goldie stopped and gazed up at the massive vaulted ceiling with its famous astronomical design in pale blue and gold. Then she took in the huge American flag hung a few days after the September 11 terrorist attacks; the information booth with its four-faced clock; the ticket vending machines along the walls. 'All these people going places,' she marveled. 'I'm gonna go someplace one day when my luck changes.'

'Where?' Anna asked gently.

Goldie raised her eyebrows and gave a wistful shrug. 'Don't know. Doesn't matter. Somewhere, that's all.' Then she shook herself from these thoughts and was all business again. 'This way.'

She led Anna down one of the wide ramps that led off the main concourse to the lower concourse.

They passed the entrance to the Oyster Bar, then descended another ramp to the platform for the number 7 subway line.

It was quiet and lonely down here, a dank, stale smell in the air. Only three people waited on the concrete platform: a middle-aged man in a dark blue suit, and two young women in short skirts and high heels. These latter two were arguing and took no notice of Anna and Goldie. The man looked half asleep.

'This way,' Goldie said softly, walking toward the far end of the platform. Here the tracks were only a few feet below where they stood. Goldie glanced back, carefully scanning the platform.

'What are you looking for?'

'Cops…and security cameras. Lots of cameras since nine-eleven. But none of them are pointing this way. No cops, either. Let's go.'

Anna frowned, taken aback. 'Go where?'

Goldie looked up at her impatiently. 'Where do you think we're going? You wanted to see Pete, right? Well, this is the way to get to him.'

Fear building inside her, Anna crouched to hop down, but Goldie stopped her. 'Now, listen to me. You heard of the third rail?'

Anna shook her head.

Goldie pointed to the subway tracks. 'You see that rail in the middle? That's it. It's where the electricity comes from. You gotta keep away from it or you're dead.'

'OK,' Anna said, apprehension in her voice, and carefully jumped down. She kept close behind Goldie, who stayed near the left wall of the tunnel as she led the way along the snaking track. From somewhere above, enough light filtered down for them to see their way.

Suddenly a low rumbling could be heard far off in the darkness.

'Stay real close, like this,' Goldie said, pressing herself against the grimy wall. Anna obeyed. The rumbling grew into a thundering roar and a train burst from the blackness, white lights blazing.

'Look down!' Goldie shouted, and they lowered their heads. The train seemed to pass inches from their faces, carrying with it a hot, musty wind. When the train had passed, Anna realized she had been holding her breath. She let it out.

'You don't want the headlights to reflect in your eyes,' Goldie explained. 'You don't want the motorman to see your face, either. These motormen got eyes like hawks, always lookin' for people on the tracks to report to the cops.'

Soon they departed the main track, heading down a narrower tunnel to the left. Goldie stopped before a large grated door.

'It's locked,' Anna said, pointing to heavy

chains running from a hole in the door to the door frame. Ignoring her, Goldie grabbed the side of the door opposite the chain and pulled hard. The door swung slowly toward her, the hinges on this side apparently having given way, the chain on the other side acting as the hinge instead. When she let go, there was only about a foot of space between the door and the wall, but it was enough for them to squeeze through.

'Careful here,' Goldie told Anna. 'There's a small drop down.'

Anna stepped down. They were in a cavernous room, some of its walls lost in shadow. 'We're gonna need those flashlights now,' Goldie said. Anna got them out and they shone them around the room. Now they could see two tattered mattresses against a far wall, and next to them, a rumpled sleeping bag.

'Heard us coming.' Goldie walked toward the right wall and another grated door came into view, except that this one hung loose on one hinge. She and Anna stepped through. They were in another large room. Here, too, were more camps—sleeping bags, mattresses, and tarps...evidence that track people had been here.

Anna had noticed that Goldie never took a wrong step, knew exactly where she was going. 'You've lived here,' she said suddenly.

Goldie stopped and turned to her. 'Yes. Not so very long ago, either. The Outreach lady I worked with till I got fed up said moving topside was "making tremendous progress".'

'You don't think so?'

Goldie shrugged. 'I still got no job, live on the streets. At least here it's safer if you're careful. It's cool in the summer, warm in the winter. I'm not so sure it's worse.'

At last the chain of rooms ended. Stepping through the last of the grated doors, they entered a sort of alcove from which rusty iron stairs descended. 'Down here,' Goldie said, and stepped on to the first step. It groaned menacingly. 'Don't worry,' she said, turning back to Anna with a smile. 'It's solid.'

At the bottom of the stairs was another tunnel which Goldie said was still in operation. 'This here's a major thoroughfare.' Thankfully, no rumbling could be heard. They moved along the tracks, then branched off into an unused tunnel. After a short while a cement wall blocked their way.

Anna shone her flashlight on the solid mass. 'Now what?'

Goldie moved to the left and crouched down at what Anna now realized was a hole near the floor about two and a half feet in diameter. Goldie shone her flashlight into it. 'Take a look.'

Anna crouched beside her, looked through, and saw a light about forty feet below. For a moment she felt dizzy and steadied herself on the cool cement of the wall beside her.

'You OK?' Goldie asked.

Anna nodded.

'You can't see it from here, but there's a floor maybe four feet below this hole.'

Goldie went first and Anna followed, dropping on to a sort of shelf, about a dozen feet wide, that ran high up along the wall of a cavern. At the far side of the shelf ran more tracks. Beyond these tracks lay the dizzying abyss Anna had seen through the hole, lights twinkling at the bottom.

Without warning, a train roared past. The two women switched off their flashlights and averted their eyes. When the darkness had returned, they turned the lights back on and Goldie started moving slowly forward, as if looking for something. Suddenly she called out, 'Pete, it's Goldie! I need to talk to you.'

Silence.

Anna said, 'Is he—'

Goldie silenced her with a sharp sweep of her hand. 'He's here. Just doesn't want to come out.' She turned to Anna. 'Gimme that money.'

Anna handed her the fifty dollars.

Goldie held it up and shone her flashlight on it. 'Just talk to us, Pete. It's worth fifty if you do.'

From somewhere—Anna couldn't tell where—came a low, gravelly voice. 'Talk about what?'

'Come out here and you'll find out. Oh, never mind,' Goldie said, turning back toward the hole she and Anna had crawled through. 'Come on, Anna, this ain't gonna work.'

'Hold it.'

They spun around. Goldie shone her light. Standing not far away was a middle-aged man, his shirt and pants ragged, his feet bare. One side of his shirt was torn and hung open, showing prominent ribs. The skin of his face not covered by shaggy gray beard was a waxy yellow. His black hair hung down in greasy ribbons. 'What do you want, Goldie?'

She didn't answer right away. She was clearly shocked at his appearance. But she recovered quickly. 'Pete, this here's my friend Anna. She and I need to talk to you about Isaiah.'

Pete spat. 'What about him?'

'When was the last time you saw him?'

Looking at her as if she were insane, he took a step forward and grimaced in pain. He faltered, nearly falling, before righting himself. 'What, you think I got a Palm Pilot down here or somethin'? How should I know?'

'How long have you been down here? When was the last time you went topside?'

'Long time ago. Weeks. Why you askin' about Isaiah?'

'He's dead, Pete. Murdered. It's no secret you and he weren't exactly friends.'

'And you think I killed him?' Pete's chest moved slightly in a chuckle. 'Would have liked to, after the way he beat me up. He had no call doing that.'

Goldie's eyes narrowed. 'You were trying to rape me, Pete. What was he supposed to do?' But she didn't wait for answer, as if realizing there had been no point in asking the question in the first place. 'Was that the last time you saw him?'

'Maybe, maybe not.'

'Let's go, Anna.'

'Wait. No, it wasn't the last time. I went back… to see him.'

'Where?'

'At the Rat Cave.'

'And what happened?'

'He was sleeping. I grabbed him by the throat. We struggled. Took a bunch o' guys to pry us apart. We were both all bloody. My arm was broken. I told Isaiah I'd be back to give him more.'

'But you didn't go back?'

'No. Too sick.'

Goldie studied him. 'You are very sick, Pete. Much worse than the last time I saw you. Why don't you go up and get some help?'

'Help?' He laughed. 'There's no help for me.'

'What do you mean?'

In response, he opened his mouth wide and stuck out his tongue. Thick, fuzzy white patches coated the top and sides. Then he grabbed his upper lip, revealing large wine-colored lesions covering his gums.

Goldie was quiet for a moment. Then she said, 'There's still help for you, Pete. Don't stay down here,' she urged.

'Gimme that money,' he demanded, taking another step forward and wincing in pain.

Goldie held out her hand and Anna passed her the money. Goldie walked up to Pete and gave it to him.

'Now get out of here,' Pete cried after them. 'And don't forget what I told you.'

The two women turned. 'What?' Goldie said.

'Tell Marie I love her. Tell her I'll be home in a few days. I got a teddy bear for Sherry.'

Goldie regarded him as if it pained her to do so. Then she took Anna by the arm and led her back to the hole in the wall.

'Who's Marie?' Anna asked after they'd passed through.

'His wife who's been dead for at least twenty-five years. Sherry was their daughter—died in a fire.'

'How awful… He hasn't much time left. He's got AIDS.'

'I know. You think that's the first time I've seen that? But that don't mean he didn't kill Isaiah. You heard him. He'd have killed him if he could.'

'You're right,' Anna said, 'but we'll never get more than that out of him.'

'Which means this was a total waste of our time.'

Moving through the unused tunnel toward the live tracks, Anna didn't respond. But Goldie was probably right.

When they finally reached the platform, three men stood waiting for the train. Anna and Goldie waited until it had come and gone, then hopped up.

Outside on Forty-Second Street, Goldie seemed uneasy about something.

'What is it?' Anna asked.

'There's something I wanted to ask you.' When Anna nodded, Goldie went on, 'I didn't tell you this before, but sometimes Isaiah kept stuff at the Rat Cave. There's a secret place there that he and

I knew about—a hole behind some loose concrete. Isaiah left something there and, well, I took it since you told me he's dead, and I'm feelin' funny about it.'

'What did he leave?'

From her pocket Goldie took a small purple velvet pouch with a drawstring. Carefully she opened the top of the pouch and poured out its contents into the palm of her hand.

Poking at the objects, Anna smiled. 'Rabbit's foot…troll doll…lucky penny…' She touched a tiny wooden carving of an arm and hand, the fingers clutching the thumb. 'A figa, I believe it's called. All good-luck charms.' She looked up at Goldie and a look of sadness passed between them.

'They didn't do him much good, did they?' Goldie said.

'He left this in the hiding place?'

Goldie nodded.

'Did he leave anything else?'

'No. Last time we were in the Rat Cave together, he put it in while I was watching, as if he wanted me to know where it was. "My good luck charm," he said.'

'He wanted you to know about it in case something happened to him.'

'Then you think it's all right if I keep it? You

know, just to have something of his to remember him by?'

'Absolutely.'

Satisfied, Goldie carefully placed the objects back in the pouch and stuffed it in her pocket.

Before they parted, Anna thanked her.

'You got no call to thank me,' Goldie said, not unkindly. 'He was my friend, too.' She gave one nod by way of saying goodbye, then turned and started down the sidewalk, head down, hands shoved in her pockets.

AT NINE FORTY-FIVE the following morning, Gerry Licari knocked on the door of Anna's office and dropped a letter on her desk. 'I signed for it,' he said, and left.

Anna frowned as she read the words at the top left-hand corner of the envelope: LAW OFFICES OF SCHUTZ FINE KOVNER. Beth's firm. The letter was addressed to Anna in care of the garage. She tore it open and unfolded the sheet of thick, cream-colored paper inside.

Dear Ms Winthrop,
This firm represents the artist known as Bonz as well as his corporation, Street Muse, Inc.

On July 5, 2008, you attended a book signing at the Times Square Bookstore at 1537

Broadway in New York City. At this event, you confronted Mr Bonz with a series of photographs of a street mural which you accused him of copying. Such a statement constitutes slander and defamation of character per se, actionable torts subjecting you to liability for both actual and punitive damages.

Mr Bonz demands that you forthwith cease and desist this and any similar assertions. To the extent that you ignore this request, you do so at your own peril, as my client is prepared to pursue all legal remedies.

Very truly yours,

Adrian Betancourt, Jr.

'That little worm!' Anna muttered, throwing the letter on to her desk. Then she broke into a slow smile. She had definitely hit a nerve.

Still smiling, she called Beth. It took Anna a full five minutes to convince her sister's secretary to put her through.

'What do I have to do to talk to you?' Anna said with a laugh.

'Sorry,' Beth said. 'That's her job. What's up?' She sounded rushed.

'Do you know an Adrian Betancourt at your firm?'

'Of course. Why?'

'I just got a scary lawyer letter from him.'

'I haven't got time to hear what his letter is about, but I will tell you to take it seriously. He's a shark.'

'That's what I figured,' Anna said, and let Beth go.

She grabbed a stack of papers from the corner of her desk and a small white envelope fell out, landing on the desk blotter. It was addressed *Anna Winthrop*.

'Now what?' she muttered, tore it open, and read:

I told u 2 stop but u wont do u really want 2 die?

She jumped up from her chair and ran out into the corridor. Hal Redmond and Gerry Licari stood a few feet away, laughing about something.

'Hal—'

He turned to her, surprised.

'Have you seen anybody going into my office—anybody you don't know?'

Hal shrugged and gave a little shake of his head. 'Me, neither,' Gerry said.

'How long have you been standing there?'

They both looked puzzled. 'About five minutes,' Hal answered.

Saying nothing, she went back into her office. A minute later she was heading out again. Allen wasn't in his office. 'Guys, do me a favor. I've got an emergency. Tell Allen for me, OK?'

She didn't wait for their reply. Out in the lot, she jumped into her car and headed east across town.

THE BRICK TOWNHOUSE on East Sixty-First Street looked no different from when Anna had been there last. Scaffolding still stood in front of the building, whose front door was wide open. Her heart pounding—she cursed herself for that—she hurried up the steps and inside.

Remembering the friendly little man with the hero sandwich, she crossed the foyer to the small unfinished coatroom at the left—and found Austin Parkhurst himself sitting at a desk, poring over a blueprint. When he looked up, his eyes bulged in disbelief. He opened his mouth to speak, but before he could, Anna slammed down the anonymous note on the desk before him.

'You get off on terrifying women half your size? First the attack me in my own building, then this. What's next?'

Slowly he took in the note, then shifted his gaze to her. 'Lady, I don't have the slightest idea what you're talking about. What are you doing back here, anyway?'

'Why did you lie to me about your father?'

'What are you talking about?'

'You said you hadn't seen or spoken to your father in seventeen years. But the truth is you spoke to him only a month ago and even promised to meet with him.'

He sized her up, as if deciding how to answer. Finally he said, 'Yeah, that's right, I did say I'd meet him. It was the only way I could think of to get him off the phone, short of hanging up. Because you know what?' he said, looking straight into her eyes. 'It's not as easy as that. You can't just pick up where you left off seventeen years ago, as if nothing has happened.'

'Who said he wanted to pick up where he left off? All he wanted to do was see you. You couldn't give him that?'

'No, I couldn't.'

'Why did you say you would meet him and then not go?'

'I told you—to get him off the phone.'

'You broke his heart.'

'Oh, really?' he said happily. 'That's great. Now we're even.'

'Why did you lie to me?'

'Because it's none of your business. Now get out of here before I call the cops.'

WHEN HER SHIFT ENDED at two, Anna closed her office door and changed into an outfit she'd brought to work: a gray cotton skirt and simple black top. Then she got in her car and drove the same route she and Lawrence had taken to the Rat Cave, except that this time her destination was a far more elegant address.

From an article she had found in *New York* magazine, she knew that the converted cardboard factory where Bonz lived and worked was The Hargreaves on Adams Street, right around the corner from the Rat Cave. How fitting, she thought, preparing to confront this rat in his own cave.

As she drove slowly past the building, a squat red-brick structure with a trendy gray awning extending to the street, a burgundy-uniformed doorman watched her, eyes narrowed slightly.

She parked her car farther down the street and walked back. The doorman had seen her coming. He smiled the phoniest of smiles. 'May I help you, ma'am?'

Her smile was equally bogus. 'Yes. I'm here to see Bonz.'

He straightened up. 'And is he expecting you?'

'Probably.' When he frowned, she went on, 'If you would just tell him his friend from the bookstore is here with some valuable new information, I would appreciate it.'

He hesitated, looking her up and down. Then he went grudgingly to the phone in the building's vestibule. After a moment she heard him muttering into the receiver. He laid the receiver on the desk and came back out. 'And your name, ma'am? I'm sorry, I forgot to ask.'

'Anna Winthrop. Just tell him, Isaiah's friend.'

'Very well.' Returning to the phone, he spoke again into the receiver and finally gave one nod and hung up. 'Bonz is unavailable, I'm afraid, but his assistant has agreed to see you. This way, please.'

The lobby was decorated with old, rusted parts from what she presumed had been cardboard-manufacturing machines. They projected a bizarre ferocity against the delicate furnishings and pastel walls.

The doorman gestured toward the elevator. 'Eighth floor.' Even before the elevator doors had slid completely shut, his smile had vanished.

After a ride so smooth she hadn't felt the elevator car moving, the doors opened on to a large foyer done entirely in blond wood. She stepped out. In the center of the wall facing her was one of Bonz's creations, a sloppy swirl of brown-and-yellow paint that vaguely resembled a lizard. Footsteps clacked on the hard wood floor and she turned.

Coming toward her was a young woman whose appearance Anna could only have described as frightening. Tall and shockingly thin, she wore a tattered black burlap dress that hung on her thin frame. Black shoes with the highest stiletto heels Anna had ever seen matched the dress. Her face, as gaunt as her body, was covered with a strange white makeup that reminded Anna of a kabuki dancer. In the middle of the white was a blood-red slash of lipstick. The woman's hair, a blue-black, hung to her neck in shaggy clumps.

Could she be related to the goth Statue of Liberty man at the bookstore? Anna wondered. Should she wish her a happy Halloween? She smiled.

The woman did not smile back.

'Thanks for seeing me,' Anna said. 'I'm Anna Winthrop. I—'

'We know who you are. What do you want?'

OK, if she wanted to play that way. 'Bonz knows what I want. Get him. And who are *you,* by the way?'

The woman glared at her, as if deciding whether to answer. Finally she said, 'My name is Glass. I'm Bonz's assistant. He's busy. You can talk to me.'

Anna let out a sigh. 'OK, you asked for it. I'm not sure how much you know.'

'I know everything—all about you. What is this "new information"?'

'The new information is that I know Bonz went to see Isaiah Parkhurst at least once, probably more than once.'

Glass crossed her arms and stared down at Anna. 'So?'

'So—'

'It's all right, Glass, I'll talk to her.'

Both women turned. Bonz stood at the end of the hallway, looking exactly as he had at the bookstore—small and wimpy.

'Should I stay?' Glass asked him.

'No.'

She nodded once—did everyone in this building nod once?—and marched away on her stilettos like a robot. When she was gone, Bonz approached Anna.

'Why do you keep bothering me? Didn't you get my lawyer's letter?'

'I got it. Don't care.'

'Who *are* you, exactly?'

'You know who I am. How else could your lawyers have found me?'

'I know your name and that you work for the Sanitation Department, but I don't know what you have to do with any of this—with Isaiah, I mean.'

'He was my friend. That's all you need to know.'

'Well, Miss liberal New Yorker who makes

friends with old bums, you'd better take my lawyers' advice and watch what you say.'

She gave him a defiant sneer. 'I'll say what I please, because the truth is never slander. You slimy little toad—you stole Isaiah's work, because you have no talent yourself. You're just a vandal with a good agent.'

'Did you come here to insult me?'

'Not primarily. I want you to answer some questions.'

'Like what?'

'Like where you were on the afternoon of June twenty-third.'

'Why? What happened then?'

'Isaiah Parkhurst was murdered.'

Looking at her in amazement, he let out a guffaw and actually smiled—not a pretty sight. 'You think I murdered an old bum?'

'Yes, as a matter of fact I do.'

'And why would I do that?'

'Simple. To prevent your secret from getting out. He wouldn't sell his talent to you, so you stole it and got rid of the evidence. Who'd miss an "old bum", right? So where were you?'

'Why should I tell you? You're not the police.' He looked at her sharply. 'Have you told them this theory of yours?'

'No.' Not officially, anyway, she thought. 'But

I will if you don't answer my question. That's one reason you should tell me where you were on the afternoon of the twenty-third. The second reason is that if you don't, my next stop will be the *New York Post*. Can't you see it? "Bonz has skeleton in his closet".'

His gaze wandered around the hallway, as if he were imagining this scenario. Suddenly, without moving, he called, 'Glass.'

She appeared instantly, as if by magic. More likely she'd been eavesdropping.

'Yes?'

'Where was I on the afternoon of June twenty-third?'

She thought for a moment, then shook her head—once. 'I'd have to check your appointment book.'

'Then do it.'

Again she vanished into the back. While she was gone, Anna watched Bonz, who had focused his gaze on the floor.

'Here.' Glass was back, appointment book in hand. She referred to an open page. 'You were at Prince Bandar bin Sultan's reception at the Four Seasons for his new clothing line. It went all afternoon. We didn't leave until well after eight that evening.'

'There,' he said triumphantly.

Anna shook her head. 'A party is the perfect

place to set up an alibi. Even you could have figured that one out. You just slip out, no one notices.
Kill Isaiah. Slip back in.'

Glass's eyes were wide in her white-white face.

Bonz said, 'The Four Seasons is at—'

'I know where it is,' Anna broke in. 'Fifty-Sev-
enth between Park and Madison.' It was in her district. 'Believe it or not, I've been there. So what?'

'It would have taken much too long for me to
get over there and come back without anyone no-
ticing I was gone.'

She leveled a steady gaze at him. 'Get over
where? I never said where Isaiah was killed.'

He shifted nervously, darting a glance at Glass.
Finally he looked back at Anna. 'If you must know,
I knew about what happened to Isaiah, where he
was killed, but it was from...people I have on the
street.'

'"People"?'

'Yes. They report to me, tell me what's going
on. Keep me fresh.'

'Ah,' Anna said, 'a lifeline to your beginnings.'

Glass spun around to face Anna, her posture
defensive. 'Those *are* Bonz's beginnings. There's
nothing criminal about it.'

'Oh, I completely agree. It's just that I don't believe it. Or,' she said to Bonz, a thought occurring
to her, 'maybe you *didn't* murder Isaiah.'

'Now you've got it,' he said.

'One of your street goons did.'

'That's ridiculous,' Glass said.

'Or maybe *you* did it,' Anna said, turning on her.

Glass drew back. 'Me!'

'Sure. You look capable of that and more.'

'All right, all right,' Bonz said, like a referee. 'You've given us your various theories. The problem is you can't prove any of them. So you'd better leave, or—'

'Or what? You'll sick Schutz Fine Kovner on me?' She laughed in disgust. 'That's it for now, Wonder Boy. But don't get too comfortable, because I'm watching you.'

Glass had summoned the elevator. Its doors slid silently open.

Anna winked at her. 'Thanks, Igor. Don't you get too comfy, either.'

Descending to the lobby, she felt her bravado drain from her like air from a punctured balloon. The truth was, there probably wasn't any way to prove Bonz hadn't been at the prince's party all afternoon and into the evening. And even if there were, it might not matter because Bonz could have sent someone else to do his dirty work.

Much more his style, she thought.

EIGHTEEN

Just after lunch on Thursday, Gerry Licari popped his head into Anna's office. 'I've got a call on my line that's meant for you. I'll transfer it.'

'Thanks, Gerry. Who is it?'

He scratched his head. 'I'm sure I got it wrong. I thought she said her name was Glass.'

Intrigued, Anna picked up the phone.

'Ms Winthrop?'

It was indeed Glass, Bonz's assistant. Anna recognized her voice.

'What can I do for you, Glass?'

'Please,' she said, 'my real name is Denise. Denise Bukowsky. Glass is my professional name.'

'Professional name? You mean, like an actress?'

'No,' Denise said lightly, 'though I have done some performance art. It's just the name I use when I work for Bonz. He likes us all to have edgy names.'

Anna laughed. '"Glass" is certainly edgy. I'd even say it's sharp.'

There was silence on the line.

'What can I do for you, Denise? I must say this

is a surprise. Has Bonz asked you to try to scare me off some more?'

'No, he has no idea I'm calling you. He mustn't ever know. Ms Winthrop, could we meet somewhere? I really need to talk to you.'

'Of course. When?'

'Whenever you say.'

'My shift ends at two,' Anna said. 'There's a Starbucks at the corner of Forty-First and Broadway. Can you meet me there at two-thirty?'

'Absolutely. Oh—you may not recognize me. I'll be wearing jeans and a pink T-shirt.'

IT WAS TRUE. Anna would never have recognized Denise—a.k.a. Glass. Standing in the doorway of Starbucks, she wore faded jeans and a pink T-shirt with a picture of Marilyn Monroe on it. The shaggy blue-black hair was now a soft brown, combed smoothly over her forehead. Gone was the ghostly white skin and the red gash of a mouth. She looked like any young woman on her day off. Seeing Anna, she smiled sweetly and walked over on sneakers.

'I know, I know,' she said, smiling, as she slid into the booth. 'I look like a completely different person. This is the real me. As I said, Bonz wants all of his people to be "different".'

'I much prefer you this way—no offense.'

'Oh, none taken. So do I. But for the money he pays me, I don't mind getting into costume. I could use some coffee.' She went up to the counter and got some for them both.

Sitting back down, Denise said, 'I appreciate your seeing me. I've been really upset since you came up to the studio. I'm sorry I was so rude to you, by the way. Part of the job. It took a lot for me to work up the courage to call you.'

'What did you want to talk to me about?'

When Denise set down her coffee cup, her hand was shaking. 'You promise you will never tell anyone I spoke to you?'

'I promise.'

'There arc some things about Bonz I think you should know. In light of this business with the homeless man. That mural isn't the first one Bonz has "adapted", as he always puts it.'

Anna raised her eyebrows in encouragement. It was all Denise needed. 'In fact, a big part of my job is to search the city for these murals. There are hundreds of them, you know. These graffiti writers, as they call themselves, spend thousands of hours creating these masterpieces in obscure places where only vagrants will see them. When I find them, I photograph them thoroughly. Then I bring in my crew.'

'Your crew?'

Denise squirmed uneasily. 'I have a group of people who sweep in and—well, obliterate the murals once I've documented them.'

'Ah,' Anna said. 'Now I see. How do they do it?'

Denise shrugged. 'Oh, just some paint, usually black, to cover it all over. That mural in the Rat Cave that you took pictures of is slated for obliteration. We just haven't gotten to it yet.'

'And how do you feel about this "obliteration"?'

Denise hung her head. 'I'm ashamed. I feel like a vandal—no, worse. I'm stealing these artists' work, painting over their beautiful pictures, and there's nothing these people can do about it. Not that some haven't tried.'

'Oh?'

'One artist, a woman named Dahl—yes, there are a few women graffiti writers—came to Bonz's studio, but she didn't have your luck. She was thrown out. Then she came again, and this time two of Bonz's men took her away. I—I don't know what happened to her.' Denise began to cry.

'What do you think might have happened to her?' Anna asked. 'Are you saying…'

'Oh, absolutely.' Denise nodded rapidly. 'That wasn't the first time someone who challenged Bonz disappeared.' She sniffed, wiped her nose with her napkin. 'He's like the mob. Cross him and you're eliminated. That's one of the reasons I wanted to see you. To warn you. You don't know what he's capable of. And the beauty of it is that he doesn't do any of it himself. He has this gang of henchmen he pays even better than he pays me to do his bidding.'

Anna took a moment to absorb this. 'Denise, do you think Bonz killed Isaiah Parkhurst?'

'Oh, sure,' Denise replied casually, 'it's perfectly possible. Probable, in fact. You see, Isaiah crossed him.'

'How so?'

'I found some of Isaiah's murals, photographed them, and then had my crew obliterate them. Isaiah found out. One night I was in Harlem photographing a mural on the side of an abandoned building by another artist when Isaiah appeared and attacked me. He was wild. He said I was a monster, that I was taking his soul.'

'What did you do?'

'I was afraid he was really going to hurt me. I got away from him long enough to call one of the guys on my crew who I knew was working nearby. He came in a hurry and beat Isaiah up pretty badly.'

Denise took a sip of coffee. 'But that didn't stop him. One day Bonz was giving a lecture at the Metropolitan Museum of Art on "Masterpieces of the People" and Isaiah stood up at the back of the auditorium. He started screaming that Bonz was a fraud and a thief. The security guards threw him out. Later, at the office, I heard Bonz on the phone talking to one of his goons. Bonz was furious that Isaiah was still around and said the old man should have been dealt with a long time ago.'

A chill ran down Anna's spine. 'Do you think he left the prince's reception, found Isaiah—probably with the help of his team—slit his throat, and hurried back to the hotel?'

'I think it's highly likely. He definitely left to do something. At one point I was looking for him so I could introduce him to someone, and he was definitely not there. When he appeared later, he looked disheveled and he was all sweaty and smelly, like he'd been exerting himself. When I asked him where he'd been, he looked at me like I was crazy and said he'd been there the whole time. Later I was talking to one of Bonz's men and he said he thought Bonz had slipped out for a tryst with a woman he met at the party. But that's what he *would* say, isn't it? The thing is, we just don't know. The reason I wanted to speak to you was to warn you to be careful. Bonz may be young but he's very rich and very powerful. It's no accident he's achieved so much so soon.'

'I'm grateful to you, Denise. I know the risk you took calling me, meeting with me.'

Denise nodded. 'Could I ask you something?'

'Of course.'

'Do you really work for the Sanitation Department?'

'Yes,' Anna said, smiling, 'I really do.'

Denise slowly shook her head. 'How cool is that? Do you think that's a field I might be right for?'

Anna had to think about this one. 'Possibly,' she said slowly, 'but keep in mind that the typical starting position in the department is sanitation worker.'

'Oh, I know,' Denise said eagerly. 'A garbage collector. San man—or san woman. I know all about it. But after a while you can take tests and try out for higher jobs, right? Isn't that how you did it?'

'That's right.'

'And anyone can apply? To be a sanitation worker, I mean?'

'Sure, as long as you're twenty-one, drug free, a resident of the City of New York or of Nassau or Westchester counties, and speak and understand English.'

'Wow,' Denise said, shouldering her purse. 'Garbage is really cool, don't you think? Edgy.'

'I've never thought of it in those terms,' Anna said thoughtfully, 'but yeah, I'd say so.'

Denise shook Anna's hand warmly. 'Thanks again.' Her expression darkened. 'Remember, be careful. And we never met here today.'

CROSSING TIMES SQUARE, Anna got a call from Santos on her cell. 'There's someone I want you to meet.'

'Who?'

'Can you come over to the station house?'

'Santos, who is it?'

'Just come over, OK? Trust me.'

'All right. I can be there in fifteen minutes.'

'See you soon.'

She walked the ten blocks to the Midtown North station house on West Fifty-Fourth near the corner of Eighth Avenue. In the waiting room, she found Santos sitting on one of the stainless steel benches. Next to him sat a boy of about fifteen with crisp black hair and handsome features.

Santos rose when he saw Anna. The boy started to stand as well, but Santos turned to him and said, 'You stay there.' The boy sat back down.

'Santos, what's going on?'

He smiled. 'Let's go in the muster room. I don't think there's anybody in there right now.' He opened a door to a back corridor and cocked his head for the boy to go through. Anna and Santos followed.

In the muster room, a drab space lined with vending machines offering soda, ice cream, and candy, they sat at a conference table.

'This is Ramón,' Santos said. The boy looked down. 'Do you want to tell her, or should I?'

Ramón didn't answer.

'OK,' Santos said with a sigh. 'Here's what we got. Ramón here's got hands that go where they're not supposed to go.' When Anna just stared, he spelled it out. 'Pickpocket. Decided to go on a little expedition at St Patrick's Cathedral today.'

The boy looked up. 'I wanted to say a prayer for my little sister,' he said in a surprisingly deep voice. 'She's very sick.'

Santos rolled his eyes. 'A woman just entering the cathedral caught him with his hand in her purse. You're getting sloppy, Ramón.'

'She bumped into me. I didn't go nowhere near her stupid purse.'

'Anyway,' Santos said, ignoring the boy and turning to Anna, 'once I got him down here I found something on him that I thought you'd want to see.' He took a wallet from his pocket and set it on the table. It was made of cream-colored ostrich leather. 'Take a look.'

Anna opened it. It was a bifold, a row of credit cards down each side.

'Bottom right,' Santos said.

She slipped this card out of its slot. It was a New York driver's license. 'Austin Blake Parkhurst', it read. Above it was a photograph of Austin's face, set in a grim stare. Quickly Anna committed his address to memory, then tucked the license back into its slot.

'Where did you get this?' she asked Ramón.

The boy looked at Santos, as if asking whether he had to answer.

'Tell her,' Santos said.

'A coffee shop called Sammy's on West Forty-Fifth.'

Santos added, 'Half a block from House of Hope.'

'When?' Anna asked.

Ramón considered. 'Maybe about a month ago. Not sure.'

'Tell the lady how it went down,' Santos said.

'I went in for a cup of coffee—'

'You mean to size up the crowd,' Santos said.

'Whatever, man. You want me to tell her what happened or not?'

'Go ahead.'

'I sat down in a booth at the back. These two guys came in and sat a few tables away from me.

One looked like he was maybe twenty-five, and the other man, he looked old. I noticed them because the young one looked rich—you know, fancy clothes, acted all snooty.'

'A good mark,' Santos said. Ramón ignored him.

'Then what happened?' Anna asked the boy.

'They ordered something and talked quietly. After about ten minutes, the older guy went wild.' Ramón threw out his hands. 'He yelled something at the young guy and stood up so fast he knocked over his coffee cup. Oh man, there was coffee all over the place. The young guy, he stood up, too, and kind of pleaded with the older guy, but the older guy just walked out. And…that was it.'

'No, that was not it,' Santos said sternly. 'When the young guy went up to the cashier to pay his tab, you took advantage of the situation.'

Grudgingly Ramón said, 'OK, so when he put his wallet back in his pocket, I brushed by him, making believe I was trying to get past, and I lifted the wallet.'

'How much money was in it?' Santos asked.

Ramón gave a little shrug. 'Not much, a couple of dollars.'

'Right,' Santos said, rolling his eyes.

'Ramón,' Anna said, 'why did you keep the wallet? Why didn't you just take what you wanted and toss it?'

The boy looked at her, eyes wide. 'Lady, this is ostrich. You got any idea what I could get for this?'

She nodded, understanding. 'Did you hear what the two men were saying?'

'Only one thing. When the older guy jumped up, he yelled, "No!"'

'And that's all you heard?'

The boy nodded.

'Did you notice anything else? Did the young man say anything after the older man left?'

'No, he just seemed mad. As soon as the older guy walked out, he went up to pay his bill.'

Santos rose. 'You stay here,' he ordered Ramón, and motioned for Anna to come with him.

'What's going to happen to me?' Ramón asked.

'You'll find out. Just cool your jets.'

At the other end of the room, he said quietly to Anna, 'You see why I wanted you to meet him?'

'Absolutely. Thank you. So Austin did meet with his father. And both men lied about it. I can understand why Austin would lie—he didn't want to admit he made contact with Isaiah, either because he killed him, or because he didn't want to be accused of killing him. And Isaiah was so ashamed and heartbroken that he told Goldie his son never showed up.

'What I need to do is find out if anyone else heard what they were talking about. What was the name of that coffee shop again?'

'Sammy's. Corner of Tenth and Forty-Fifth.'

AT FOUR IN THE AFTERNOON, Sammy's Coffee Corner was relatively quiet, only two of its booths occupied. A man behind the counter was setting down a cheeseburger and fries in front of a heavy woman surrounded by shopping bags. He smiled at Anna as she came in. 'Sit anywhere you like, hon.'

She sat at the counter, two stools down from the woman. The counterman came over. 'Noticed your uniform. We don't get you people in here very often.' He set down a cup and saucer in front of her. 'Regular or decaf?'

When she hesitated, because she hadn't planned to order anything, he said, 'It's on the house. I figure it's the least I can do for SDNY.'

She smiled. 'Regular. Thanks.'

He filled her cup. 'Something else? Piece of pie? We got a nice French apple today.'

'No, thank you. Actually, I came in to speak with you about something.'

He pulled his head back in surprise, pointing to himself. 'Me?'

She nodded. 'It's about an incident that took place here about a month ago.'

The man leaned forward, grinning. 'You with the Sanitation Police?'

'No, I'm a section supervisor at Manhattan Central Thirteen Garage.'

'Ah,' he said, though he looked as if he didn't understand at all. Even so, he gave a firm nod. 'Happy to help the Sanitation Department in any way I can, uh…'

'I'm sorry,' Anna said, putting out her hand. 'The name is Anna. Anna Winthrop.'

'Hi, Anna Winthrop,' he said, taking her hand in his. 'The name is Sammy. Sammy Rosenberg.'

'Hi, Sammy Rosenberg.'

They laughed.

The woman with the shopping bags turned to them. 'I hate to spoil a beautiful thing, but do you think I could get a refill?' She held out her cup and cocked a brow.

Sammy gave her a forced smile. 'Of course, darlin'.' He filled her cup, then turned back to Anna. 'So, about a month ago, you said?'

'Right. Two men came in. One of them was twenty-five. Dark blond hair. Well dressed. The other man would have been older. Longish hair. They had an argument. The older man jumped up and tipped over his coffee.'

Sammy thought for a moment, then his face lit up. 'I do remember them. Why are you asking?'

'The older man was a friend of mine.'

'Was?'

'He's dead. Murdered. That's why I'm asking questions.'

The woman two stools down turned to Anna. 'Hey, Columbo, would you let the man do his job? I don't have all day.'

Sammy turned on her. 'Lady, what the heck is your problem?'

She drew back, stunned. 'All I want—'

'Is to bust my chops. But you know what? I own this place and I don't have to put up with that kind of behavior if I don't want to.'

'Behavior?'

'Yeah, you're rude.'

The woman's jaw dropped. 'What about these people?' she said, twirling on her stool and pointing to the two occupied booths. 'Has it occurred to you that they might like some service?'

Anna looked over. The two couples were staring in bewilderment.

'You folks OK?' Sammy called to them.

They nodded.

'Guess they're all right. As for you,' he said, ripping a page off a pad from his apron pocket and tearing it up, 'your lunch is on the house.'

'It is?' she said, puzzled.

'Yeah. That's your payment for never coming back here again.'

The woman looked down at her half-finished burger and fries, thought for a moment, then snatched up her shopping bags and stormed out.

'New Yorkers,' Sammy said, watching her pass the front window. 'Now, where were we?'

Anna laughed. 'Thanks. I was asking you about those two men. Do you remember anything about them?'

He thought for a moment. 'Only that, like you said, the young one was dressed nicely. They only had coffee. The older guy left after he spilled his.'

'What did the young man do?'

'Looked pretty embarrassed, for starters. He had coffee on his shirt. He grabbed some napkins from the dispenser and dried himself off as best he could. Then he came up to the register to pay the bill.'

'That's all you remember?' Anna asked, disappointed.

'Well, yeah. What else do you wanna know?'

'Did you overhear any more of what they were saying, for instance?'

'Oh, why didn't you say so? I only work the counter, Anna. That day I had Sophie working that side of the shop.'

'Where can I find her?'

'You can find her right over there,' he said, and pointed to a swinging door at the back. It flew open and a waitress came through carrying aloft a fully loaded tray. When she neared the two occupied booths, she used her free hand to unfold a stand, set down the tray, and served the couples.

'Yo, Soph, c'mere a minute, will ya?' Sammy called.

Wiping her hands on her apron, Sophie came over. In her late twenties or early thirties, she was small and slim, with dark hair pinned on top of her head and pale, pretty features. 'What's up?' she asked, a little breathless.

'You remember that day those two guys came in—one of them was young, fancy clothes, and the older one knocked over his coffee?'

'Yeah, I remember. What about it?'

Anna asked, 'When you were at their table, did you overhear anything they said? Other than when the older man said "No!", I mean.'

Sophie bit her lip, trying to remember. 'Gee, I don't think so—no, wait. There was one thing. I kept coming back to their table to see if they were ready to order, and they kept saying no, but one of the times I heard the older guy tell the young guy he was his father, not his cash cow. Funny thing to say, huh?'

'Yes, it is,' Anna said thoughtfully.

'Any idea what it means?' Sammy said.

'Possibly,' Anna said. 'Anything else?'

'No, I don't think so. Not long after that, the older guy jumps up and his coffee goes flying.'

Anna thanked them.

Sammy smiled. 'Hey, you be sure to come back here, OK, Anna Winthrop? 'Cause I like you. There's a free cup o' joe here for you any time you want to come in.' He nodded toward her uniform. 'Always happy to serve our men—I mean our women—in…what would you call that color?'

She smiled. 'Spruce,' she said, and gave him a wink before she went out the door.

WHEN A CARPENTER AT Orchid told Anna that Austin wasn't there, she went to the address she'd memorized from his driver's license.

It was a townhouse on the Upper East Side, not far from the Bentley Gallery. Ringing the bell, she peeked through the sidelight and saw plants and part of a staircase. After a few moments, she heard footsteps coming down the stairs. Then the door opened.

Anna thought that if Austin Parkhurst's eyes hadn't been connected to his head, they would have fallen out.

'You!' he said.

'Mm, me,' she said, and gave him a little smile.

'How did you get my address?'

'Don't worry about it.'

He glared at her for a moment, then said, 'What do you want?'

'I want you to stop lying to me.'

'About what?'

'You told me you never went to meet your father, but that's not true. You did meet with him—at Sammy's Coffee Corner, to be exact.'

'How do you know that?'

'Connections.'

'What of it?'

'Why did you lie?'

He shifted his weight to one hip. 'Lady, are you stupid or just pretending? Why do you think? He was murdered. You know as well as I do that if he's dead, my mother's money goes straight to me. That gives me a motive.'

'I see you've been giving this a lot of thought. Yes, I am aware of that. But you left out one detail. For your mother's money to go to you, she's got to die, too.'

He stared at her. 'Obviously.'

'And maybe you're trying to help that along a bit, too. Sawing through balcony railings...'

'If you were a man, I'd beat the living daylights out of you.'

Fury rose in her and she drew herself up to her

full height. 'Go ahead and try. I may be small but I'm strong. I'd love a crack at you.'

The dislike between them was almost palpable.

'All right,' Anna said after a moment, 'so you're saying you lied about seeing your father so you wouldn't be suspected of killing him.'

'Now you're catching on.'

'Why did your father tell you he was your father and not a cash cow? Why did he yell "No!" and leave the restaurant?'

'If I tell you, will you leave me alone?'

'Yes...probably.'

'All right, I don't mind telling you. I told him I would agree to have a relationship with him, which was what he wanted—*if* he did something for me.'

Anna waited.

'I told him I wanted him to make some paintings for me to sell.'

She scowled at him. 'Why did you ask him to do that?'

'Do you have any idea how much his paintings are worth? I've been hearing rumors that collectors are paying upwards of a quarter of a million dollars apiece for them. Can you imagine how much someone would pay for a *new* Isaiah Parkhurst?'

'Yes, I can imagine. And you need money, don't you?'

He regarded her shrewdly. 'That's no secret,' he said at last. 'I'm an entrepreneur. Of course I need money. I told my father that here, finally, was something he could do for me. So what did he do? He jumped up and stormed out.'

She gave him a pitying look. 'You don't see why, do you?' When he looked blank, she said, 'It's because he realized that was all you really wanted from him—to use him. As a "cash cow", as he put it. He knew you weren't really interested in a relationship. He was a smart man, your father.'

Austin shrugged uncaringly. 'So that plan didn't work. No big deal. He's dead now, so like you said, all of my mother's money now goes directly to me. And she can't live for ever.'

She stared at him in horror.

'Now,' he said, bending so that his face was inches from hers. She smelled his breath, minty and sharp. 'You're going to keep your end of the bargain and never bother me again.'

'Or else what?' she said with a little laugh. 'You'll attack me again under the stairs?'

He slammed the door so hard the glass panes shook.

THE WAITING ROOM was tiny, barely large enough to hold a fully stocked magazine rack and the loveseat on which Anna sat. On the floor, a white-noise machine generated a soothing whooshing sound that didn't quite mask the voices of the doctor and her patient beyond the inner door.

At precisely 6:51, that door opened and an obese young woman emerged in tears. Without looking at Anna, she crossed the room and let herself out.

A moment later, Esperanza Trujillo appeared at the door, a sheet of paper in her hand. 'Anna Winthrop,' she read, then looked up. When she saw Anna her brows lowered in a little frown. 'I know you. I *thought* this name was familiar.'

Anna smiled pleasantly. 'Yes, Dr Trujillo. I met you about three weeks ago, outside your mother's townhouse.'

Esperanza thought for a moment. 'Yes, right.' But she still looked puzzled. 'Is *that* why you're here?'

'To be honest, yes. The only way to see you seemed to be to make an appointment.'

'What is it you want?'

'If you don't mind, I'd like to talk to you about your mother.'

Esperanza hesitated, then gave an uneasy nod and gestured for Anna to come into her office.

In the small room filled with books and plants, they sat facing each other in worn armchairs. 'What about Maria?' Esperanza asked. 'You said you didn't know her.'

'No, I didn't, but— Let me explain. It appears

your mother was…friends with a man the police think may have killed her. This man was a friend of mine.'

'Was?'

'He was killed less than a week later. Murdered, like your mother.'

'And who was this man?' Esperanza asked, her features impassive.

'His name was Isaiah Parkhurst. He'd fallen on hard times, but years ago he was a well-known painter. Your mother recognized him…wanted to help him. They became intimate.'

Esperanza's face grew red. 'They were intimate all right. Your friend Isaiah was nothing more than a gigolo. Maria was his sugar mama, as I said when you and I met.'

'It sounds as if you already knew that the man your mother was seeing was Isaiah.'

'Sure, I knew,' Esperanza admitted. 'But I didn't know if you did.'

'Why do you think Isaiah was only using Maria, that they didn't really care for each other?'

'I didn't say Maria didn't care for him. That was just like her, taking in the neediest cases. But this man was a vagrant. He was mentally ill. Think about it. How long do you think it had been since anyone had shown any interest in him? As soon as Maria did, he stuck to her like glue. He saw what he could get out of her…and he got a lot.'

'Like what?'

'Like those expensive clothes you saw me throwing away. Money. She was even going to take him to an art festival on Cape Cod to "re-kindle his passion for painting". How long do you think it would have been before he convinced her to marry him?'

Anna was silent for a moment. Then she said, 'Who do you think murdered your mother?'

'Isaiah,' she said with an easy shrug.

'But that wouldn't make sense in light of what you just said. If she was his meal ticket, why would he kill the golden goose—if you'll forgive my mixed metaphors?'

'I don't think killing her was in the game plan. I think things got rough in bed and he accidentally killed her. I don't think he meant to do it. But he was a sick man.'

'How do you know all these things about him?'

'Maria told me. I went to her house for dinner one night long ago and we went to get groceries for the meal. While we were out she told me about her new friend. She wanted so badly for me to approve, but I told her she was messing up her life because she was such a bleeding heart, and not to come to me if things didn't work out.' Esperanza shrugged. 'I was the only family she had.'

'Your father left your mother a lot of money, is

that correct? He was in the import/export business?'

'That's right. But Maria wasn't my mother.'

Anna looked up in surprise. 'I beg your pardon?'

'She was my stepmother.'

Which explained her referring to her as Maria rather than her mother, Anna thought.

Esperanza went on, 'She married my father when I was a little girl. But as I said, I was the only family she had left.'

'So am I correct in thinking her money would have gone to you...*has* gone to you?'

'That's rather personal, don't you think? Like I said when we met, you're nosy. But it doesn't matter. Yes, her money comes to me. The collections my father left to her come to me. That's all as it should be. For years I put up with her nonsense.'

Anna studied Esperanza carefully. Then she said, 'If your stepmother had married Isaiah, her money would likely have gone to him if she had died, isn't that true?'

Esperanza returned Anna's shrewd gaze. 'You can't be implying what I think you are.'

Anna said nothing.

Esperanza said, 'So you're saying I killed my stepmother before she had a chance to marry him?'

'Or marry anyone else.'

'The answer is yes—if she had married, of course her money would have gone to her husband if she died. But I didn't kill her. I didn't much like Maria, but I wouldn't have murdered her. Besides, I'm not exactly poor myself. My father left me some money, too. No,' she said, shaking her head confidently, 'Isaiah did that himself.'

'When I met you,' Anna said, 'why did you pretend you hadn't spoken to your stepmother in over a year?'

Esperanza blinked, as if flustered by the question. 'You figure it out. If your stepmother was sleeping with a hobo—a man she met in a homeless shelter, a man who ultimately strangled her to death—wouldn't you be mortified? I certainly am. Mortified to have had anything to do with her.'

'When I spoke to you a few days after Maria was killed, you said you thought her boyfriend had killed her, but you didn't mention Isaiah specifically—though you knew about him. Why?'

'Same reason. I was ashamed.'

Anna nodded, satisfied for the moment with her answer. 'Who do you think killed Isaiah?'

'What an odd question,' Esperanza said, giving a shrug that said it didn't matter. 'One of his fellow vagrants. A thief who wanted the money Isaiah no doubt had on him, thanks to Maria. Or maybe it had something to do with drugs. I don't know, and I really don't care.'

'You don't seem to have much sympathy for the homeless.'

Esperanza laughed. 'Oh, another bleeding heart like Maria. No,' she said, leaning forward slightly, 'I don't. These people need to get their act together and work, the way the rest of us do, instead of expecting the world to take care of them.'

'But many of them are mentally ill. It's not their fault they're homeless.'

'Then they should get help for their mental illness. But they usually don't, do they? Or they get help, get drugs prescribed for their problems, and then for whatever reason they stop taking them. I see it quite often in my practice. It's exactly what appears to have happened with Isaiah. No,' Esperanza said, a look of distaste on her face, 'I have no sympathy.'

Esperanza rose. 'Listen, if he was your friend, that's your business, and for your sake I hope they find out who killed him. But that has nothing to do with me. And now,' she said, glancing at a clock on a table beside Anna's chair, 'I'm afraid we're out of time.'

NINETEEN

ANNA GRABBED a fried won ton filled with minced chestnut and topped with fresh sage. It was her seventh. She always overate when she was bored or nervous, and tonight she was both.

Gloria and Donald were now married, the ceremony having gone without a hitch. Cocktail hour was more than half an hour underway, and the newlyweds still hadn't shown up. Perhaps that was for the best.

What was she so nervous about? Her parents had been more than gracious when they met Santos, though the introductions hadn't lasted more than a minute or two. They couldn't possibly grill him here, at Gloria's wedding…could they?

Gazing across the noisy room, she saw Santos coming toward her, a drink in each hand. In his tux he was the handsomest man in the room—handsomer even than the amazing Donald, she decided. Their eyes met and she smiled. Then she saw her parents just behind Santos, heading her way, and her smile melted away.

'Here you go.' Santos handed her her drink, then

used his free hand to tug at his collar and wipe his brow. 'Hot in here.'

And it looks as if it's going to get a lot hotter.

'Darling,' Tildy said, floating over in her robin's-egg-blue gown. She looked from Anna to Santos. 'Beautiful ceremony, wasn't it?'

'Beautiful,' Anna echoed.

Her father came up behind Santos and worked his way into the group. 'One down,' he said, all smiles. 'Now I just have to get rid of you and Beth.' He looked at Santos. 'What do you say, old man?'

'Daddy...' Anna growled.

But Santos took it sportingly. 'I say I'm ready when she is.'

Anna felt her face flush hotly.

'Oh, Jeff,' Tildy said in mock reprimand, 'you're embarrassing her.'

'Well, how about it?' Jeff said, not backing down, and Anna realized he'd already had far too much to drink. He turned to Santos. 'You think I'm joking?'

'No, sir,' Santos said respectfully, 'I don't think you're joking at all. Anna is a wonderful woman. Any man would be lucky to have her as his wife.'

'There, you see that?' Jeff said to Anna. Then he said to Santos, 'But would Anna be lucky to have you as her husband?'

There was a sudden silence.

'Daddy,' Anna said, stepping forward, 'why don't you go see if Gloria and Donald are here yet?'

He clenched his jaw as he did when he was angry. 'Don't patronize me, young lady. I'm your father and I have a right to know all about the man who wants to marry you.'

'He hasn't said he wants to marry me.'

'He just said he did!' Jeff insisted.

Santos simply stood there, eyes round. He realized Jeff was waiting for him to speak. 'I'll tell you anything you want to know, sir.'

'All right.' Jeff's tone was haughty. 'What was it you said you were? A policeman? You couldn't have said that.' He was beginning to slur his words.

'Actually, I did say that, sir.'

'Stop calling me *sir*.'

'I did say that.'

Poor Santos, Anna thought.

'I am a police officer, in Manhattan.'

Tildy spoke up. 'Jeff, would you be a darling and get me another glass of wine?'

'Don't try those games on me, Mathilda. So,' he said, turning back to Santos, 'a cop. I guess that's a fitting match for my daughter, since she's a garbage collector.'

Anna grabbed Santos by the arm and tried to lead him away. 'Come on, let's get some air.'

But Santos didn't move. When Anna looked at him, his face was red.

'Your daughter, Mr Winthrop, is not a garbage collector. Not that there's anything wrong with that. She was a garbage collector at one time, but she's a garage supervisor now, and I think that if you really cared about her as much as you say you do, you would respect what she does and not ridicule her.'

Jeff moved closer to Santos so that their noses nearly touched. 'When have I ridiculed her?'

'You just did. And the rest of you are no better. Gloria badgers her every chance she gets. Right now she's trying to line Anna up for some job she doesn't want at Citigroup.'

'I'm doing what?'

They all turned. Gloria, in her wedding gown, stood a few feet away, a beautiful smile on her face. Then she sensed the tension and her gaze darted from her mother to her father to Anna to Santos. To him she said softly, 'What am I doing?'

Santos started to speak, then stopped himself.

'No, say it,' Gloria said.

'You're hounding your sister to change careers—not because you think she would be happier, but because then you wouldn't be ashamed of her.'

Gloria stared at Anna and her mouth dropped. 'Is that what you think, Anna?'

'I—' Anna stopped herself. It was what she thought, but she wasn't about to say so—not here, not now, at Gloria's own wedding.

But it didn't matter. She might just as well have said it. Gloria burst into tears. 'I'll never forget this, Anna. How can you be so cruel to me when all I'm trying to do is help you? Well, you know what? Forget it. Stay in your filthy, smelly old job, for all I care. Waste your brain—waste your life. And do it with this—' she turned on Santos '—this cop!' Then she took up her skirts and ran off. Donald stood as if paralyzed.

Now Santos took Anna's arm. 'Come on. We do need some air.' He propelled her out to the club's plush lobby.

'Oh, Santos,' Anna said. 'I am so sorry.'

'What do you have to be sorry about?'

'My family.'

'You did warn me.'

'I don't know why I do this to myself. A therapist would say I'm a masochist. But they are my family and I love them. I just wish they…'

'Would leave you alone?'

She nodded, on the verge of tears.

'Let's walk,' he said.

They crossed to the rear of the lobby and—not knowing where they were going, not caring as long as it was away from everyone—passed through a door on the right that led into a narrow corridor with doors on each side.

'I don't think we're supposed to be in here,' Anna said.

'Doesn't matter,' Santos replied, and they walked through a door at the end of the hallway into a library. It was a quiet sanctuary—walls of dark wood, built-in bookcases overflowing with books, thick carpets, comfy armchairs and sofas scattered about.

'How beautiful,' Anna said. 'Do you think we could stay here during the whole reception?'

'I wouldn't advise it,' he said with a wink. 'If we do, that will be the end of what's left of your relationship with your family. But we could stay here a few minutes, give everyone a chance to cool down.'

They sat on a sofa in the center of the room and she nestled against him. 'You watch,' she said. 'When we go back in, it will be as if nothing happened. That's how it always is. Typical WASPs.'

'Meaning what?'

'Meaning the height of dysfunctional. Hold it all inside. Avoid conflict at all costs.'

'I don't know…your father was doing all right in that department just now.'

'He's drunk.'

Santos conceded this point with a nod. After a few minutes Anna reluctantly stood. 'Time to face the music.'

'And dance,' he said with a smile. 'Will you dance with me?'

'You know I will,' she said, taking his hand. She started toward the back hallway through which they had come, thought better of it, and turned in the opposite direction, toward a wide windowed hallway that ran past the library. 'Better this way.'

Leaving the room, they started down the hallway…and stopped short.

On the wall directly in front of them hung a large painting. It was a garden party scene: ladies taking tea, gentlemen watching as they smoked their pipes, young men and women dashing across tennis courts, children playing croquet.

'Isaiah,' they said in unison.

Anna moved closer, peering at the lower right-hand corner. There, hidden in the grass and flowers, nearly invisible, she found it: *Parkhurst*.

As they stood marveling, a waitress passed with a tray of canapés. 'Fun, isn't it?' she said, stopping.

They both agreed.

Anna said, 'And worth a lot more now than when the club bought it, I'm sure.'

The woman gave her a bewildered look. 'They only bought it last week. Paid a fortune for it, I understand. Oops—better run.' She hurried off.

'Last week?' Santos said.

'How is that possible? Those clowns at the Bentley Gallery said the one they showed me was one of only a few left. They said they wished there were more to sell.'

'Maybe this is one of the few left,' Santos said reasonably. 'Or maybe the club didn't even buy it from the Bentley Gallery—have you thought of that?'

'Then we'd better find out, hadn't we?' She turned and walked back down the hallway, Santos not far behind. In the main lobby, she went to the reception desk. A woman asked how she could be of service.

'I'm looking for information about one of your paintings.'

'Information?' The woman looked confused. 'Such as?'

Anna shook her head impatiently. 'Who's responsible for buying the art here?'

'That would be our manager, Mr Lowell.'

Anna asked to see him. As it happened, he was in his office in another part of the club. He agreed to come out and, after a few moments, was crossing the floor toward her.

'Miss Winthrop?' He looked puzzled. 'Winthrop...the bride in the wedding reception going on now is named Winthrop.'

'She's my sister,' Anna said, and rushed on. 'You have an Isaiah Parkhurst painting on the wall at the other side of the club, near the library. What can you tell me about it?'

He paused, looking uneasy. 'Why don't we go to my office.'

Anna introduced Santos. Then they followed Mr Lowell to a small room not far from Isaiah's painting.

'Now,' he said, closing the door and moving behind his desk, 'what was it you wanted to know, exactly?'

'Where did you buy that painting?'

He looked at them. They waited, standing at the edge of the desk.

'Why do you want to know?'

Something was definitely wrong here, Anna thought. 'Why can't you just tell us?' she countered, smiling to soften the question.

'How about this,' he said at last, 'you tell me why you want to know, and then maybe I'll tell you where I bought the painting.'

'All right. The artist, Isaiah Parkhurst, was a

friend of mine. He was murdered. I'm trying to find out who killed him.'

'Oh, dear. That's awful. But I hardly see what that has to do with where I got the painting.'

'I thought we had a deal.'

'I said *maybe* I'd tell you.'

Anna blew out her breath and cocked her head to one side. 'Let me guess,' she said. 'You bought it at the Bentley Gallery in Manhattan. But Mr Meltzer and Mr Kavanaugh asked you not to reveal where you got it—to maintain privacy, or discretion, or something of that sort that makes no sense at all. Am I getting warm?'

'Yes,' he said, 'as a matter of fact, you are.'

'But you didn't keep it quiet, did you? You hung it right here in the open for all to see.'

'All right,' he said, meeting Anna's gaze. 'I fell in love with the painting the moment I saw it. You've just seen it. It's perfect for a country club, isn't it?'

Anna shrugged. 'I suppose.'

'Anyway,' Mr Lowell went on, 'I had to have it. If the only way to get it was to pretend I was a private collector and promise not to tell anyone where I got it, so be it.

'But these men have no right to tell me who I can tell and can't tell. It's my money—*ours,* I should say. The club bought it as an investment.'

'And I bet you spent a lot for it.'

'We did, indeed. Nearly three hundred thousand dollars. And for that kind of money, I'm not keeping it under wraps. I want our guests to enjoy it.'

'Which was what you intended to do all along.'

'Yes,' he admitted, 'it was.'

Anna thanked him. 'Let's go,' she said to Santos, and they left Mr Lowell's office. In the corridor she said, 'It seems there are more Isaiah paintings than Mr Kavanaugh and Mr Meltzer led me to believe.'

'Why would they have lied?'

'You're a cop—think about it. If they keep the sales a secret, they don't have to pay Lara.'

'Ah,' he said, nodding. 'But what can you do about it?'

She gave him a devilish look.

'Anna…' His tone was warning. 'Don't do anything crazy.'

'Why, Officer Reyes,' she said, angelic, 'when have you known me to do anything crazy?' And she led the way back to Gloria's wedding reception, thinking about how Santos would react if he knew she had been down in the Catacombs. But he wouldn't know, because she had no intention of telling him. At least, no time soon.

TWENTY

NOT LONG AFTER roll call Monday morning, Anna heard raised voices outside her office. Hurrying out, she found Kelly and Brianna shouting at Jay and Winston.

As soon as Anna appeared, Kelly turned to her. 'Anna, I'm not going to take this anymore. You've got to do something.'

'What happened?'

'I was getting into my truck,' Kelly said, 'and Winston pinched me!'

Anna looked at Winston, whose gaze wandered around the garage. 'Is that true, Winston?'

Jay spoke up. 'So what if it is true, boss lady? Don't you think we're big enough boys and girls to handle this ourselves?' His words were angry but there was a smile in his eyes, as if he was intentionally baiting her.

'Obviously, you're not. Both of you,' she said to the two men, 'in my office. Now.'

They followed her in. She slammed the door and spun on them. 'I've had it with you two. You're like children. I'm writing you both up.'

'Thought you already did that, boss lady?' Jay said, a challenge in his voice.

'I did. I haven't had a response yet. This time I'm going to recommend disciplinary action.'

'Like what?' Winston looked alarmed.

'Like transferring both of you to other garages. Separate ones. I don't think keeping you together is a good idea.'

Jay mumbled something.

'What?'

'I said, you can't do that.'

'Oh, really? Why not?'

'Because that would be improper punitive transfer.' Jay said the words carefully from memory.

'Got the terminology down, haven't you?'

He nodded. 'A friend of mine just went through the same thing. Got transferred because it was his supervisor's time of the month. My friend hadn't done anything wrong, either.'

She worked to keep her fury under check. 'You don't think you've done anything wrong? Winston, do you think it's OK to pinch Kelly?'

'Oh, I think it was more than OK,' Winston replied. 'I think it was great!'

Both men burst out laughing.

'Get out,' she said, opening the door. They trooped out. A moment later, Hal Redmond came out of his office next door and into hers. 'Everything all right?'

'Nothing I can't handle.'

Hal glanced out to the garage. 'Those two are trouble. I don't know how you put up with them.'

'I won't be putting up with them for long. I want them out of here.'

'Out of here, or terminated?'

'That'll be for the department to decide. I just don't want them on my team anymore.'

Hal nodded. 'Let me know if there's anything I can do,' he said, and went back to his office.

The rest of the morning passed uneventfully. As she worked, she remembered the horrible scene at Gloria's wedding. Taking Santos had been a terrible idea, she saw that now. Now that he had met her family, would he think twice about their relationship?

She forced her thoughts back to her work. Finishing her tonnage reports, she came to the conclusion that Jay and Winston were her poorest performers—not surprising. Another good reason to get rid of them.

Today she had brought her lunch from home and, craving company, decided to eat it upstairs in the break room. There she found Pierre and Tommy chatting over sandwiches at one end of the long conference table, and Jay sitting alone at the other end. As she entered the room he looked up at her, his face expressionless. Tommy and Pierre both greeted her cheerfully. She sat down at the table's halfway point and took out her sandwich and an apple she'd bought at Mr Carlucci's.

When she was nearly finished, she heard a thump and a groan out in the hallway. Then Winston appeared in the doorway, his face contorted in pain, and limped into the room.

'What happened?' Jay asked him.

'Oh, man,' Winston said, easing himself into a chair. 'Bad accident.' He extended one leg, cuffed up his trousers, and rolled down his sock. Carefully he touched his ankle, which looked perfectly normal to Anna.

'What kind of accident?' she asked.

'I was all sweaty from our route this morning, so I decided to take a shower. There's water on the changing room floor and I slipped and fell. Broke my ankle, I think.' Winston adjusted himself in his chair, wincing. 'I think I hurt my back, too. Better report the flooding to BBM,' he said in a helpful tone, referring to the Sanitation Department's Bureau of Building Maintenance.

Without answering, Anna left the room and went directly to the men's bathroom and showers. 'Anyone in there?' she called through the outer door. When there was no answer, she went in and looked around. Just as Winston had said, water had pooled in one of the showers and overflowed on to the edge of the changing area. Something on the floor of the flooded shower caught her eye and she carefully stepped closer to get a better look.

A washcloth had been jammed into the drain, preventing the water from escaping. With considerable effort she was able to dislodge it. Immediately the water began running out.

There was no way that washcloth could have gotten into the drain without help. But how could she ever prove it? She sighed and headed back downstairs. Soon she would be rid of them both.

Downstairs, sanitation workers were heading back out on their routes. The white collection trucks rumbled past her as she made her way to her office.

Suddenly there was a loud crash of metal against metal. She spun around. Directly in front of her, Pierre's truck was rammed into the truck before it. She could see that considerable damage had been done to both trucks.

Pierre jumped out, took a look, and shut his eyes. The door of the truck Pierre had hit flew open and Jay hopped down, his expression furious.

'You idiotic kid, I told you to be more careful. Now look what you've done!'

'You stopped short,' Pierre said. 'What was I supposed to do?'

Jay's eyes bulged in amazement. 'Don't you try pinnin' this on me, Jamaica boy.' Jumping forward, he gave the younger man a hard shove in the middle of his chest.

Pierre reacted immediately, coming at Jay.

'Whoa, stop it!' Anna wedged herself between them. When they were quiet, she said, 'I want you both to go home.'

They shot each other dirty looks before heading in opposite directions.

'Winston—' Anna called. He came around from the passenger side, no longer limping. 'You've got to do your route alone today. Take another truck.' Winston groaned and walked away.

She could see that the compacting mechanism at the back of Jay and Winston's truck was no longer operable. She took another look at the front of Pierre's truck. This damage wasn't as bad. The truck could go out, but she would have to call the Central Repair Shop about both vehicles.

Tommy was now standing at the driver's door of his and Pierre's truck. Anna told him, 'You need to go out on your own today. Sorry.' In contrast to Winston, he nodded curtly and hopped in.

She headed back to her office to call Safety and Training to arrange more driving instruction for Pierre.

AT LUNCHTIME ANNA TOOK a cab from the garage to the Bentley Gallery on the Upper East Side.

'Ah, Miss Winthrop,' Neal Kavanaugh greeted her. 'I was so glad to hear you were coming.'

Yeah, I'll bet. She smiled sweetly. 'Thank you so much. And where is Mr Meltzer?'

'Bert isn't here at the moment, unfortunately. I know he would have liked to see you.'

'He's left you all alone?'

'Yes, that naughty boy. Now,' he said, business-like, 'I take it you've made a decision about the Parkhurst?'

She gazed at him thoughtfully. 'I'd like to see it again, if you don't mind.'

'Of course I don't mind.' He led her to it. 'Marvelous, isn't it?' he said, his gaze on the painting.

'Unquestionably. As you've said, it's a shame there aren't many of his pieces left.'

His eyes slid to her, narrowing slightly. 'What do you mean?'

'Nothing. You told me you wished you had more of his pieces to sell, that's all.'

'Yes, of course. That's true. A shame. But look at it this way. The fewer pieces there are, the more yours is worth.'

'Then again, I would be paying dearly for it, wouldn't I?' She laughed.

He laughed with her. '"Would", you said, rather

than "will". Does that mean you still haven't made up your mind about purchasing it?'

She regarded the painting once more. 'May I use your ladies' room?'

'Of course. This way.' He led her back out to the reception area and pointed to a door beyond the desk. 'It's just in there.'

Once inside the ladies' room, she whipped out her cell phone and dialed the gallery's number. After a few rings, Neal answered.

'Bentley Gallery,' he said in his refined tones.

Anna pinched her nose with her free hand, held the phone about a foot from her mouth, and lowered her voice. 'Yeah,' she said, 'listen. This is the Fire Department. We been bangin' on your door. You aware there's a fire in your place?'

'A fire! What are you talking about?'

'I got no reason to make these things up, sir. If you'll come out to the street, I can show you the window it's comin' out of.'

After a few distressed gasps, the phone went dead. Anna heard the gallery's front door open and close.

She dashed out of the room, across the quiet reception area, and into the corridor leading to the back of the gallery. At the end of this corridor was a heavy white door. She pulled it open and slipped through.

The room in which she found herself was as shabby and rough as the gallery was chic and smooth. It was a large combination workroom and storeroom. Cardboard cartons stood in high stacks against the far wall. Nearby stood a dirty upright vacuum cleaner. To Anna's right was a small kitchenette with sink, cupboards, and a small microwave oven. Someone had spilled instant coffee on the Formica counter and not bothered to clean it up.

She swept her gaze farther into the room. The opposite side was the workroom section. A wooden workbench against the back wall ran the entire width of the room. On it sat a broken light fixture…a pile of empty frames…

Anna blinked. On the workbench, leaning against the wall, was a large painting that was unmistakably by Isaiah Parkhurst. She knew it by its style but not by its subject, since the canvas had been repeatedly slashed. Ribbons of stiff, vividly colored canvas hung to each side. She crossed the room to it, reached out to touch it.

'Perhaps you'd like to buy that one?'

She started, spun around.

Neal had come through a door she hadn't seen in the far right corner of the room, only a dozen feet from where she stood.

TWENTY-ONE

'ALL RIGHT, HONEY, what's your game?' Neal's voice was low and dangerous. All traces of refinement were gone from his voice, replaced by a distinct Brooklyn accent. He waited, watching her.

She inhaled, stood up straight. 'You're going to answer some questions, that's my game.'

'I am?' he said, amused. 'And why is that?'

'Because if you don't, I'll tell Lara Parkhurst that for years you've been selling her husband's paintings and not giving her a penny of the proceeds.'

Bull's-eye. He glared at her, speechless.

She said, 'Why else would you ask everyone to keep the details of their purchases private? A ridiculous request, by the way. But as long as people complied, there was little chance Lara would ever find out what you were doing.'

'I have no idea what you're talking about.' She hadn't seen him moving slowly to a telephone at the edge of the counter in the kitchenette. He was punching out a number. 'All I know is that you're a fraud and you're trespassing. We'll see what the police want to do with you.'

'I'm not a fraud. I'm everything I said I was—Anna Winthrop, daughter of Jeffrey Winthrop of Greenwich. Speaking of Greenwich, your client at the country club has broken his word. His Parkhurst is hanging in the club for all to see.'

He made no response.

'What I didn't tell you about myself is that Isaiah Parkhurst was my friend. He didn't die in 1997. He died on June twenty-third, 2008. He was murdered. I'm trying to find out who did it, and you and your partner are near the top of my suspect list.'

He stopped dialing, put down the phone. 'What do you want?'

'The truth.'

'And if you get it, will you leave us alone?'

'Certainly—if I decide you and Bert aren't murderers.'

He let out a mirthless laugh. 'We're not murderers. We're simply trying to make a living. Business has been bad for some time. Yes,' he admitted, 'we do have a number of Parkhurst pieces, but he's one of the few artists we can sell for decent money.'

'Which you don't share with Lara.'

'She doesn't need it!' he shouted. 'The woman was rich before she even met Isaiah.'

'Whether she needs it or not isn't for you to decide. As his wife, and now as his widow, she's entitled to the sale price, less commission, of every Isaiah painting you sell.'

'Aren't you Miss High Principles,' he said, disgusted. 'Easy for you. We know all about you. Trust fund…'

She shifted uncomfortably. 'That's none of your business. And don't change the subject. When was the last time you saw Isaiah? The *truth*,' she said, glancing at the slashed painting.

'A month ago,' he replied sullenly.

She waited.

'We hadn't seen him in eleven years. We'd thought he was dead.'

'*Hoped* he was dead, you mean.'

He ignored this. 'We were surprised at how well he looked, how he'd cleaned himself up since the last time we'd seen him.'

'What did he want?'

'He'd found out we were selling his paintings. I don't know how he found out, but he did.'

'What did he think had happened to them?'

'He thought they were all in storage at Lara's house. Why he thought this, I don't know. Oh, wait, yes, I do!' he said sarcastically. 'He was a drug-addicted maniac who didn't even know his name.'

'But he wasn't when he came here a month ago, was he?'

'No. He demanded his share of proceeds from the paintings we'd sold.'

'What did you say?'

'We told him that legally he was dead, and that by rights, that money went to Lara.'

'By rights,' she repeated with a chuckle. 'It didn't go to her, either.'

'It was academic, anyway. There was no money. What do you think Bert and I have been living on for the past eleven years? We offered Isaiah a little something to help him out, but he flew into a rage. He ran back here. Unfortunately, we had that painting of his on the workbench. We were reframing it to show it to a potential buyer. Isaiah grabbed a pair of scissors and slashed it to shreds.' He indicated the painting's remains. 'Can you imagine? His own painting.'

'You're unbelievable,' she said. 'Can you blame him?'

At that moment the door from the gallery opened and Bert Meltzer stood gaping at them, baffled. 'What's going on?'

'I'll explain later,' Neal told him, and turned

back to Anna. 'So where does that leave us? Do you still think we're murderers?'

'Murderers!' Bert cried. Gone, too, was his refined accent. The Bronx, if Anna wasn't mistaken.

'Shut up, Bert,' Neal said.

'You're not off my list quite yet,' Anna told them. 'You had a strong motive to kill Isaiah. He knew what you'd been doing and was in a position to not only stop you but also get you in trouble with Lara Parkhurst and the law. Killing him would have solved your problems.'

'That's ridiculous!' Neal scoffed. Then, 'So what are you going to do?'

'I don't know yet.'

'We made a deal.'

'I said that if you told me truth, I would leave you alone. That doesn't mean I won't tell Lara Parkhurst and the police what you've been doing.'

The two men stood watching her, silent.

'What *you're* going to do,' she said, 'is stop selling Isaiah's paintings. You will put together a list of all of his paintings you've ever sold, and another list of all the paintings you still have.'

'And what will we do with these lists, may I ask?' Bert said.

'You will give them to me. In the meantime, if I find out you've sold another of his paintings, the police will be here before you even get to the bank with the check.' She turned to go.

'Wait!' Neal said, and she turned. 'Are you going to buy *Surf's Up?*'

Her eyes widened in amazement. 'Unbelievable,' she said, and made her way out of the gallery.

Outside, walking toward Fifth Avenue, she thought about Isaiah trying to put his life back together, turning in every direction he could think of…only to be rebuffed again and again. Despite the heat of the day, a cold, lonely sadness washed over her.

As soon as she got back to the garage, Anna wrote up her reports on Jay and Winston. At two o'clock, weary, she headed home.

As she neared the corner of Ninth and Forty-Third, she heard someone calling her name. Looking around, she saw Mr Carlucci crossing the street toward her. As he reached the sidewalk, he shot a glance back at the shop. 'I can't talk long. The wife—she gets upset when I talk about these things. She says it's because she doesn't approve of gossip, but I know it's really because this murder stuff upsets her.'

'What murder stuff? You mean Maria Trujillo?'

'Sort of,' he said. 'It's really about her daughter, that monster Esperanza I told you about. This morning I was chatting with Mr Eberhardt—he comes in once in a while for his pistachio nuts— and he asked me if I'd ever found out who that man was who ran out of four-twenty-seven West Forty-Fifth Street, and why there had been police cars there a few minutes later. Well, first I say to myself, Why does that address sound familiar? Then I remembered, it's where Esperanza lives and has her office. You know how I know? The last time she and her mother were in, she paid with a credit card. I went and found her receipt and checked her information, and I was right. So I asked Mr Eberhardt when this was, and he says it was the day Mrs Olson had the fire in her kitchen.'

Anna stared at him, confused. 'I'm afraid I don't see...'

'The night Mrs Olson had the fire in her kitchen,' he explained, 'was June twenty-third, the same day the police say that homeless man was murdered in the courtyard of your building. Do you think there's a connection?'

'I don't know. It does seem an odd coincidence, doesn't it?'

'I thought so.'

'Gianni!'

He froze, his back stiffening, and slowly swiveled to look across the street. Mrs Carlucci stood at the curb, her hands on her ample hips. 'You think the shop is going to run itself?'

'Coming, dear,' he called out, gave Anna an apologetic shrug, and hurried back across the street.

An odd coincidence indeed, Anna thought, and changed her route, making her way instead to Esperanza Trujillo's building on West Forty-Fifth Street. She rang the buzzer, got no response, and rang it again. When there was still no answer, she pressed the button and held it down. Soon an angry voice blasted out of the intercom. 'Who is it?'

'It's Anna Winthrop. I need to speak to you. It's important.'

'You can't just show up here. I'm with a client.' There was a click and the intercom went dead. Anna held the button down again. The intercom came back to life. 'Stop it or I'll call the police!' Anna kept her finger on the button, the harsh buzzer grinding away.

After a few moments, Esperanza hurried down the staircase and whipped open the door. 'What is your problem? I told you, I'm with a client.'

'Your client can wait. I need to ask you two questions, and I would advise you to answer them truthfully.'

'Oh, yeah? And what are these questions?'

'Who was the man who ran out of this building on June twenty-third? And why were there police cars here a few minutes later?'

Esperanza looked at Anna as if she were insane. 'I haven't the slightest idea what you're talking about.'

'That's the day Isaiah Parkhurst was killed.'

'Oh, really?'

There were footsteps above and a thin woman with pale orange hair called down, 'Dr Trujillo, is something the matter?'

'No, I'm sorry, Greta, just a little emergency. I'll be right up. Please wait for me in my office.' Esperanza turned angrily on Anna. 'All right, I'll tell you, since you seem to have an ability to find things out anyway. It was Isaiah.'

Anna's mouth fell open. 'Isaiah? What was he doing here?'

'He actually had the nerve to come and see me. He said he was in terrible trouble and begged me to help him.'

'What kind of trouble?'

'He said the police were after him because they thought he'd killed Maria. He wanted to tell me what really happened, then he wanted me to go with him to tell the police. He was afraid to do it alone. He said I was the closest thing he had to family because of his relationship with my step-mother.'

'What did you say?'

'I screamed at him. I told him he'd come to the wrong place because I wasn't buying any of his lies. That he had some nerve coming to me, since he *did* kill Maria, and that I was happy to take him to the police. Then I went to the phone and called them.'

'What did Isaiah do?'

'He went into a panic. He started crying, talking back to some voice he was hearing in his head. I told you, the man was seriously deranged. He started to run out. I dashed to the door and locked it and stood in front of it. He pulled at me and we struggled. He was stronger than I am and he pushed me away and ran down the stairs and out of the building.

'The police got here a few minutes later. One of them was working on my stepmother's case, a Detective Rinaldi. I told her Isaiah had been here and she and the other officers ran after him, but he got away.' Esperanza shook her head. 'I see now that I should have handled it completely differently.'

'What do you mean?'

'I should have pretended to believe Isaiah, then slipped out and called the police without alerting him. Oh well, it doesn't matter now.'

'Why not?'

'Because as I told you,' Esperanza said, anger

rising in her voice, 'he did kill Maria. One way or another, he was going to die for what he did. Someone performed the execution a little early, that's all.'

'And what if—just what if—he didn't do it?'

Esperanza regarded Anna as if she hadn't heard a word she'd said. 'I don't have time for this. I've got to get back to my client.' She started back inside. 'If you're not gone in thirty seconds, I'm calling the police again.'

Anna watched Esperanza climb the stairs and disappear on the upstairs landing. Then she let herself out. Poor Isaiah. Nowhere to turn...

As she walked, her mind wandered. Could Esperanza, in actuality, have followed Isaiah herself and killed him? And if so, why? Because she truly believed Isaiah had killed her stepmother and she wanted revenge? That didn't seem likely. Or perhaps because Esperanza herself had killed Maria and wanted to silence Isaiah, the prime suspect, before the police got hold of him and perhaps believed he didn't do it?

Her cell phone rang. It was Allen Schiff. 'Anna, I hate to bother you, but something's come up that I think you'll want to deal with sooner rather than later.'

'What is it?'

'I got a call from a Mrs Yolanda Sanchez at the CSC.' The Citizen Service Center fielded nonemergency calls from residents regarding city services. 'She said she'd had a complaint call—some guy who said his garbage hadn't been picked up. Whenever possible I like to deal with these calls quickly, show people we're responsive. So would you mind…'

'Say no more, Allen. What's Mrs Sanchez's number?'

She took it down and punched it out as soon as she'd finished with Allen.

'Oh, yes, Anna, thanks for getting back to me. We've had a three-one-one call from a gentleman in your section, a Mr Bobby Kline on West Forty-Third between Ninth and Tenth.'

Jay and Winston's route.

Mrs Sanchez went on, 'He claims his trash wasn't picked up last night. You wanna give him a call?'

'Sure,' Anna said, though not really wanting to. She took down the number. When she called it, a man with a pleasant, educated-sounding voice answered.

Anna introduced herself. 'I understand you have a problem with your trash pickup?' she said, walking toward her apartment building.

'Yes, last night. Worst time to skip my building, believe me. Mrs Malone upstairs turned ninety-eight yesterday and her family threw her a party. They put a ton of garbage out afterward—lots of food scraps—and the bags didn't all fit in the trash cans. I saw four rats tearing into the bags this morning.'

Anna shivered. 'I see. I'm sorry about this, Mr Kline. I'll look into it immediately and see that it doesn't happen again.'

She expected that would be that, but he went on, his tone petulant. 'It's not just last night, you know. Your guys have really been falling down on the job.'

'What do you mean?'

'One night last month a garbage truck sat at the end of my block for hours. I took down the truck number and the license plate number. I've been meaning to call and give them to you. You want them?'

She said she did and took them down. Unlike Gerry Licari and Hal Redmond, she didn't know the truck numbers by heart. She would find out whose truck this was the next time she was in the office.

She had come down Ninth Avenue after seeing Esperanza. But when she reached West Forty-Third, instead of turning left to go home, she turned right toward the garage. She wanted to know now who that truck belonged to.

As she entered her office and fired up her computer, her cell phone rang yet again.

'Hey,' Santos said. 'Had a minute to breathe, thought I'd check in. How was your day?'

'I paid another visit to the Bentley Gallery. It was extremely fruitful.'

'What did you find out? Have they been doing what you said—secretly selling Isaiah's paintings?'

'Oh, yeah. I'll tell you all the details when I see you.'

On her screen was the list of truck numbers. She scanned it, looking for the one Bobby Kline had given her...and grew perfectly still.

'...so do you want to?' Santos was saying.

'What?' she said absently.

'Anna, are you listening to me? What are you doing?'

'I have to go. Talk to you later,' she said, and hung up.

Could it be...?

My good luck charm...

She picked up the receiver and dialed her mother.

'Anna, darling, this is a lovely surprise. I'm on the patio lunching with Helen Lippincott. You remember her, don't you? Her son, Jeremy—'

'Mother, listen to me.'

'What's wrong?'

'Nothing. I just want you to do something for me. Can you do that?'

'Depends on what it is,' Tildy said airily.

'I'm serious. Here's what I want you to do. Go into the bathroom off Daddy's study and look at all the medications on his vanity. Get me the one that starts with T-I-M.'

'Tim? What kind of a joke is this?'

'Just do it.'

'All right, dear, all right. Hold on.'

Anna could hear her mother apologizing to Mrs Lippincott. Anna was thankful Tildy hadn't put Mrs Lippincott on the phone—the kind of thing Tildy was likely to do.

Tildy was gone several minutes, during which time Anna stared at the truck number she'd found on her computer monitor. After a while it began to strobe, as if trying to speak to her.

'All right.' Her mother came back on. 'I have it.'

'What's the full name?'

'Let's see…Timoptic. Is that all you need to know?'

'What's it for, Mother?'

There was silence on the line, then, 'Oh, you know your father with all his petty ailments. Every other minute he's taking something. I'm sure it's nothing important.'

'Mother...' Anna said ominously.

'Oh...' Tildy fretted. 'We were going to tell you, dear, but we just haven't found the right moment.'

'Tell me what?'

'Your father has glaucoma. It's actually quite bad. His sight is deteriorating badly. This medication is his eye drops.'

'Oh, Mother, I'm so sorry. Poor Daddy.'

'Is that what you wanted to know? About the medicine, I mean?'

'Yes, but I already knew it.'

'What? Then why have you put me through all this?'

'I had to be sure. Tell Daddy I love him. I love you, too, Mother.'

'I love you, too.' Tildy sounded confused.

As Anna hung up, her cell phone began to vibrate on her desk.

Frowning, she picked it up and saw that she had a text message:

something in catacombs u need 2 c. come 2 where pete is. huryy. goldie

Anna punched out the number of Goldie's cell phone. A recording said the customer Anna was trying to call was unavailable.

TWENTY-TWO

ANNA HURRIED FROM Grand Central's main concourse down a ramp to the lower concourse, then down again to the platform for the number 7 subway line.

Unlike last time, the platform was crowded with people. She made her way to the end and waited until a train came. Its doors opened and passengers poured out, their attention focused on the exits. When the last of the passengers had alighted, the people waiting on the platform poured on to the train. *'Please stand clear of the closing doors,'* boomed the conductor's recorded voice. The doors whooshed shut again, the train took off, and for the moment, at least, Anna was alone. After checking for police, she hopped quickly down to the level of the tracks.

She stayed close to the tunnel's left wall, keeping as far from the third rail as she could. A familiar rumbling began. This time, knowing what to expect, she turned toward the wall, pressing herself against it. Suddenly the train was rushing past her, the wind it created so strong it nearly dragged her along with it. But just as suddenly it was gone, disappearing around a bend in the tracks with a rhythmic clacking sound that died away. She continued along the tunnel.

Finally the grated door appeared. She managed to open it by its hinges, as Goldie had done, and squeezed through, the chains on the lock side jangling.

On the far side of the door, in the blackness of the cavern, she took out her flashlight and switched it on. Where last time there had been two mattresses now lay five. She hurried on, finding the loose grated door in the right wall and stepping through. More mattresses, sleeping bags, tarps, flattened appliance boxes... But where were the people who had put them there? Probably watching her, she thought with a shiver.

She passed through several more rooms, finally reaching the rusty stairs. She ran down, the metal letting out a loud, sharp squeal.

As she proceeded down the tunnel at the bottom of the stairs, her cell phone began to vibrate in her pocket. She took it out.

anna hurry

She did, moving along the tracks and bearing right into the unused tunnel that ended in the cement wall. She found the low hole, put her legs through first, and slid down on to the shelf-like ridge running high along the wall of the cavern.

This was where they had found Pete. She shone her flashlight all around. She was completely alone, only the lonely sigh of a train somewhere far away to keep her company. An enormous rat appeared as if from nowhere and headed straight toward her, veering away at the last moment and shooting around her.

Then she saw Goldie, far ahead—farther away than where Pete had stood. The younger woman was racing toward her, waving her arms. 'Anna!'

'Goldie?' she called back, frowning in concern. 'What's going—'

From behind, two strong arms grabbed Anna around the waist and slammed her to the concrete floor. She sprawled forward, scraping her hands on the rough, gritty surface. She turned her head and found herself looking directly into the muzzle of a gun barrel.

Just beyond it, Jay Rapchuck was smiling. 'Hey, boss lady.'

'Anna, I'm so sorry,' Goldie said, stopping a few feet away, gasping for breath. 'He took my phone. He wouldn't let me leave here.'

'It's all right,' Anna told her.

'Shut up,' Jay growled, and kicked Anna viciously in the ribs. Pain shot through her and she winced. He smiled. 'You got no idea how long I been wantin' to do that.'

'Leave her alone!' Goldie shrieked, and lunged for him, leaping on to his back. For an instant he was caught off guard, nearly dropping his gun, but he recovered quickly, grabbing Goldie by the hair and giving his body a powerful shake that sent her flying toward the abyss. Inches from it, she managed to regain her balance and right herself. She backed away from the edge, crying now.

'Sit over there—now,' Jay ordered her, pointing to a spot against the wall about ten feet from where he stood.

Goldie obeyed, sinking to the floor, tears streaming down her cheeks.

'Goldie,' Anna called to her, 'where's Pete?'

Goldie's face contorted. 'He's dead, Anna.' She pointed at Jay. 'He killed him...pushed him over the edge.'

Jay chuckled. 'I needed his spot. Now,' he said to Anna, 'you're gonna start talkin'. You're gonna tell me how much you know and how much anybody else knows.'

She gave him a look full of loathing. 'What do I know? I know it was you who killed Maria Trujillo and Isaiah. I know it all...except for the link.'

He knew exactly what she meant. 'Oh, I can

tell you that,' he said amiably, 'before I kill you. "The link", as you call it, was a letter I found in Trujillo's garbage. It was from a coin dealer on Forty-Seventh Street. Guy named Sturges. The letter mentioned a "generous offer" he'd made the old lady for her late husband's coin collection, but she'd turned him down. In this letter he was upping his offer. You can learn so much about people from their garbage. That's where I also found a computer printout with details of reservations for two at a hotel on Cape Cod. That's where she was supposed to be on the night I broke in. Obviously, for some reason she didn't go. Her tough luck.' He prodded Anna with his foot. 'Who else knows it was me?'

Before Anna could answer, Goldie let out an air-rattling shriek and was running at Jay. Before he knew what was happening, she was upon him, clawing at his face like an animal. *'Run, Anna!'*

She only hesitated for a second before jumping to her feet. She looked to her left, toward the spot where Pete had appeared from the shadows. As far as she could tell, no way off the ledge lay in that direction. And not far behind Jay, a wall jutted all the way to the edge of the ridge, blocking any possible passage. So she scrambled back to the hole, grabbing at the floor of the passage above and working her legs wildly in an effort to lift herself up.

Strong hands grabbed one of her legs and pulled. She screamed, kicked out her free leg with all her strength, and felt her shoe connect with Jay's face. He let out a harsh grunt and let go.

Once through the hole, she ran along the un-used tunnel and on to the tracks, rushing toward the rusty stairway. As it came into view, a gun-shot rang out, followed by a woman's scream. It echoed through the endless tunnels and chambers of the Catacombs. Then Anna heard hard footsteps slapping the concrete close behind her.

She reached the stairs and nearly flew up them. She had never run so fast. But he was right behind her. When she was halfway up the stairs she felt him grab the hem of her pants leg and yank hard. Almost losing her footing, she managed to twist around, her ribs aching, and free herself from his grasp. On his face was a look of madness, his eyes bulging, blood mixed with saliva running from the corners of his mouth where she'd kicked him.

She remembered the flashlight. She pulled it out of her pocket, swung back her arm, and smashed it into his face. With a deep, guttural grunt, he lost his footing and clattered down the stairs, face-down. She didn't wait to see the damage.

At the top of the stairs was the last of the rooms

connected by iron grates. She knew she'd never outrun him if she had to work at opening each of them. So as his footsteps slammed the metal of the stairs, she made the split-second decision to run past the door. The tunnel widened, stretching in a straight line far beyond her. From behind her came the sound of Jay's heavy breathing as he reached the top of the stairs.

She ran.

Where did this tunnel lead? Its walls were solid—no doors or holes that she could see. There was nowhere to go but forward. His shoes smacked the concrete behind her.

Suddenly the tunnel intersected at right angles with another tunnel. She ducked to the right and kept running, hoping he hadn't seen which way she went.

Ahead on the right was a rusted door. She yanked on it and it opened easily. She slipped through. Before her, a staircase led down into blackness. Brandishing the flashlight, she headed down, stepping carefully, trying to lessen the protesting cry of the metal under her weight.

It seemed the stairs would never end, but at last they did and she was in another tunnel, this one straight, vanishing into infinity in either direction. Would she ever find her way out of this maze? What had Jay done to Goldie?

'Anna,' came a hoarse whisper. She spun around, shining the flashlight, but saw nothing. 'Anna, over here.'

This time she found the source of the voice: an iron ventilation grill near the floor, about ten feet from where she stood. She ran to it and shone the flashlight through. Goldie's head and shoulders were visible. She was peering through from a lower level. 'This comes off,' she told Anna, 'but I can't move it. Kick it in.'

'All right, stand back,' Anna said, and with her foot she pushed the grill with all her might. It popped out on the other side and hit the floor with a dull clang. She winced, casting her gaze about, but there was no sign of Jay.

'Slide through,' Goldie said.

Anna slipped through legs first and landed on the floor of this new room with painful impact. She shone her flashlight on Goldie, who now sat on the floor, holding a piece of cloth torn from her shirt against a gunshot wound in her side. 'Goldie!' She ran to her.

'It's OK, Anna.'

'OK?' Anna whispered harshly. 'You'll die if we don't get you to a hospital.'

Goldie let out an ironic laugh. 'Get me to a hospital? We're never going to get out of here alive.' She turned her head to look at something far away.

'Pete's over there, Anna.' She began to cry. 'That's where he fell when that guy pushed him. Anna... he's still alive.'

Anna's gaze flew to Goldie, then in the direction she had indicated. 'I'll be right back,' she said, and walked that way, lighting the tunnel before her.

Pete lay on his back. Both his legs were twisted under him at unnatural angles. His arms, which appeared to have escaped injury, rested peacefully on his chest. He gazed up at Anna with watery eyes that squinted in the harsh light. She saw now that tears ran down his cheeks.

She knelt beside him. 'Pete...'

'It's all right,' he said softly. 'I was going to die anyway. Just—' he winced in sudden pain, waited for it to pass '—please, just get Goldie out of here. I love her. Tell her that, OK? Tell her I never meant to hurt her.'

Now Anna began to cry. 'I will tell her, Pete, I promise. What can I do to make you—?'

But at that moment an immense wave of pain overtook him, seeming to grab him by the chest and lift him upward, and he gritted his teeth and pulled back his lips in agony. His whole body jerked several times. When the pain finally released him, he went limp, his arms falling from his chest to the floor. His head lolled sideways, his gaze fixed on Anna, tear stains on his cheeks.

With a deep sigh, Anna rose. Looking up, she saw the ledge, high above, from which Jay had thrown Pete. She turned and went back to Goldie.

'How is he, Anna?'

'He's gone. He asked me to tell you he loved you.'

'He had a strange way of showin' it…though I guess he ain't the only man with that problem.' Goldie lowered her gaze. 'He's the lucky one. He got out of here.'

'What are you saying? You know your way around this place. We'll get out.'

'Sure I know my way around, but I'm not gonna get very far with a bullet in my side. Not to mention that maniac who's looking for us. Anna, I'm going to tell you how to get out. If you keep really quiet and do exactly as I say, you can do it. Then, once you're out, you can get the cops and come back here for me. Whether I'm alive or dead by then, I want to get out of here. I don't belong in this place anymore.'

'Don't be ridiculous. We'll wait a little while until you feel you can—'

They froze. The faintest whisper of footsteps came from the blackness somewhere beyond where Pete lay.

In an instant Anna switched off her flashlight, turned, and ran silently in the direction of the sounds. 'Anna!' Goldie called hoarsely after her, but Anna paid no attention.

She ran around Pete's body and beyond it, listening. Then she heard it: another footstep, followed by silence. Jay was listening for her, too.

Noiselessly she ran away from where she thought he stood. In the near-blackness she hit a wall and let out a grunt. Then she turned, hearing the footsteps again, knowing he was after only her now and that for the moment, Goldie was safe.

She ran.

He was gaining on her.

She came to a set of tracks and carefully crossed it, avoiding the third rail. As she did, a rectangular patch of white appeared before her in the darkness, glowing softly in the far wall. Arriving on the other side of the tunnel, she saw that the shape was a door, painted white. She pulled at it and it opened easily. She dashed through. Ahead of her lay a narrow walkway, solid walls on each side.

Behind her the door burst open, slamming into her back. She lurched away as Jay came through, panting heavily, and started toward her. She turned and ran.

Quickly the concrete beneath her feet became slippery black metal. But she'd realized this too late. Running at full speed, she felt her shoes slide on the metal as if it were ice. She hurtled forward into a vast black cavern, the largest yet. It looked as if she would slide right into the nothingness when something hard and cold against her shins stopped her with a painful jolt. A low metal railing.

She was at the edge of a long, narrow catwalk that extended far over the cavern. Below, dizzyingly far away, lay a tangled network of subway tracks. A hot, fusty wind blew across her face. From somewhere far away came the eerie wail of a train.

Slowly, so as not to fall, she turned around. Jay stood at the edge of the catwalk. Blood ran from his mouth down his neck on to his sweat-stained shirt. Panting hard, he smiled, but it was a smile of hatred. 'Game over, boss lady.'

He started toward her.

It can't end this way, she thought…and had an idea.

Fixing her gaze on the emptiness behind him, she cried, 'Goldie—*now!*'

He spun around, and in that split second she rushed forward and hurled herself against him. Thrown off balance, he teetered near the edge, arms flailing.

She gave him a shove.

His calves hit the railing and he flipped over it

into the blackness, letting out a shriek of terror that went on and on—and then stopped.

She peered over the railing. Far below, Jay lay faceup on a set of tracks. Miraculously, he was still alive, his left arm moving slightly. He saw her looking down at him and his mouth formed the words 'Help me!'

Then, at the far end of the cavern, a train hurtled out of a tunnel, lights blazing. On the same tracks as Jay, it bore relentlessly down on him.

Anna turned away, but not fast enough to miss seeing a spray of blood shoot out from under the train in a crimson fountain.

'Anna?'

She turned. Goldie stood just beyond the catwalk. Blood ran from the wound in her side, soaking her jeans and sneaker. She came toward Anna, limping badly and grimacing with pain. Tears still rolled down her cheeks, but now she was smiling.

Anna gave Goldie her arm. Together they made their way toward daylight.

TWENTY-THREE

LATE THAT NIGHT, at a sidewalk café just off Times Square, Anna took a long sip of wine. 'All right,' she said, setting down her glass, 'I'm ready.'

Santos smiled. 'OK, let's have it.'

'It was the connection,' she said. 'There was a piece missing…a piece that would have put it all together for me. Once I had it, I knew everything.'

'And that piece was…?'

'A letter, from a coin dealer to Maria Trujillo. He'd made her an offer for her late husband's coin collection—an offer she'd turned down. In this letter he was raising his offer.'

Santos shook his head quickly, confused. 'But I don't get it. Where was this letter? How was it the connection?'

'It was in Maria Trujillo's trash…and Jay Rapchuck found it. That's how he knew about the coin collection. He told his pal Winston—'

'Who's been arrested,' Santos said.

'—and they made their plan. Jay would break into Maria's house at a time they believed she would be away and steal the coin collection.

'On the night of June eighteenth, during Jay and Winston's run, Jay broke into Maria's apartment through the window in the alley. The plan must have been that after he grabbed the coins he would escape via the back of the townhouse and through the alley to Forty-Third Street, where he and Winston had left the truck a few blocks down.

'He thought Maria would be on Cape Cod because of a reservations printout he'd found in her garbage. But Maria postponed her trip "due to illness", as Isaiah told me. She had a bad cold. So to Jay's surprise, she was there, in bed. Most likely she started screaming and he panicked and strangled her. As he ran out, he heard someone in the next room. He didn't see that other person, and didn't know if that person had seen him.

'Jay and Winston had planned an alibi. While Jay was breaking into Maria's brownstone, Winston went into Mrs Intile's building, ostensibly to get her chair, and intentionally jammed the elevator. He made a point of calling to Mrs Intile that his name was Jay Rapchuck. The two men have the same build and knew that the glaucoma-blinded Mrs Intile wouldn't have been able to tell that "Jay" was really Winston.

'The person Jay heard in the next room was, of course, Isaiah. He'd been showering. Ironically, he never saw Jay. But he heard Maria's scream, hurried out, and found her dead. He knew he would be blamed. He ran out the back of the building and through the alley that led to Forty-Third Street. Brianna happened to be walking there and saw him. The next morning, in my office, she mentioned to Kelly and me that she had seen Isaiah running out of an alley on Forty-Fourth Street the previous night. At that moment Winston was coming in to ask Kelly for a cigarette and overheard Brianna. Later he told Jay what she had said. Could Isaiah possibly have been the person in the other room? Jay wondered. He couldn't take any chances.

'Isaiah was desperate for help. In his distraught state he'd stopped taking his medication. He was crazed, hearing voices in his head. When Esperanza refused to help him, he came to me, one of the few people who had been kind to him…but Jay got to him first, forcing him into the courtyard and cutting his throat.'

Santos nodded sadly. 'Oh—I meant to tell you, our friend Bonz has been arrested. Seems he's been involved in the disappearance of several other graffiti writers. Someone who worked for him came to the police—a woman by the name of Bukowsky.'

Anna smiled. Looking at Santos, she saw concern come into his eyes.

'Anna,' he said gently, 'listen to me. Maybe Gloria's right. Maybe you shouldn't be in this line of work. Next time, things might not work out so well.'

'No,' she said. 'This is the perfect line of work for me. I see that now.' She had called Pam Young at Citigroup and canceled her interview. 'I can protect myself. I'm strong—one of New York's Strongest, remember? When I rushed at Jay on that catwalk, I knew I'd be able to push him off.'

'And why is that?' he asked.

'Because,' she said, mischief in her eyes, 'I've had a lot of practice throwing garbage.'

Santos raised his wineglass. 'To garbage!' he cried, drawing stares from the people around them. They clinked glasses and drank, gazes locked.

The waiter brought their dinners and they ate quickly. As soon as they were finished, they would go back to New York Presbyterian Hospital to see Goldie.

Two weeks later, Anna stood at the railing of a ferry crossing Long Island Sound from City Island to the mile-long piece of land known as Hart Island to some, Potter's Field to others.

As they approached the island, she scanned the shore, taking in a sad conglomeration of abandoned buildings among scrubby vegetation. A sign painted on a gray concrete wall warned 'PRISON— KEEP OFF', a relic from the various times the Department of Correction had housed convicts there. On a hill stood a tall white tower bearing the word 'Peace'. Nearby, nestled in a bed of yellow flowers, rose a stone cross inscribed with the words 'He Calleth His Own by Name'.

Standing just behind Anna, Correction Captain Marilyn Blakely, a tall, trim woman in her mid-forties, recited softly, 'To him the porter openeth; and the sheep hear his voice: and he calleth his own sheep by name, and leadeth them out. And when he putteth forth his own sheep, he goeth before them, and the sheep follow him: for they know his voice.'

Anna turned to her.

'From the Book of John,' Blakely said. 'I memorized it years ago, the day I first saw that cross. It's right next to where they bury the babies and children.'

When they reached the dock, Blakely disembarked first, followed by Santos, who carried a bouquet of flowers Goldie had brought. Then Anna climbed ashore. She and Santos both assisted Goldie, Anna holding her crutches while Santos helped her out of the boat.

A large blue pickup truck driven by a Correction

Department guard was waiting for them. Goldie sat up front with the guard. Anna, Santos, and Blakely sat in back, Blakely letting her legs dangle from the tailgate. After a bumpy ride past the granite cross, over high weeds and broken concrete, they got out in front of a long, narrow area of newly turned earth.

'This is it,' Blakely announced, leading the way over.

Goldie looked confused. 'But where's Isaiah?'

Blakely pointed to a white stone grave marker. 'Your guy's in here, I know that, but I can't tell you exactly where. We got a hundred and fifty people stacked up at each marker.'

Horrified, Goldie turned to Anna.

Anna gave her a reassuring little smile. 'They have records that tell exactly where each person is buried.'

'Then they do know where Isaiah is?' Goldie asked.

Anna nodded. 'They'd better. I've decided to have him buried in a real cemetery. I'm ashamed I didn't think of it sooner.'

Blakely, who had overheard, came over to them. 'What name, did you say?'

Anna and Goldie looked at her, confused.

'Your party.' Blakely pointed at the mass grave.

'Oh,' Anna said. 'Isaiah Parkhurst.'

Blakely took a small spiral-bound notebook

from her back pocket and flipped a few pages. 'Thought so,' she said, nodding. 'You don't need to move him. Someone's already doing it.' When Anna and Goldie looked at her in surprise, she read, 'A Lara Parkhurst. He's got family, then.'

Goldie smiled at Anna and tears welled up in her eyes and flowed down her cheeks. 'Yes,' Goldie told Blakely, 'he's got family.' She took the flowers from Santos and, balancing on her crutches, laid them on the ground before her. Then she gave Anna and Santos a nod and they headed back to the pickup truck.

Anna took Santos's arm and squeezed it. 'Thanks,' she said softly.

He gave a little shrug, as if their visit to Potter's Field had been easy to arrange. In truth, it had taken a massive amount of bureaucratic maneuvering.

Back on the ferry, Anna felt a sense of relief at leaving the lonely island. Standing beside her, Goldie said, 'I don't suppose I'll ever see you again.'

'Of course you will. We do have a friend in common, after all. And,' Anna said, gazing toward the approaching shore of City Island, 'there's someone I want you to meet.'

GOLDIE FOLLOWED ANNA along Forty-Seventh Street, past windows ablaze with diamonds.

Halfway down the block, Anna consulted a scrap of paper, nodded, and opened a door situated between a diamond-and-jewelry exchange and a watch company. 'In here,' she said, gazing up a narrow stairway. 'Take it slow. Do you want me to hold your crutches?'

'Anna, *what* is up here?'

'Can't tell you that yet.'

'Don't they have an elevator?'

'No. Sorry. Are you coming or not?'

Letting out a sigh, Goldie turned around, sat down on the first step, and began scooting her way up. 'Gonna take a while.'

'I can wait.'

When at last Goldie reached the top, Anna led her through a set of double doors into a narrow, stuffy corridor on to which several doors opened. Anna stopped at one labeled 'STURGES—COIN DEALERS. WE BUY COINS. APPRAISALS.' 'In here,' she said, pushing open the door.

They found themselves in a tiny, cluttered office where a man sat at a paper-covered desk. Small and frail, he had piercing blue eyes over a sharp little beak of a nose. Anna judged him to be in his late nineties.

He took them both in. 'Can I help you?' he asked in a high, reedy voice.

'Mr Sturges, I'm Anna Winthrop. I called you yesterday.'

'Right, right.' He leaned forward across the desk. 'Let's see it.'

Anna turned to Goldie. 'May I please see your good-luck pouch?'

'What?'

'The purple pouch Isaiah gave you.'

'Why?'

'Trust me.'

Goldie fished the pouch from her pocket and handed it to Anna, who pulled it open and spilled its contents carefully into her hand. 'Here you are,' she said, and handed Mr Sturges the penny.

'Anna, what are you doing?'

'Shh.'

Holding the penny by its edge, Mr Sturges peered at it through a black jeweler's loupe. Time passed as he flipped it over, then over again, the office silent but for the faint ticking of a clock on a dusty shelf behind him. At last he looked up at Goldie. 'Where did you get this?'

'It was…a gift,' she said.

'I've seen this coin before,' Mr Sturges said.

'Yes, you have,' Anna said. 'It was part of a collection Maria Trujillo showed you. You made an offer for it, but she turned you down.'

'That's correct,' he said, remembering. 'Then I sent her a letter increasing my offer, but she never replied. So what are you doing with this coin? Where's the rest of the collection?'

'Mrs Trujillo gave this coin to a friend of ours,' Anna said, 'and he in turn gave it to Ms Russell here. Mrs Trujillo has since passed away, and her stepdaughter has the rest of the collection. What she'll do with it, I'm afraid I don't know.'

'Passed away?' Mr Sturges said. 'How sad. She was a lovely lady.' He broke from his thoughts, back to business. 'Your friend gave you a very generous gift,' he said to Goldie. 'Do you know what it is?'

'Yeah, it's a penny,' Goldie said, and laughed.

Mr Sturges gave her a tolerant smile, then answered his own question. 'It's a 1969-S doubled die. It's extremely rare, and it's in excellent condition.' He set down the coin and the jeweler's loupe, pulled several books from a shelf beside his desk, and spent the next few minutes flipping pages and jotting notes on his desk blotter. Finally he looked up at Goldie. 'I'll give you thirty-five thousand.'

She looked at him blankly. 'Thirty-five thousand what?'

'Dollars.'

Goldie rolled her eyes. 'Anna, let's get out of here. Guy thinks he's a comedian.'

'Young lady,' Mr Sturges said, 'I hope you will be serious, because I assure you, I am being perfectly serious.'

'Anna, what's he talking about?'

Anna threw her arms around Goldie and hugged her tight. 'I knew it. The reason Isaiah wanted you to know where he hid his good luck charms was that he wanted you to have them if anything happened to him. Because this particular charm—' she indicated the penny on Mr Sturges' desk '—was worth a lot of money, and he knew it.'

'But where did he get it?'

'From Maria Trujillo. She gave it to him from her husband's coin collection. If something should ever happen to her, she wanted to make sure Isaiah would be taken care of...as Isaiah wanted to make sure you were taken care of.'

Fortunately, there was a chair behind Goldie. She fell into it, looking dazed.

'Well, young lady,' Mr Sturges said, 'what is your decision?'

Anna reached over and carefully took the coin from his desk. 'Thank you for your time, sir, but she needs to think it over.'

'My offer isn't good forever!' he called after them as they went back out to the corridor.

Anna handed Goldie the purple velvet pouch.

'My good luck charm,' Goldie said in wonder.

Anna nodded rapidly and wiped a tear from her eye. 'I'd say your luck has changed.'

* * * * *

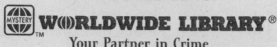